TEXT ME FROM YOUR GRAVE

Pamela Cartlidge

Books by Pamela Cartlidge

Bluebells and Tin Hats
Rhubarb without Sugar
Restless Yew Tree Cottage

Text me from your grave

Chapter One.

Rachel hovered at the edge of the broken stone wall that circled the abbey cemetery. She was waiting for her mother to come away from the funeral. She glanced around her. No-one had noticed her hanging about. Only once, at a burial, had someone perceived her presence. When Rachel had realised that, she had spirited herself very quickly to another spot.

Some of her friends advised her not to linger too close at funerals but she was fascinated observing the behaviour of the bereaved. She liked listening to the snippets of gossip shared amongst those who attended. It was a good way of finding out what was happening on the 'other side'.

Rachel's mother was taking her time getting away. Always gregarious and sociable, Anna Bellis was behaving true to form. She weaved in and out of the mourners; examined the names on the wreaths and silently sympathised with family and friends. Her wistful gaze followed each of the bereaved as they left her grave side to get to their cars. Finally Anna drifted across to join Rachel.

"Hello darling. I would love to give you a hug." Anna gesticulated a greeting. Her raised arms, swathed in the blue silk

sleeves of her cocktail dress, fanned thin air.
Rachel nodded. "Me too. Her eyes roved over Anna's clothes. I see you have come out in style mum. Did you choose that get up?"
"Yes. Your father followed my instructions to the letter." She gazed down at her outfit taking joy in her white nylon tights and blue shoes that matched her dress. "I hoped you liked those clothes I chose for you. It was such a horrible, terrible time. Planning your unexpected funeral was not easy. It isn't nice for anybody in those circumstances, I know. But you were young. You shouldn't have gone so soon."
Looking down at her ripped jeans and her 'Save the Orangutan' T shirt Rachel grinned. "I was chuffed with your choice. Thank you. But mum, why did you put my mobile phone in the coffin? Surely you didn't think you could contact me in the grave?"
"I did ring you. I could hear it calling you."
Rachel stifled a grin. "I didn't hear it, but I saw the 'phone vibrate and the light flashing telling me there was a call coming through. Not bad considering I was buried six feet under. But obviously I couldn't respond! There was nothing I could do about it. I was unable to touch it let alone answer or make a call."
Anna pursed her lips. "Well I instructed your dad to put my own mobile in my coffin just to see if I could communicate with him.

Anyway I wanted him to make sure I was dead. I had a fear of being buried alive."

This time Rachel burst out laughing. "Oh mum, I'm so sorry, but that wasn't going to happen. I'm sure dad would have checked everything. There is no way he was going to let you be buried alive." She softened her voice then added, "I don't think he will try to use the mobile."

"If he follows my instructions he will. He promised!" Anna retorted assuredly.

Rachel smiled at her mother. She let that comment pass. "Mum I am pleased to see you even though I'm sure you would have preferred to be on the 'other side' a bit longer. You aren't that old. God, fifty five. I wasn't expecting to see you again so soon!"

"I know. I thought I would have had at least another twenty years, but that heart attack left me very weak. However, I had time to make some plans and leave instructions. I have left unfinished business."

"Have you asked dad to carry on investigating my murder? I heard him swear to me at my own funeral that he would get justice for what they did to me. He visits me a lot. Gavin comes too."

"Yes of course! He will. It was my dying wish." Anna hesitated. "Please tell me. Did you know the brutes who killed you?"

Rachel shook her head. "No. They were complete strangers."

"Well that's some relief. I always dreaded that it might have been someone you knew. Anyway Gavin will help your father to try to find your killer, as soon as he flies back from Budapest. He will be leaving shortly after the wake."

"Budapest! What is Gavin going to do there?"

Anna smiled. "He is going to see if any of your friends can help. They will be endowed with some power just like you. He knows someone who is a psychic. His name is Phil. Do you remember him? They were in college together a few years ago. Apparently he and his then girlfriend went on a ski-ing trip there and fell in love with the place. They're married now living in Transylvania of all places! They keep in touch with Gavin by email and face book.

Rachel frowned. "Yes I remember Phil vaguely. But I don't have any friends in Transylvania nor anywhere in Romania. And I don't have any power."

"Your *special* friends. You know like you are now. In fact like me too." Anna chortled somewhat nervously.

"Oh I see. Just because we are all dead doesn't mean we are all 'universal friends' you know. And in any case I don't think those dead people in Romania or Transylvania have any more power than us either. All that vampire stuff is just a myth. Besides that, I can't get there to find out for myself. You need special agreements to go there. It is a very complicated system to get permission. In fact it is also very complicated to get permission even to venture outside your relevant zone."

"Zone? What do you mean by zone? I thought ghosts could go anywhere they like."

"That's just it. We aren't ghosts. We are spirits. We are only ghosts when we get the powers to re-visit a place and, in rare cases, be seen by someone living."

"I'll soon get the powers. I'm quick to learn."

"It doesn't work like that."

"What do you mean? Now I'm dead, I can do what I like."

"Sorry mum but you can't."

"I don't see why not." Anna looked earnestly at her daughter.

"You need permission to be a ghost."

Anna frowned. "So do you mean to tell me that even though I am dead, I need some kind of agreement to allow me to go wherever I want?"

"Sort of. It depends on your death. I qualified to be a temporary ghost because I was murdered. You wouldn't be able to be a ghost because you died naturally."

"That's a shame." Anna sighed. "I was planning on haunting a few people I don't like."

She made a pulling motion at her white gloves to smooth out the creases, yet despite her efforts they remained still wrinkled. She hadn't got the hang of being dead yet.

"That's being malicious and not encouraged." Rachel replied. "Even though I have been granted status as a ghost, I still need special authorisation to wander further afield."

"Special permission, rights to roam, this is beginning to sound like Brexit!" Anna groaned.

Rachel ignored her mother's complaint.

"As I am now designated a ghost, I'm sure I will get permission to roam. But I don't think I will need to explore too far away from here, because I think the evidence we need is right here in this town. I just need some help to find it."

"Really? So you do know who killed you? I thought you said you didn't."

Rachel shook her head. "No. What I mean is, I didn't know either of them, but I'm pretty sure they're from round here. They seemed to know their way around the cathedral grounds. They looked familiar yet they were strangers to me. If that makes sense."

"So there were two. The police thought there may be two murderers."

This time Rachel nodded.

"And you think they are locals. It's not nice to know that murderers live in this area. Yet I always suspected your killers were from around here, in Holywell. I said that to your father numerous times. He on the other hand, always thought it would be someone passing through and took the opportunity to to…" Anna faltered over the words. She couldn't bear to say out loud what had happened to her daughter a year ago.

"Attack, rape and kill me you mean." Rachel finished for her flatly. She had got used to being dead and was able to control her anger. She could discuss the manner of her death in a calm way.

Anna nodded. Her expression sad. "Yes. That." She paused reliving in her mind that terrible evening when the police had informed her that her daughter was dead.

"If you can bear it, can you tell me what happened?"

"Are you sure you want to hear about it today? You have only just got here from your own funeral."

Anna took a deep breath and Rachel caught the aching heartbreak in her mother's eyes. She tried to cheer her up and repeated her welcome. "Mum I'm so pleased to see you, even though I'm so sorry you had to leave sooner than you expected."

Always methodical, practical and organised, even in her grief Anna rallied herself. "Tell me as much as you can. I need to know to help me come to terms with it. Take me as close as we can get to the place it happened. Maybe between the two of us we may pick up some clues to help us figure out who murdered you."

Rachel motioned to her mother to follow her across the abbey graveyard. They passed through wide flower beds and strategically placed benches for visitors before arriving at the ancient well of St. Winefride. Close to the well was a cluster of pine trees. Mother and daughter floated over the trees, then hovered above a high stone wall. Here they remained just within the boundaries of the abbey. Behind the wall they could see a grassy slope that spread itself widely as it stretched downwards to border St. Winefride's Lake.

"We can't go any further." Rachel explained.

From their high position Rachel pointed out the lych gate and the network of footpaths. She then drew her mother's attention to a thicket of shrubbery close to a small section of the lake. The herbaceous border appeared to be rooted in the water, but in actual fact there was a two metre gap between the bushes and the water's edge.

"That's where you were found!" Anna gasped.

"Yes. The place where the brutes dragged me, half killed me then dumped me in the lake."

"And you really didn't recognise any of them?" Anna asked again.

"No. Like I said, I just had a feeling I had seen them before. I barely had chance to see their faces as they pulled me to the ground. It all happened so quickly. I struggled and I might have got away if one of them hadn't hit me on the side of my head with his fist. It knocked me flying. My arm hurt too where he grabbed me. They were both calling me some terrible names like… stuck up bitch! And…and slut! And even worse words than that! I couldn't understand why. I didn't know them. Why would they say that? I was confused and trying to make sense of what was happening. The first one kept thumping me like some kind of a maniac. I think I broke my arm when he dragged me to the ground. I was only half conscious then of what was happening. When I realised what they were doing, I was lying face down with most of my clothes ripped from me. My head hurt and I felt as if my lip had been split in two.

After they had turned my body over, I knew I was going to be raped. One of them did his horrible deed whilst keeping one of his arms on my head to stop me moving. He held back my uninjured arm with his other hand. The other guy held my feet. I had no strength anyway to scream or struggle. My cheek hurt and my mouth tasted of blood. I knew my lip was bleeding and I had a sensation of two brittle objects rolling around on my tongue. I realised two of my teeth were broken. I was helpless and terrified. Then his evil friend was determined to rape me too. I tried to scream when they changed places. But the second one bashed me again. He must have picked up a big stone from somewhere. I could feel blood from my head trickle down my face. Again my head and mouth was held fast with an arm to stop me screaming.

After they had finished with me sexually, they both kicked me continuously to roll me down the slope into the lake. They left me alone and bleeding in the water and walked away laughing. There was no-one about to help me and anyway that particular spot was almost concealed by the bushes. It was also dark."

Rachel paused as she observed the impact her words had made on her mother. "Are you sure you want to hear the rest?"

Anna nodded. "Please go on. I have to know."

"I supposed they thought I would drown. But I was still alive when those other two young men found me. One of them had gone behind the shrubbery to pee and must have heard me moaning. It wasn't very deep where I had been dumped. The water hadn't carried me out to the centre of the lake or pulled me down, like I think my attackers hoped. I merely ebbed back towards the edge and became trapped in mud. I was very weak, and if I had drifted out to the centre of the lake I wouldn't have had the strength to keep afloat. All I could manage to do was to use my fingers on my good arm to swish some water. Perhaps my rescuers thought I was an animal. Anyway it was too late. He and his friend pulled me out and then very soon after… I died."

"At first, your father and Gavin were convinced that those young men who said they had found you, were responsible for your death. I wasn't so sure. I'm glad I was right. They seemed so genuinely shocked."

Rachel nodded. "They tried their best. They were really scared. One of them held my hand whilst the other used his mobile to call an ambulance and the police."

Anna stared for a long time at the spot. "I think the police suspected them at first. But there was no forensic evidence to incriminate them. Everything had been contaminated. The murky water was mostly to blame. That, plus the fact that those two men who rescued you, had moved you, made everything unfathomable. In fact there was no forensic evidence to use to incriminate anyone! They had no other suspects."

Anna sighed again. "I have visited this spot many times to try to get a clue. But I don't understand why you were here. I thought you said you were meeting Emma and Jade outside Saint Winefride's Abbey well. That's the other side of the abbey away from the lych gate."

"Yes. I know. I actually got to the well on time. Then Emma texted me that she was going to be twenty minutes late. She also said that Jade had changed her mind. So rather than hang around at the well I strolled along the short cut from the well towards the lych gate. I'd planned to walk back to the well again, on the outside of the abbey just for something to do. More or less from here where we are hovering. The light was beginning to go by then but I could see my way clearly around the abbey walls. I was a bit preoccupied with what Emma and I were going to do. I felt if she was very late we would miss the beginning of the film at the Odeon."

"Emma was riddled with guilt after you died. She kept saying if she hadn't been late it might not have happened." Anna said quietly. "I found it difficult not to think that way too. The poor girl was a mess."
Rachel shrugged.
"Anyway go on." Anna urged.
"Well as I got close to the lych gate, I heard someone shout 'there's that bitch!' Then this horrible man pounced on me from behind and started to manhandle me. I managed to shake him off and ran up here, but he followed me. When I looked over my shoulder I saw that there were actually two men chasing me. I couldn't get the lych gate to open quickly, so by the time I got to the pathway that leads down to the town square, they had overtaken me and dragged me down the opposite direction to the lake. By this time it was dark. There was no-one about. I couldn't get away and…..well you know the rest." Her gaze rested on her misshapen arm which had been broken in the struggle. Meanwhile her mother contemplated Rachel's neck which had also been broken. She recalled seeing her daughter's limp body where her head had been twisted out of line with her torso.
Mother and daughter's eyes met. Neither said a word. Rachel wouldn't know that her parents had paid a fortune for a bone-setter to put her body into a good shape again.
"That area used to be one of your father's favourite spots for fishing. He hasn't been there since you were murdered. When I

knew that I was going to die, I told him he ought to come here again to try to come to terms with your murder and my death. I hoped he would find some peace. It didn't seem fair that your murderers should get away with violating the spot which we all loved."

Rachel nodded. "I hope he does start fishing again. I might be able to reach him somehow when I get permission to roam. Then I will be a fully-fledged ghost."

Together they glided over the headstones of several graves towards the front of the ancient shrine known as St. Winefride's. They passed a few rambling spirits on the way. A few said hello to Rachel.

"Maybe I will get special permission to roam too seeing as I am your mother and the murderer hasn't been found." Anna suggested cheerfully. Anna was an optimist and she liked getting her own way. She also liked to organise things and people. In her previous life as a deputy head teacher she had earned a reputation for being disciplined and efficient. She had been well respected and liked by her colleagues and students.

Rachel shrugged. "It's worth a try. Come on, I will show you where the Assessors gather every month. Then we can go to *The Bench* where you will meet my friends Desmond, Margareta, Laticia and Big Steve. I suppose Tomtit will be there too. He usually turns up causing mischief."

"I suppose I won't be able to catch up with my deceased family, because we moved away from Lancaster where most of them are buried." Anna observed miserably. She was only half listening to the list of names Rachel was reciting.

"I'm afraid not mum."

The Assessors discussed their business around a grassy knoll that bore the tomb of St. Winefride. Set apart in a corner of the cemetery the tomb was enclosed by eight straggly overgrown yew trees. On the first day of every month, the eight Assessors assembled themselves around the tomb. Each of them took up a position in front of a yew tree. This meant that all the Assessors faced each other.

"Why do they meet here? Anna asked.

"In honour of St. Winefride I suppose." Rachel shrugged. "I don't really know. I hadn't given it much thought. Maybe it is because this is a convenient spot in the graveyard. It being on raised ground and she being a saint and all that."

"So does she make an appearance at these meetings?" Anna asked. Being inquisitive by nature, the questions that spilled from Anna were those that had never even crossed Rachel's mind to ask.

"I've never seen her here. I don't know if her spirit is part of the conclave. There would be a language problem for a start. She being seventh century and the Assessors being nineteen and twentieth century. They change on a regular basis."

"So how do you get to make a request to roam or be a ghost? Anna asked. She had a number of questions to ask.

"You have to go to St. Bueno's stone and ask three times for permission. You also need witnesses who will attend the hearing when your turn comes up. The witnesses represent you and inform the Assessors of your request."

"So Bueno's stone? Is that the statue that is in the flower garden in front of the well? I've seen it several times."

Rachel nodded. "Yes, I will show it you later. First, I will take you to meet my friends and other spirits at '*the bench*."

Rachel led the way towards the ancient abbey, then turned her head towards her mother to add "I've already made my request. I'm waiting for the next stage now. Hopefully it will be very soon. Then I can start searching for my killers."

Chapter Two

The Bench

Anna followed her daughter into the crypt of St. Winefride's Abbey. She was expecting to see a row of marble coffins and stone tombs, but there were none. Between the stained glass windows that reached high up to the arched ceiling, there were several granite niches and ledges. Spirits assembled themselves in little groups along the ridges. They adopted sitting positions even though they couldn't feel the cold stone beneath their bony frames.

Rachel drifted her way to a corner behind a colonnade and beckoned her mother to join her.

"Mum this is Desmond and Big Steve."

Both male spirits nodded a welcome to Anna.

"It was mum's funeral today." Rachel explained. "So she needs to know the ropes."

"Happy to help." Desmond said. "I've been here many, many, years now. Natural causes. I was seventy nine. Shame I missed out on the celebrations for my eightieth, but that's how it goes."

"I was only fifty five." Anna returned. She noticed that Desmond had a full head of hair. It was completely grey and hung in waves around his still handsome though wrinkled face.

"I was forty two." Big Steve sighed. His black silk shirt strained across his wide chest. It was easy to see why he was referred to as Big Steve. "Knocked down by a hit and run a year ago. The Assessors are still deliberating about giving me my freedom to roam because they said I was drunk and disorderly at the time."

"Do you know who killed you?" Anna asked. She was fascinated.

Big Steve shook his head. "Not exactly but I remember the car registration. If I had freedom to roam I'm sure I could find it! It's a local number."

"But what would you do if you found the driver?"

"If I had enough time on my freedom pass, I would haunt that bastard as much as I could."

"If you acquired the skills to do it you mean." Desmond interrupted scathingly. "It could take a while. I'm told by other spirits who have been able to roam as ghosts, that a lot of concentration was required to be able to do even the simplest of things. For example lifting pieces of paper. To be able to lift or move small items also took some strength of mind. And more skill was required to try to communicate in other ways. As regards causing some mischief, well….you know you are not allowed to seek revenge." Desmond spoke sternly.

"It can be done though." Big Steve returned defiantly. "I don't mean try to kill him. I just want to put the wind up him; make life uncomfortable for him and maybe find some clues for the police."

"Hmm!" Desmond muttered. He wasn't convinced that Big Steve's intentions were as innocent as he claimed.

"Where's Margareta?" Rachel asked. She had heard about Big Steve's plans for revenge many times. The Assessors were taking their time with his case. She guessed that they were delaying things because Big Steve was still full of anger. She understood how he felt. She too was angry that her life had been taken away from her so soon. But she wasn't looking for revenge, she wanted justice.

"She's with Laticia. It's her third hearing. Let's hope she gets her pass." Desmond said.

"Laticia is from the West Indies." Rachel explained to her mother. "She came to live here five years ago when she married a man from Manchester. He started to beat her up almost as soon as she got to Britain. She ran away to a friend's house in Connah's Quay but he found her. Then when she ran away again he followed her here to Holywell and killed her. She wants to go home to be with some of her dead family in the Caribbean."

"Which part?"

"Barbados. That's where she met her husband. He was on holiday with some of his mates. A whirlwind romance and wedding apparently." Rachel replied.

"Then violence and death." Big Steve added morosely.

"So where is her husband now?" Anna asked anxiously.

"Prison. Hopefully for a long time." Rachel replied.

"Look." Desmond said. "Laticia and Margareta are coming, and behind them it looks like the Tuesday night bell-ringers are coming too."

The little group were joined by two enthusiastic spirits. They gathered together beside a concrete monument in the shape of a Celtic cross. They watched as six human forms were observed walking up the aisle. The bell-ringers stopped close to the altar where one by one they slipped through a side door leading to steps up towards the bell tower.

The spirits were distracted momentarily by Laticia looming before them. "I've got it!" She cried jubilantly. "I can go at the end of the week."

"That's in three days' time." Margareta added. She was pleased for her friend but was now preoccupied thinking about the bell-ringers.

"Let's go and see if Tomtit gets up to his tricks again. It could be funny." Margareta suggested.

"Tomtit?" Anna looked perplexed. Do you mean a bird?"

Rachel grinned. "No. We call him Tomtit or sometimes Tomtwit. He's a spirit like us."

They glided enmasse upwards to gather together on a bench near the belfry. On the way Rachel introduced her mother to the rest of the group and Margareta explained about Tom.

"Long before he died, Tom had two knee replacements made from titanium. After the operation it seemed to give him a new lease of life and despite his age he went for long walks and even cycled a lot. He's quite athletic considering he was eighty one when he died. Of course now, his body has perished, yet the mobility that he enjoyed before his death is still with him. It's like as if he is still wearing the titanium knees." Margareta laughed.

"So where are the metal replacements now?" Anna asked. She was worrying about her contact lenses. Her eyesight she noticed was still good.

"All the metal is still in his sarcophagus. A waste really." Margareta remarked. "Though I sometimes wonder if there is some lingering traces of titanium lurking in his resting place that seeps into his bones. He argues that because he lies in the coffin every night with the titanium replacements he gets re-energised."

Anna frowned. Rachel laughed. "You will soon see mum."

As anticipated Tomtit the aged spirit began to sway in between the bells trying to distract the bell-ringers. He desperately wanted them to see him, but no-one could. Despite his antics and pulling faces, the bell ringers were oblivious. However he did manage to distract one of the younger members of the troupe. A teenage girl was wearing a metal watch and each time Tom sashayed over her hand, the watch began to twitch on her wrist. The young bell-ringer was obviously feeling some discomfort but valiantly kept on pulling her rope. The spirits assumed that the watch was causing her skin to itch. Tom felt some sympathy for her and turned away to select an older victim. But it was too late. Just when the girl could no longer stand the itching, she used her chin to try to scratch her wrist. Unfortunately this movement unbalanced her and she tumbled into her neighbour. He in turn became unbalanced and the resultant domino affect caused the bells to clang in a thunderous, tuneless din.

Having achieved his objective, Tom took up position at the top of the belfry and looked down as the group tried to re-assemble themselves. The young girl apologised profusely whilst the spirits above laughed.

Desmond told Tom off. "That was mean. Why didn't you target some of the older ones?"

"It was an accident. I had already meant to leave her alone, but the connection with the metal of her watch with my titanium legs was stronger than I realised. Her watch is probably made of a combination of steel and titanium. Whatever it was I felt a very slight current. Enough to cause her an irritation. Or maybe she's allergic to the metal." Tom didn't look very remorseful. "Still, it was funny wasn't it?"

Several other spirits who had crowded in to the belfry to watch the bell ringers agreed with Tom that the incident had been amusing. It was a way of passing time. Desmond shrugged.

When the bell-ringers prepared to leave, Margareta passed on a message to Rachel that she had been summoned to the bench the next day.

"They are having an extra session tomorrow to clear up a backlog of requests. Your name has been called." Margareta explained. "So you have to take your three witnesses. It's a good job Laticia isn't going until the end of the week. Otherwise you would have to start again. She's one of your witnesses, isn't she?"

Rachel nodded. She turned towards her mother her face displaying her relief and excitement."

"Can I attend too?" Anna asked.

Desmond nodded. "Yes they don't mind observers but you are not allowed to say anything."

Inwardly, Rachel thought with a smile tracing her face that it would be very difficult to restrain her mother from saying anything.

"Tom is coming too." Desmond advised them. He turned towards Anna to give her some more information about Tom. He died five years after his second operation on his knee."

"I hope he doesn't try any funny business." Anna said.

"He won't. I promise you. He just likes a bit of fun with the living." Margareta assured Anna. "The living provide our entertainment."

"I'm coming too." Big Steve said. "Just to remind them I'm still waiting for their decision on my case. See you tomorrow. I'm going now to follow these bell-ringers as far as the boundaries, just to see if I can catch any gossip."

"Where do you go at night?" Anna asked everybody else. She noted that Tomtit had accompanied Big Steve out of the cathedral.

"Well we normally hang around here and chat for a while before getting some rest. I usually go back to my coffin." Rachel replied. "You could go to yours. Some spirits usually hang around in here or they go up to the chapel at the side of the cathedral and rest on the pews. Others float around on the roof top. In fact that's where most of them go during the day time. They people watch. Trying to get a glimpse of human beings."

Anna seized on that piece of information quickly. "Did any of them see what happened to you? They must have a good view up there."

"Unfortunately no. A few said they saw me near the well, but as I was hanging around doing nothing, they lost interest. It was getting too dark to see anything clearly after that. A couple of spirits who chanced to glance towards the lych gate said they could just make out the backs of two men chasing me but couldn't distinguish anything else. All they could see of their clothing, was trousers and jackets. They were sure they wore casual clothes and not suits but they couldn't tell me anything else. Once I had been dragged down to the ground, I was out of sight and by then the sun had gone down."

Anna sighed.

Later, Rachel accompanied Anna to her graveside. On the way they passed a grave that had been dug out several months before Anna's. It still looked relatively fresh.

"So who is in there?" Anna asked.

Rachel shrugged. Apparently it is the half leg of someone called Stefan Kadinsky. He was killed in an explosion. His body was blown out of a car just when he was driving past a house where a gas cooker blew the kitchen into bits. Half of his leg went up in the air, the rest of him was mangled up with the metal from his car. His family were allowed to bury that part of his leg. It might take some time to find the rest of him, if they ever do, poor sod. I'm not sure what will happen next."

"So does his leg roam around here?"

"Not that I have seen. I'm not sure how he would communicate. Maybe it goes around when we are all 'resting'.

"I recall reading about that explosion in the local newspapers. The name rang a bell with me. I think Gavin mentioned that he knew him slightly through a computer course they both attended. It's an unusual name for around here."

The whole area surrounding Anna's grave was laden with wreaths. Roses and carnations were already beginning to wilt. It had been another unusually warm April day. Together they passed through the flowers and peered in to Anna's casket. Inside it, Anna's mobile was blinking a message.

"You see. I told you your father would ring me." Anna said triumphantly.

Rachel shrugged. "Well I don't know how you are going to make contact with him. You've probably got about two days to make a plan before the battery runs out. Good luck with that. I couldn't come up with anything when you sent me a message. Though it was a nice thought mum."

Anna sighed. "It was just an idea."

Rachel turned towards her mother, "I've been wondering why you didn't get me cremated. You always said that you felt burials an inefficient way of disposing of dead bodies. Not forgetting how depressing they are especially in bad weather."

"Your father and I felt that if the police came up with some evidence, that they may need to exhume your body. We hoped that would be the case, so we decided not to cremate you. In the end I asked to be buried too. Good night love."

Rachel watched her mother make herself comfortable and then sashayed back to her own resting place nearby. Thinking hard on her mother's words she allowed her eyes to rest on her headstone.

Rachel Elizabeth Bellis beloved daughter of Daniel and Anna Bellis
Born 23rd February 1999
Died 20th March 2018.
Rest in Peace.

Presently she settled down to rest. At her feet on the pink silk interior of the coffin lay her mobile 'phone as lifeless as herself.

Chapter Three

Daniel Bellis

After the funeral, various friends, distant family members and ex work colleagues hung around in awkward groups. They were struggling to find words of comfort to offer Dan, a man who had lost his wife and daughter within a year of each other. Whilst a few quietly drifted away, other mourners accompanied Dan along the street to the "*Saint Winefride's Head Hotel*. Conveniently located on the edge of town, the hotel was able to offer guests easy access to the lake, the cathedral, the town square, and the famous Saint Winefride's well. Just a stone's throw away from the cemetery it was the obvious choice for anyone requiring refreshments after funerals.

Dan left the wake as early as he could. He wanted to be alone with his sadness. He was feeling the strain of holding himself together. If anything, he was fed up of putting on a smile and giving a light hearted answer to well-meaning friends who asked "how are you?" and "how are you coping?" He sometimes wished they didn't ask.

At home he poured himself a glass of whisky and took it with him to his bedroom. He sipped at the drink whilst he removed his suit, then lay on his bed hoping to get some rest. But, he couldn't unwind. Too much was going around in his head. In the space of thirteen months he had first lost his daughter in a horrendous attack and then his wife died. Meanwhile his son was on his way to Romania on an outlandish notion to try to communicate with the dead. All Dan had for company was the dog Leo.

The warmth of the evening, and the alcohol eased Dan in and out of a restless slumber. As the hours passed the setting sun gently slipped through the undrawn bedroom curtains and flooded the room. During a spell of wakefulness, Dan sat up to admire the ethereal beams of light cresting the distant hills. Closer to home the peal of church bells suddenly pierced the silent twilight. Tuesdays, he knew was the bell ringing practise. He recognised the tune of 'Oranges and Lemons' though it sounded a bit off that night he thought. He yawned, then drew the curtains together before treading downstairs to feed the dog. After he had made the house secure he poured himself another whisky. He returned to his bedroom with his drink then got properly ready for bed. Aided by more alcohol he very soon fell into a fitful sleep.

At six a.m. Dan gave up trying to get any more rest. He got out of bed, pulled on his old clothes and went downstairs. He was greeted by an enthusiastic dog eagerly anticipating an early walk. The excited animal wasn't disappointed.

There was a network of footpaths and country lanes at the rear of the crescent, where Dan lived. One of the lanes led down to St. Winefride's cathedral. That particular lane eventually linked up with another spidery web of pathways.

Dan chose a well-trodden dirt track that skirted the cathedral and led directly to the famous well. The trail sometimes became muddy and flooded during heavy storms, but today it was firm under foot. The unseasonal dry April weather had seen to that.

Presently he arrived at the well. He stood at the side of it staring gloomily into the vast expanse of water. The shape of the well was more like a small swimming pool, unlike the traditional wells depicted in children's story books. Visitors came from all over the world to bathe in the water which purported to have healing powers. The source of the water was from a spring which centuries earlier had been captured into a star shaped font. From that stone construction the water cascaded into the pool below.

Dan had never believed in any of the myths associated with the so called magical healing power of the water. Nevertheless, a few months earlier he had taken a container of the water back to his wife's sick bed. There he had bathed her face and neck in a desperate attempt to revive Anna's weak body. But it hadn't worked. She claimed she had felt better after his administrations, and though she did rally for a week or two, she eventually died. He was never sure if the water had kept her alive a little longer or whether it was just coincidence.

Dan dipped his fingers in the water to dab his face. He felt refreshed. Straightening up he let his eyes rove around the silent cemetery. Unhappily he walked across the grass to his wife's grave. There, he contemplated morosely the already drooping flowers where his wife's body lay. After a few minutes he pulled out his mobile phone and pressed Anna's number on his contact list. He knew it would be useless. But he had promised he would try at least three times.

The sound of Anna's message service jolted him a bit, just like it had when he had tried the day before. He reasoned with himself, just as he had then, that the message was not coming from an ethereal sphere. Despite himself he smiled. Poor Anna. At least I can hear your voice once more.

Leo was sniffing at the flowers and digging at the freshly dug soil. Dan realised that the dog's sensitive hearing could probably detect the mobile ringing yet couldn't figure out where the sound was coming from.

"Come on Leo. Time to go."

Eventually the dog gave up and followed Dan to the lych gate. The church clock struck seven. Glancing at his watch to check for accuracy, his eyes then scanned the path towards the town square. Everywhere was quiet. Sighing heavily he decided that now would be the best time to fulfil another promise he had made to Anna. He would walk down to the lake. It wasn't far from the lych gate. He braced himself for something he knew he had to do.

Each step that brought him closer to the lake, his anguish increased. Finally he forced himself to gaze at the spot where Rachel's mangled body had been found. His breathing was becoming heavier. Anger and grief engulfed him. He steadied his breathing with deep gulps of air, willing himself to linger hoping for some kind of cathartic effect. Eventually he moved some distance away to a picnic bench and sat down. It was such a beautiful area. For him it had been spoiled by the evil that had taken place there and robbed him of his daughter.

The police were still investigating but he realised as time went on and the case became colder, there would be less public money spent on trying to find the murderer. He and Gavin had vowed to investigate the murder themselves. Then Anna had become seriously ill and all their time was concentrated on making her comfortable.

He wished Anna hadn't put Rachel's mobile in her coffin. He hung on to a possibility that there was a clue amongst her contacts that the police may have missed. They didn't know her like he had known her. He would just have to visit her old friends one by one and start again. He knew where they lived. All he needed was some energy. Two bereavements in the space of one year had taken its toll.

Grief seemed to have the opposite effect on his son. Gavin vowed to stop at nothing to find out who killed his sister. Dan allowed himself a rueful smile as he recalled his son's resolute expression, when he had left Anna's funeral to go to Manchester airport. What he hoped to gain from a trip to Transylvania Dan had no idea.

Gavin had always been fascinated in the supernatural. The occult, was just one of many of his interests. He was a very gregarious man who played football every Sunday morning with his mates and enjoyed a few pints at the local pub in the evenings. It seemed incongruous to Dan that his son could believe in vampires and ghosts. Dan believed that when you are dead, you are dead. End of story.

Leo was getting restless, so Dan got up. Then he heard the town clock strike the quarter hour. Automatically he checked his watch.

"Come on Leo. Time to go home."

Later that same morning Dan strolled to the front garden of his house to look into his garden shed. Hanging up on the wall was his old fishing rod. He took it down and gave it a rub with his thumb. The dust came off thickly on to his skin. He had vowed to Anna before she passed away that he would go fishing again in the lake. He wouldn't allow those people who had violated his daughter to ruin his favourite pastime.

On his way to the kitchen to get some cleaning cloths, the telephone rang and Dan rushed to answer it.

"Dad?"

"Gavin. Are you alright?"

"I'm fine. Listen dad. I've been talking to my friend Phil. You know, the guy I told you about who I was in school with. He left six years ago to live in Transylvania. The one who is a psychic? He's visited us a few times since, though it's been a while."

"Yes. I remember him. He's the one who has been working on a thesis for his Ph.D. in Romanian culture and history. You told me that he was also interested in horror movies. That's why he went to live in Transylvania, to get some atmosphere. I haven't forgotten. My memory isn't failing me yet."

"Sorry dad. Actually his wife is more interested in horror movies, though he likes them too. He is interested in all genres of film. Anyway, Phil said he is prepared to take a few days off work to come back over and help us look for Rachel's killers. He works part-time in a pub to supplement his income, such as it is. I said he could stay with us. Is that ok?"

Dan was about to say that it was a waste of time, but he could hear the hope in his son's voice and so he relented.

"Alright. If that's what you want."

"Isn't that what you want too? To catch the person or persons who killed Rachel?"

Dan sensed the disappointment in his son's voice and tried to make amends. "You know I do, but you also know that the police have done everything they can. How could this Phil do anything? I'm more than happy for Phil to come, but I don't hold much hope in him finding any new clues."

"Phil senses things. It's worth a try dad." Gavin said earnestly. "If you don't want him staying with us he is happy to stay with his sister and brother-in-law, or his parents in Mold. I just thought it would be more convenient for all of us if he stayed in Rachel's old room. He might be able to pick up a vibe."

"When are you both coming?" Dan asked. He wondered what Anna would have thought of Phil sleeping in Rachel's room. Probably she would have welcomed it, he acknowledged. She had been a bit more indulgent with Gavin's leanings towards mysticism. As for Rachel, he was unsure how she had thought about matters beyond the grave. He was aware though, that she used to enjoy teasing Gavin about his interest.

"We'll fly back tomorrow to Manchester. See you tomorrow afternoon."

Dan put the kettle on and made some coffee. Presently he went up to Rachel's room and removed the old sheet that covered the bare mattress. Taking a deep breath he made up the bed with clean sheets and a duvet. He lightly dusted the furniture and then stood back to survey his work.

Satisfied, he strode to the dressing table at the side of the bed where he picked up the box that the police had returned to him. It contained Rachel's personal things. The police had checked Rachel's messages on her mobile, they had run checks over her email account and Face Book page, and had found nothing sinister. Interviewing her friends had got them nowhere either. Searching through her old address book; her diaries and notebooks also proved to be unproductive. The police concluded that Rachel had been the victim of a random attack.

They had been sympathetic when Anna explained she wanted to put Rachel's mobile in her coffin. Her mobile hadn't contained anything suspicious as far as they could tell and had returned that quickly. As far as Dan knew, the Police had interviewed all the contacts on the mobile. Not that there were many.

Rachel's lap top and her tablet had not given the police a starting point they hoped for either. All that had been revealed, was some websites she had used for her university work. There were also some websites of a few pubs, restaurants and cinemas in Cardiff. Dan doubted she had been to the majority of those places. Rachel was only just nineteen, and had little money. She and her friends rarely went to pubs, they spent what little money they had, going to the cinema. He guessed she had researched a list of places out of curiosity, or possibly for a future event. The police were inclined to agree.

Rachel had often said she would get a part time job to supplement her loan when she started university, but they had persuaded her not to do that. They promised that they would help her to pay back the loan. They felt her time was better spent studying rather than having to take on part-time work.

Dan sighed and lifted up the lid of a small jewellery box to have a quick glance inside. The silver locket that Rachel had been wearing the evening she was killed lay at the bottom of the box. Anna had not wanted to put that in the coffin. She had intended to wear it herself. She felt it would bring her closer to her daughter. But when the police returned it she found she couldn't bear to touch it. The locket was a rectangular shape and had been an eighteenth birthday present from Gavin. He had bought it in Bucharest on one of his holidays abroad. Rachel had liked the size and shape of it because she said it meant she could put a 'decent' image of her favourite people in it. She said that the usual sized lockets were too small for photos and it meant massacring a photograph to get them to fit.

Dan replaced the jewellery and notebooks in the box, keeping back Rachel's address book. He took it downstairs with him, where he made some more coffee. Settling himself in an armchair he began to look through the address book. Maybe there was something they had missed. All thoughts of his fishing rod had been pushed to the back of his mind.

Chapter Four

The Hearing

Rachel was excited about her pending meeting and her enthusiasm kindled vigorous discussion amongst the rest of the group. Laticia, who had already been given a pass to leave Holywell was buoyed up with anticipation of her imminent departure. She knew she had a lot of organising to do to transport herself to Barbados but she was free to roam wherever she wanted, so she didn't envisage any difficulties in reaching her destination.

Rachel led her group of supporters to the Assessors' meeting place around St. Winefride's tomb. It was midnight. The sky was clear and many stars were visible. A late night visitor to the graveyard with extra sensory perception may have witnessed shimmering shapeless forms as the moonlight outlined those spirits gathered around Rachel. As instructed, Rachel's supporters formed a triangle leaving Rachel at the apex point facing the Assessors.

Each Assessor scrutinised Rachel for a few seconds then the first one read out her request to roam as a ghost to try to find her murderer.

"You were murdered a year ago and the police have not found your killer. Is that correct?"

"Yes." Rachel replied.

"Do you have any clues who did it?" Another Assessor asked.

"No. I'm afraid not." Rachel admitted. "But I have a few ideas where to start looking."

A third Assessor asked what she would do with the evidence if she were able to find it.

"I will try to find a way to get the evidence to the police or to my father."

There was some silence for a few seconds then another Assessor asked if she realised it would be difficult to communicate with the living.

Rachel confessed that she did. "But I know it can be done if I concentrate hard."

"Have you considered making contact with the living through a medium?" The next Assessor asked.

Rachel shrugged. "I will use any means possible. Within reason. She added. "I won't attempt to employ dark forces or use evil means."

The silence that ensued was an anxious few minutes for Rachel. She felt that if she was human again she would be sweating and biting her nails in frustration. However she was a spirit and only just a ghost, the latter in name only, so she couldn't do any of those things to relieve the suspense.

Eventually the Assessors reached an agreement. The first one who had questioned Rachel turned towards her.

"As you know, most of us on the Assessors Panel have been victims of murder and so we understand your plea. Those of us who were murdered, knew the killers. It made the task easier to find the evidence for the police. You on the other hand do not, and so whilst we sympathise, we feel we can't give you the maximum amount of three months to find your attackers. We therefore award you one month as from Friday at sun down. We wish you success."

Rachel felt that if she could cry she would. She would have spilt tears of relief, joy and exasperation. She had just one month to find her killers.

Anna on the other hand wasn't impressed. "Surely you should give her longer time, not shorten her allowance!" She challenged the Assessors fiercely.

"Who are you?" The first Assessor asked.

"I am her mother. I just got here and I want to help my daughter."

"Very commendable. How did you get here? Were you murdered too?"

"No. I had a heart attack. I had a malingering death if you must know!"

"I'm sorry about that, but we have made a decision."

"Can't we appeal?"

All the Assessors nodded their heads.

"Mum come away! The appeal takes ages. They have given me a month. That amount of time is probably enough. If I can prove I am making headway they will give me an extension."

The Assessors confirmed this statement with another inclination of their heads.

Anna wasn't convinced but she followed her daughter and the rest of the group back to their niche at *the bench.*

"Wecangotogether! I canelp ya?" Laticia's excitement made her speak in such a fast Barbados patois that no-one could understand her.

"Slow down." Margareta said.

Laticia tried again. "I said, that, we can go out together and I can help you."

"But you are going to Barbados!" Margareta and Desmond cried simultaneously.

"I can wait a day or two." Laticia replied. A huge grin spread across her face making her statement barely distinguishable. Her friends were used to Laticia's accent but when she got too excited they sometimes had difficulty making out what she was saying.

"How are you going to get there?" Rachel asked.

"Well I will catch a train to Chester, then another one to Manchester airport. After that I will find a plane to Grantley Adams airport."

"Will you have far to go from there to the cemetery?" Big Steve asked.

"No, not really. There will be plenty of buses I can hop on to. The cemeteries there are more like parks and animal sanctuaries so there will be plenty of public transport. The local council provide transport for visitors. You have to pay of course, but as you know I won't be paying." They all laughed. "It's a well-kept area, just like this is."

"Well this abbey or cathedral as some people refer to it, is preserved because of Saint Winefride." Margareta said. "It's a holy shrine, and visitors to the well, bring in revenue for the whole area. Other cemeteries in Britain are not maintained to such a high standard as this one."

Desmond agreed. "The local council and the Roman Catholic Diocese of Wrexham make sure this is cared for properly. We can thank our Saint Winefride's legend for that."

"That's true." The others agreed nodding their heads in agreement.

"That reminds me!" Anna said excitedly. "Why don't we ask Saint Winefride for some help? She was murdered too. And she was given healing powers and other stuff."

The spirits groaned.

"Do you think we haven't tried?" Big Steve asked. "She doesn't speak English for a start. Nobody here can translate. Her language is like a mixture of Latin, Gaelic and Welsh and god knows what else! One or two words are familiar but we can't understand anything she says. Not that she says much. She doesn't mix with the likes of us, we are too modern. She regards us with a lot of suspicion. Actually I'm not sure who she mixes with. I doubt if there are any spirits here from the same century as her. I think her interment was the first and only one for a very long time. Centuries probably."

"When was she interred?" Margareta asked. She had never been interested in St. Winefride's background, because she thought she was aloof, notwithstanding the language barriers. However, now, despite herself she was curious.

"There is some dispute about that. Some say it was in the seventh century other scholars have said it was much later." Desmond informed them.

"In any case, it was her uncle Bueno who found the murderer. That bastard had attacked her and chopped her head off. Bueno washed it with holy spring water and stuck it back on her neck again and brought her back to life. For that reason she claimed to have acquired special healing powers from the spring water."

Margareta snorted. "Tosh. If you believe that, you believe anything!"

"A lot of people do." Desmond said. "You've seen the pilgrims coming here in the summer to take the so called holy waters."

"Bueno created a font to capture the spring water and then he made a pool they call the well." Anna chipped in. She knew this because she had studied it and had included it in the history classes that she had taught in the local school.

"As a matter of interest, what happened to the murderer?" Rachel asked. This was a bit of history she had never known. Now she was dead herself all kinds of historical stories were coming to her attention. Whether they were facts or myths she had no idea. She turned to her mother for information. Before Anna could reply, Desmond supplied the answer. He too had done some research.

"That would be old Caradoc the bad. Apparently he disintegrated when Bueno restored Winefride back to life. No-one has seen anything of him ever since."

"So that's why we have to plead on Bueno's stone to ask to be a ghost!" Rachel declared.

"Forget them girl. We need to plan what we're gonna do on Friday night." Laticia drawled. She was easily bored and her mind flitted from one thing to another. She was also anxious to move on. "We've got two more nights here." She said. "First, I think we should visit the spot where you were murdered and re-trace your steps from there to your house. Do you think that's a good idea?" Laticia looked from one of their friends to the other to check their agreement.

"Yes." Rachel agreed. The others nodded their approval.

"It's a pity you can't go back in time for a few minutes." Tom said. He had been silent for a while, deep in thought thinking how to help.

"Yes, I was thinking that." Anna said.

"Does anyone time travel?" Rachel asked eagerly.

Everyone shook their heads. "Not allowed." Big Steve said. "Not even the Assessors can do that."

"Who are the Assessors to say we can't do this and we can't do that?" Anna asked. She was getting impatient.

"The Assessors are appointed by us. We can change them every two years. In fact you can put yourself up for election if you have been murdered yourself." Big Steve advised.

"So that means I can't ever be an Assessor?" Anna said with disgust.

"It helps if you have been murdered, you would get more votes, but anyone technically is eligible." Tom said cheerfully. "But who would want that responsibility?" He chuckled.

"Why do I need their permission to wander where I want as a ghost?" Anna said defiantly.

The small group except Rachel looked appalled at such a question.

Desmond shrugged. "You don't really need their approval, but you wouldn't be welcome back into the fold if you tried to do it alone. As the saying goes. 'You are a long time dead', so best to have some friends. Besides you would have to break the barriers down yourself, whereas the barriers would be open for you easily if you have their approval."

"So who guards the barriers?" Anna asked. She wasn't put off by Desmond's statement.

"A treble layer of spirits whose combined strength provide an impenetrable wall for a lone spirit." Big Steve answered. "I've actually tried and got nowhere."

"That's why the Assessors are taking so long with your case." Margareta commented. "They are making you wait, some kind of a penance."

Anna wasn't discouraged. "Well I don't think that should put you off Steve. Why should we be controlled by a load of stupid rules? We are dead now. We shouldn't be hampered by these silly so called laws. There must be a way to get through."

"Mum. It doesn't matter. I have permission to roam." Rachel tried to placate her mother. She knew that Anna was the kind of person who would flout rules in order to get her own way. 'Rules are there to be broken' she always said.

"When the time comes perhaps you could vote for me as an Assessor and then we could change the rules – legally." Rachel finished the last sentence in a wheedling voice.

Anna sighed. "Well maybe that's not such a bad idea." She conceded.

"Why don't we concentrate on how we can help Rachel find her murderer?" Laticia suggested.

The others agreed. "First of all tell us everything about the night you were killed." Margareta said." The full story. As much detail as you can."

"Well I can help there too." Anna offered. "Rachel's told me what happened, but there might be bits in her story that I missed."

Despite learning of her daughter's horror, Anna felt that hearing the story again would be useful. Any clue that Rachel could give them may lead to the identity of the killers. She was experiencing the same frustration of not being able to find Rachel's killers during the time when she herself was alive, as she was feeling now she was dead.

The spirits gathered around Rachel as she related the events of the evening that led up to her death.

"You already know that I was murdered not far from here. I had arranged to meet my friends, Emma Winterton and Jade Lucas."

Anna agreed. "Yes. That's what I told the police."

"Did they turn up?" Margareta asked.

Rachel shook her head. "Not both of them. Emma was coming, but I didn't see her. She was running late."

"She turned up too late." Anna confirmed. "She was waiting for you at the well you see."

"Does the friendship go back a long way?" Desmond asked.

"Yes." Rachel replied.

"Did you have a boyfriend?" He asked.

Rachel nodded.

"Was it a serious relationship?" Laticia asked.

Rachel glanced at her mother before replying.

"Don't look coyly at me. I'm sorry to say the police told me that though you had been raped, that you hadn't been a virgin."

"Mum! Don't embarrass me!"

"I think we've all got past that stage." Laticia soothed. "We need to know everything about you so that we can look for clues."

Somewhat placated but not without a glare at her mother, Rachel proceeded.

"His name was, or rather, is, Josh Watkins. Emma was seeing Dave Baldwin at the time. But I wasn't that serious about Josh!"

"They were both interviewed by the police." Anna confirmed. "Josh and Emma, I mean."

"What did they say?" Big Steve asked.

Anna shook her head. "I don't know for certain what they said to the police. I only know what both Emma and Josh told me. They came to see me after they had given statements. They were a bit shook up. Obviously the police were not going to tell me the outcome of their interviews. All I know is they were free to go."

"Do you think these two boyfriends, Josh and Dave had friends who might have murdered Rachel?" Laticia suggested.

"What, you mean contract killing?" Margareta said. "Don't be daft."

"I think that is one theory that the police considered. But if the boys told their friends to attack and kill Rachel," Anna paused as she recalled the incident, "and I don't see why they should, then no evidence has come to light. At least they still haven't arrested anybody." Anna said.

"I wasn't thinking of contract killing, I was thinking of jealousy as a motive." Laticia protested.

"Is there some secret you aren't telling us?" Desmond asked.

Rachel shook her head. "No. Absolutely no."

"So who found Rachel's body?" Laticia asked.

"Two very kind boys found me. I was still alive, but I knew I was dying. I was barely conscious. They called the police and an ambulance and stayed with me until they arrived. But it was too late."

"What exactly happened?" Laticia asked gently.

Rachel sighed and prepared herself to tell her friends the story she had previously related to her mother.

"I didn't see the two men who assaulted me until it was too late. Or rather I saw them from a distance but ignored them. Maybe that was my mistake."

Rachel paused and glanced at the attentive faces of her audience then continued her story. "Before I realised what was happening one of them had grabbed my arm and called me a load of rotten names like bitch and slag and..and. Well you name it."

Rachel glanced at Anna and hesitated. "And mum other terrible words I can't bear to repeat. Just use your imagination. Why would they say that? I was confused and trying to make sense of what was happening. I couldn't understand why they were hurling such abuse at me. But then it got much worse. It all happened so quickly. I was only half conscious of what was happening."

"There's no need to give them every detail of the rape darling." Anna said. The others agreed solemnly.

Rachel nodded. "Eventually they rolled me into the lake using their boots, carefully though, so as not to make a splash that would call attention. I suppose they thought I would float away and drown. But although my body was completely submerged in water, I drifted back to the lake's edge. It was quite muddy there and so I was stuck with most of me in dirty water and my head resting in the slimy edge of the lake. I was still alive when those other two young men found me."

"Can you recall anything about their faces? The rapists I mean." Laticia asked slowly. She shuddered. She had painful memories of her own brutal murder.

"No. I was too battered and scared to focus on their faces. In any case they wore sun glasses even though by that time it was quite dark. It had been a sunny day, so they were still wearing them. Even though the sun had definitely set by then. They'd also pulled up the hoods on their jackets."

"If they were wearing hoodies and sun glasses, it sounds as if they planned it." Big

Steve suggested. He spoke slowly trying to make some kind of sense of the terrible event.

Rachel shook her head. "I've thought about this a lot. I don't think it was planned. They didn't know I was going to be there. As I have said it had been an unusually sunny day though not very warm. It was after all the middle of March. They were probably trying to look trendy wearing the sun glasses. All very convenient for them but not for me." Rachel added.

"I also considered that they may have been high on drugs. I don't know. I suppose it was possible. Whatever the reason, they saw their chance with me."

"And this happened about seven o clock?" Laticia asked.

Rachel nodded. "It was about seven or just after, and it was going dark. You know, that stage when light rapidly fades. It was also getting very cold. There was no-one around to help me. No dog walkers or people taking evening strolls. No-one except those two brutes."

"And you've no idea who they could be?" Desmond persisted.

"All I can remember is that they were both tall and one was a much heavier build than the other. I caught sight of their jackets which were light blue. Both of them the same. They looked similar to the ones the lifeguards wear at the boat and sailing club."

"That's something the police didn't know." Anna said excitedly.

"The thing is mum, the boat club sells jackets to the public, so there are a few of them around."

"Not so many that I have seen. They are quite expensive." Anna retorted.

Rachel sighed and conceded that point. It was expensive to join the sailing club too, she recalled.

"Do you think there would be blood on their clothes?" Laticia probed. Again she recalled the amount of blood running from her head when she was killed. Hers had been a bloody attack too.

"I don't know, possibly on the sleeves if anywhere." Rachel replied. She recalled the horror of her assailants' arms covering her face to keep her head down.

"She had cuts and bruises on her face and she also had internal injuries besides her broken neck. I doubt there would have been a huge amount of blood to stain their clothes, if that's what you are thinking." Anna remarked. She recalled that terrible night when she and Dan identified Rachel's body. "I suppose some traces may have come off her face on to their clothing somewhere. Just a small amount."

"Mum, I know my face was bleeding. The blood may have washed off in the lake."

"We haven't got much to go on, but at least something to start us off." Laticia commented. She changed the subject dramatically. "By the way on Friday night there is going to be a full moon. It should help us a bit when we get out of the cemetery."

Chapter Five

Plans

"Your suggestion to re-trace my steps from my house to the place I was killed is a good one." Rachel said to Laticia the next day. "It's better to do it that way than the other way round."
"Great! And when you are in your house try to find something in your belongings that might give you a clue. Something like a diary, notes to yourself. Did you have a notebook?"
"We looked through all those and the police did too." Anna said.
"You may have overlooked something though." Laticia persisted. Something that may appear totally meaningless but something important to Rachel."
"I can't think of anything of significance. Off hand." Rachel admitted. She pulled a face so that the tiny bones in her cheeks showed up the cracks where she had been beaten up. Despite the handiwork of the bonesetter, these were sometimes visible through the thin and delicate film that sheathed the skeletal form of the spirits. The morning light bore easily through that flimsy camouflage revealing her fragile looking frame. "I often used to write notes to myself that had hidden meanings." Rachel said slowly.
"I wondered about that." Anna said.

"Out of interest did you look in my old school satchel?"

Anna looked perplexed. "No. At least I didn't, but the police would have gone through everything in your room."

"I doubt they would've found anything significant. Even if they looked in some of the old letters I used to keep there, they wouldn't find any clues to my murder. I'm sure of it. But I may have confused the police with all the memory notes in my old satchel. I'd also stuck a few in my jewellery box. I rarely threw anything away and used an old purse with the catch broken and a shoulder bag a bit worse for wear for storing things. I kept them for sentimental value, so I used to keep bits and bobs in them. Mostly I kept old notes to remind me to do something, or call someone. Meaningless to most people except to me."

Anna nodded. "Yes those things are still in your bedroom. I suppose the police looked at them. I was too distressed at the time to notice. I just let them do what they had to do."

"Is there anything you wrote down that might give us a clue?" Laticia asked.

Rachel shook her head. "I can't think of anything I did that may have led to my murder."

"What did you do the few days before you died?" Laticia probed.

"I can't remember everything, but I know, before I died, I was researching various organisations that might be looking for part time staff. You know, temporary work for summer time and all that. I don't think there was anything on my tablet that would suggest I was going to be killed."

"What kind of organisations?" Laticia asked

"Cafes, restaurants, supermarkets. That sort of thing. I'm not qualified to do anything else – I never will be qualified to do anything now." Rachel paused, bitterly contemplating her cruel fate.

"I also considered working in a pub until I finished my degree." Rachel allowed herself to be side tracked. "I was studying politics and philosophy."

"Fat lot of good that would do you." Desmond said sarcastically.

"Did you go to any of those places?" Anna asked. She ignored Desmond with a withering glance.

"Sort of. I didn't tell you mum. I just thought I would go and have a look at them first from the outside. I wasn't sure really what I wanted or what was on offer. I would have told you eventually." Rachel added the last few words when she saw her mother's surprised expression. Anna didn't know whether to be offended or amazed at her daughter's subterfuge.

"Maybe the police visited some of those places to make enquiries." Anna suggested.

"If they did, they wouldn't have discovered anything, because I didn't get very far in making contact. There were only two cafes that had vacancies. The day I decided to do something positive, the cafes were closed. So I left it until the next day, but by then I'd changed my mind about the whole thing."

In an attempt to avoid conflict, Rachel rushed on. "The night before I died, I saw an advert in the local paper from a pub looking for a barmaid. I copied the number and then made a note on the back of the photos in my silver locket. It was in my own sort of code. Did you see it?"

"We saved your locket. The police looked at the photos and they asked us about the jottings on the back. We couldn't help them. You'd drawn a heart on one of them I recall. I assumed it was because you loved the people in the photo, namely myself, your father and Gavin. Was I wrong? I couldn't explain the numbers though. I was sure it wasn't the birthday of anyone I knew. What did it mean?"

"I can't remember properly how I wrote it down but it was a kind of code. Probably a few initials to remind me of something and a time or maybe a 'phone number. I spread the information across the two photos so that if someone stole my locket they wouldn't know what it meant. Not that it was important. It meant nothing to no-one except me."

"Well that worked. Because your father, Gavin and I didn't have a clue, and neither did the police. In the end we assumed they were obscure dates in history that you wanted to remember. Maybe for an essay you might be writing. And as the dates seemed to be so far in the past we thought no more about it."

Rachel smiled. "They were meant to look like dates. Actually they were telephone numbers dissected. I discovered that most of the places around this town have land line telephone numbers that start with seven, so I took that as given. I made the second and third digits in the phone numbers to convert into a date, then used months of the year to signify the fourth digit. January would be 1, June would be six and July seven and so forth. The last two digits would form the year. For example a phone number such as 716496 would look like 16.April.96. But I sometimes used initials, usually a compressed form of the name of the place I wanted to visit or where I had an interview."

"It's all very elaborate. Why didn't you just store the numbers in your mobile?" Big Steve suggested.

Before Rachel could answer, Laticia jumped in. "To stop your mother snooping!"

Anna glared at Laticia venomously. Rachel grinned sheepishly at her mother. "Actually it was also a bit of fun too. Just to see if it would work."

Anna looked affronted.

"Snooping! How could you say such a thing?"

"Come on mum. You know you were always snooping around in my diary and my notebooks. If I had left my mobile lying

around, you wouldn't have been able to resist picking it up."
Anna shrugged. "Only because I cared about you."
"If you'd found out I was going for an interview in a pub or a club you would either have tried to persuade me not to go, or 'phone them to find out what kind of conditions they were offering. That would have been embarrassing. That's why I only stored the mobile numbers of my friends, the ones that you knew and none of my newer friends.
All the mobile numbers of friends I made at Uni are all in code in the back of my address book in the form of birthdays. Actually not that many, only four. Two of them being old boyfriends."
Anna didn't know whether to be shocked, astonished or hurt. This was part of her daughter's life she knew nothing about and she didn't know how to deal with it. She finally assumed an indignant stance.
"So you defaced those photos of your parents and your brother?" Anna admonished.
"It was in pencil and only very light so that I could see it. I intended to erase everything afterwards. As I wrote those numbers down the night before I was murdered I didn't get much chance to erase them."
"The police checked your mobile for the calls you made." Anna began.
"The police wouldn't have found the number in my mobile because it was on charge. I

had used up the battery sending messages on Facebook, so I went out to a public 'phone box to make enquiries about the position. The manager invited me to go straight away to the pub for an interview."
"Did ya go girl?" Laticia asked excitedly.
Rachel nodded. "Yes. They offered me the job there and then. But I said I would think about it, because the hours were long. I'd never been there before. I didn't even know it existed until that night. There are a lot of pubs in this area."
"Don't I know it." Big Steve grumbled.
"Which one is it?" Desmond asked. "I've lived here all my life. I reckon I know the names of all the pubs."
'The Sacred Heart'.
"I know it!" Desmond said. It's across town. The beer was good, but the place was a bit run down. Mind you that was a few years ago. I've been dead nine years."
Big Steve agreed. "Yes I've been there too." He turned towards Desmond. "I was there two years ago not long before I was killed. Actually it has had a makeover. It's a very trendy pub now. Ruined it I reckoned when they modernised it. But they still have good beer. Real Ale. The landlord is friendly, but it does attract some unsavoury customers especially on a Thursday."
"Why Thursdays?" Margareta asked. "I've never heard of it. It sounds like it doesn't live up to its name. I assume it refers to our sacred Saint Winefride."

"On Thursday nights they have live bands playing, and the pub gets a licence extension for drinking until midnight. Some punters get drunk and invariably there is some drunken behaviour." Big Steve replied. "Saturday nights too, sometimes." He added. "But not every Saturday."

"It sounds a lively place." Rachel said. "The landlord told me I would have to work late on a Thursday but would organise a taxi for me free of charge."

"But something put you off about the place. Do you think it had something to do with your murder?" Laticia suggested.

Rachel shrugged. "I don't know. It was busy when I went for my interview. There seemed to be a mixture of people. You know, groups of women, couples, some young some older. I noticed in one corner there were a few men drinking. A couple of them were leering at me. One of the older men wolf whistled. I couldn't stand that. It put me off. So I ignored him and walked out."

"You did the right thing." Big Steve said.

"Anyone in blue jackets?" Laticia persisted.

"I can't remember properly. But now I think about it, I did catch sight of something blue amongst a pile of discarded jackets lying on the bench at the side of one group of men. It was quite warm in the pub. I didn't look at them nor the men properly. They seemed to be staring at me. I avoided eye contact. When I passed them on the way to the door, one of the younger men made some sexist remark about my breasts, though that is not the word he used!

The women shared an expression of disgust. Big Steve and Desmond shrugged.

"Anyway I ignored him and hurried past. I assumed he had probably had too much to drink. But the remark made me feel uneasy and I was anxious to go and meet Josh. As soon as I got out of the pub I saw a couple of people waiting nearby for a bus. So I waited with them. I was lucky that one arrived within a couple of minutes. Josh was waiting for me outside the Odeon."

"Hmm. That's not much to go on. Besides blue jackets are ubiquitous." Margareta commented.

"Not light blue ones though." Big Steve remarked. "Most people go for navy or even darker."

Anna nodded in agreement. "Yes. The employees at the sailing club tend to wear light blue jackets."

"But we don't know if they were from the sailing club." Rachel reminded her.

Laticia sighed. "Well never mind. When we get to your house we can have a look for more clues. But we could also have a look in that pub too. Maybe we should start from the telephone box where you made the call and then the journey to the pub and to where you met Josh. That's a thought. Do you think you were followed from the Sacred Heart?"

"I don't think so. I didn't look back. The bus stop was very close to the pub and as I've said there were people waiting. If I had been followed by those men from the pub they would probably have been put off by seeing other people standing with me. That's if they had evil intentions I mean."

Anna sighed. "I don't suppose you knew the people at the bus stop?"

Rachel shook her head. "I didn't recognise them."

"Did Emma or Jade know you were going to that pub?" Anna asked.

"No-one knew I was going to the 'Sacred Heart' except Josh because I had previously arranged to meet him that night. I had to tell him I would be later than planned. I sent him a quick text. I told him more about it afterwards.

"What was Josh's reaction when you told him about the interview?" Anna asked. "He didn't tell me that he knew about that."

"He was fine with it. He said he'd been to that particular pub once before with some friends. I don't know who they were. Anyway he offered to pick me up on his motorbike to bring me home on Thursdays if I wanted. And I suppose he didn't tell you because he probably thought it didn't matter. I'd already made my mind up I didn't want to work there and said as much to Josh. The landlord told me that if I hadn't contacted him by lunch time the next day, he would assume I didn't want the job. So I didn't bother ringing him back. Josh probably forgot about it and didn't bother telling you seeing as I was never able to go there again."

"I wonder if he told the police. They didn't mention anything about that to me." Anna mused thoughtfully. "Would the police visit all the pubs looking for the killer do you think?"

"She wasn't a missing person. Why waste time visiting pubs as part of their inquiries?" Desmond commented.

"If she was a regular at a particular pub, the landlord would get to know her and her friends. They could give the police some clues." Big Steve suggested.

"We didn't go to many pubs because we couldn't afford it. Emma and our other friends, Jade and Lara usually went to each other's houses to watch a DVD or something on Netflix." Rachel replied.

Anna agreed. She knew that was true, because she had played hostess to many of Rachel's friends. Supplying them with hot or cold drinks and snacks had been a way of life for several years. She had watched them grow from school children to teenagers and knew them and their parents very well.

"All your friends confirmed this. They came to see me and told me what they had told the police. They usually shared a bottle of wine and if they went to a pub it was usually to celebrate one of their birthdays. You could hardly say they were regulars."

Everyone fell silent after Anna had finished speaking.

Three days later at the stroke of midnight, Rachel and Laticia floated through the spiritual barriers that separated the cemetery from the living world. The guards formed a passageway for them. At the exit they were enviously cheered on by Anna, Desmond, Margareta, Big Steve and Tom.

"Good luck!" Anna cried. "Don't forget to keep us updated."

"I would normally have said "Take care' when someone was to leave on such an adventure." Big Steve said, but no harm can come to them anymore. So what's the point? I hope they find what they're looking for."

"Meanwhile, we must try to think of a way of helping them from this side." Anna said.

"And how do you propose to do that?" Margareta asked. She eyed Anna thoughtfully. The woman had only been with them a few days and already she was trying to change the way things were run. She was obviously a loving mother though somewhat overbearing all the same. No wonder Rachel felt it necessary to hide information from her. The girl was nineteen years of age, she needed her privacy.

However, Margareta liked Anna despite her controlling personality. There was something warming and comforting about being in her presence. She acknowledged that she must have had a terrible shock to discover her beloved daughter had been murdered.

"I'm not sure yet." Anna replied. "I need to think. I'm going to wander around the cemetery to try to come up with something. You can accompany me if you like."

Margareta grunted. "I've nothing better to do. Though I was thinking of going to hover over that grave with the one leg in it. It looks like they are opening it up again."

"Why? Do you think a relative of his is going to join it?" Anna asked.

"No idea. Shall we go and have a look?"

"Alright. It might help me with some inspiration. We may as well take advantage of the moonlight."

Chapter Six

Power Games

Whilst Anna and Margareta made their way towards the grave of the one leg, Rachel guided Laticia along the mile and half stretch to her father's house. She guessed that he and her brother Gavin would now be asleep.

Getting into the house was no problem, but Rachel had not expected the dog to sense the two ghosts. Leo began to whimper excitedly when Rachel floated in front of him, but his excitement turned to a bark as soon as Laticia approached. She backed away so as not to disturb him. Rachel bent towards the dog. He began to wag his tail.

"Do you think he can see us?" Rachel asked.

"I'm not sure. Try moving from side to side to see if his eyes follow you."

"His eyes will follow me anyhow because he senses me. I know, I will wave my hand above his head to see if he jumps."

Leo jumped immediately.

"That doesn't prove anything. You need to go to the opposite side of the room and wave to him to follow you."

To Rachel's delight Leo followed her across the room. He lay down contentedly at her feet.

"I'm not convinced, but at least he's stopped barking." Laticia commented. "He's a lovely dog."

"Yes he is. I wish I could cuddle him like I used to do. I don't think he can see me you know. Otherwise he would jump at me and try to get me to hug him. It's just our presence he is aware of."

"I thought it was just cats that could do that." Rachel laughed. "Well obviously dogs can too. Come on let me show you my bedroom. At least Leo can't get through the living room door to follow us to the stairs. I hope he doesn't start barking again."

When both ghosts passed through the door, Leo whimpered at first, then went back to his dog basket. He remained silent but didn't sleep though. His eyes were fully alert.

Laticia followed Rachel up the stairs. On the landing she pointed out her father's room and then Gavin's. Gentle snoring was coming from both rooms. Rachel turned towards Laticia excitedly. "Did you hear that?"

"Yes. Does that mean we'll be able to hear them talk?" Laticia was as enthusiastic as Rachel.

"We can hear humans in the graveyard so why not here?" Rachel replied. She frowned thinking over what Laticia had said.

"I dunno. It's a bit funny like. Now we're ghosts and in a house. Maybe we can hear the snoring because the sounds are made

through different air waves in the body." Laticia suggested.

"Interesting theory but I don't buy it. Think about it. If we can hear them snoring then we'll be able to hear them talking. What difference does it make whether humans talk in the graveyard or in this house? We will still be able to hear them. If we can't, then it will make our task even more difficult." Rachel pointed out.

Laticia shrugged. "Alright. I get it. Which is your room?"

Rachel led the way across the landing to her old bedroom. Outside the door she stopped. "That's funny. I can hear snoring coming from here too."

"Maybe it's your ghost girl." Laticia giggled.

"Don't be daft. I'm the ghost!" Impatiently Rachel passed through the door and was shocked to see a form underneath the duvet on her bed.

"Who is that?" Laticia asked as she placed herself beside Rachel.

"I've no idea."

Rachel glided towards the end of the bed and peered into the sleeper's face. Then she shrank back as she recognised the slumbering countenance.

"It's Phil Redwood. My brother's friend from Transylvania."

"What's he doing here?"

Rachel shrugged. "At a guess I would say Gavin invited him here to help discover my murderer. Mum mentioned that Gavin was flying to Budapest to see Phil. She didn't

say that Gavin had asked him to come here."
"Does he have special powers?"
"According to Gavin he does. Phil claims to be a psychic, or clairvoyant or whatever you want to call him. He's not really from Transylvania, he just lives there."
"Let's wake him up and see if he can sense us. Or better still see us!" Laticia whispered.
"Why are you whispering?"
Laticia giggled. "I don't know. Considering I want to wake him up, that's a bit dumb isn't it?"
"Have you always been mischievous?" Rachel asked suddenly. She realised that she knew nothing about Laticia's background other than she was murdered by her husband, and that she came from a big family in Barbados.
"I suppose so. It was a means of survival living in a big family like mine. My brothers and sisters were always playing tricks either on me, or on each other and our friends. Nothing bad you know. It was just fun. Sometimes we did go a bit too far and the neighbours got angry with us. When that happened, my mum and dad got stricter with us. We behaved for a while, but it didn't last." She laughed.
Rachel laughed too. "Gavin and I used to aggravate each other but he was six years older than me, so it was a bit different. When I was twelve he started going out more and I didn't see much of him. Then he

went away to university and I only saw him on occasional weekends and the holidays. We were quite close though despite that."
"I was one of six. There was always one of my brothers or sisters around. I miss them." She turned her attention to the still shape in the bed. "Shall we wake him or not?"
"How?"
"Well blow on him or something, or whisper down his ear maybe?"
"I don't think it's such a good idea to do either of those things you suggest."
Rachel glanced at her digital alarm clock that was still perched on her old dressing table. It was two o clock. "If we wake him now, that's if we can, I don't even know how we would do it, we don't know what effect we will have on him. He might think he's dreaming. Let's wait until tomorrow morning when he wakes up naturally. I'm looking forward to hearing what they say to each other over the breakfast table."
Laticia shrugged. "Suit yourself. I can't wait to see what power we can summon up. Let's make ourselves comfortable in this room. I like it. You were lucky to have such a nice bedroom. That rug on the floor looks soft and inviting. I will hover down there and you can rest on that arm chair in the corner. It looks like a recliner."
"It is. Some of my best friends have slept on that over the years. It turns into a bed." Rachel glided across to perch herself on the armchair.

"We ought to practise our powers of levitation, now we are free of the cemetery." Laticia commented. She was restless and very excited. "It's all very well that the Assessors said we would learn them gradually as soon as we passed through the barriers, but they could at least have given us a few tips."

Rachel agreed. "One of the Assessors said to practise on something light first, like a piece of paper. There's plenty of loose computer printer paper in those desk drawers, that's if my mum hasn't removed it. The thing is I doubt I have the strength to open them." She fixed her eyes on the desk and concentrated on trying to open a drawer. Nothing budged. After a few minutes she gave up. Her eyes roved around the room and then fell on a 'Save Wild Animals' calendar hanging on the wall. It was the type that had one page to a month. The days of the month were displayed under the picture of an animal in danger of extinction. Each month depicted one of many threatened species.

April 2018 stared at Rachel still with all her coded notes written on various parts of the animal. She knew that on each calendar month was hidden the mobile numbers of past boyfriends. The initials of each had been carefully written in either the ears or another convenient part of an animal depicted on the calendar. Copied from small pieces of paper tucked into her jeans pockets, then disposed of, the numbers were kept secret. Rachel smirked. Her mother would never have guessed to look there when she came snooping in her room. Apart from lectures about "safe sex" and "don't do it until you meet the right one," Anna always looked for clues in her daughter's room for signs of new boyfriends.

If Anna had known about the two she had slept with during the first term at Uni, she would have probably lectured Rachel about the dangers of sleeping around. Rachel had no remorse. It had been safe experimental sex. Nothing serious. Besides, how was she to know if she had the 'right one' as her mother put it, if she hadn't tried sex with them?

Anna had lived through the permissive sixties and seventies, Rachel doubted that her mother hadn't had sex before she met her dad. Dan was ten years older than Anna and she was well into her twenties when they married. Rachel had seen some of the photographs of her mother with her friends, all of them in hippy clothes. She grinned. One day she would tackle her mother about that.

"I'm going to try to lift that Tiger on the calendar." Rachel decided.

"OK."

Nothing happened. Rachel sighed and shrugged at Laticia. "It's hopeless."

"Keep trying."

Again nothing happened.

After a few minutes Laticia said she would try. However before she could get into position and concentrate on her task there came a groan from the bed. Both ghosts swivelled their heads towards Phil. They watched as he began to move his arms in a swaying motion over his head.

"Do you think he can sense us?" Rachel asked. She was whispering despite herself.

"I don't know. It seems a strange thing to do to wave his arms around like that. It's like as if he is trying to grasp something. Maybe you've willed him to get the calendar."

"That doesn't make sense." Rachel said doubtfully, allowing her eyes to stray again from Phil to the wall. The calendar faced the bed, and Rachel was hovering at the side of the bed where Phil lay.

"I suppose my energy could have got miss-directed." She muttered. "I don't know what I'm doing. Maybe if I got up closer to the wall I could try again."

Laticia nodded. She was distracted as she drifted over Phil watching his face twitching. They both observed him for a while, until he relaxed again. "Perhaps he's having a bad dream." Laticia drawled.

"Maybe." Rachel agreed. "Anyway I have an idea. Why don't we both try to lift April on the calendar? Our combined strength might do it. If we both get closer to it."

"OK. Good idea."

Both ghosts moved position so that they hovered at the foot of the bed and faced the calendar.

"After three." Rachel instructed. "One, two three."

After a few seconds the page began to lift. "It's moving! Laticia said excitedly. Her excitement caused her to lose concentration and the page dropped back in place. In the same instant Phil began to raise his arms again. This time they were stretched towards the calendar. Both ghosts glanced at him and exchanged a puzzled look. When Phil settled back they tried again. This time the page with the Tiger flipped up quite high. Simultaneously Phil sat up in bed. His eyes were closed but again his arms were flailing around. As soon as Rachel's and Laticia's attention was distracted from the calendar, Phil flopped back on his bed. Both ghosts floated over him examining his face.

"He's sound asleep." Rachel observed. "Did we make him do that, or was it a coincidence?"

"Let's do it again, to see if it works." Laticia was enjoying herself.

Together they concentrated on the calendar. Again the Tiger page lifted, higher this time. Phil also shot up in bed as he did before. Gently they released the calendar and allowed him to fall back in bed still asleep.

"We did it. Yet I can't feel the power. I don't know how to gauge the strength. Let me try

on my own." Laticia said. She positioned herself in front of the Tiger. Rachel observed her ally from the arm chair as once more Laticia concentrated on the picture. Then very slowly it began to flap about. Phil stirred slightly but otherwise remained flat on his bed.

"That's better. Now let me try." Rachel said. "I'm going to do it from here."

After a few minutes Rachel too achieved the same affect. This time, though, Phil turned over in his bed. His face protruded from under the sheet opposite Rachel's reclining form on the arm chair.

"Did I cause him to do that, or was that a natural sleep movement?"

"I'm not sure. Try it again."

Rachel concentrated hard on the majestic beast in the calendar. Suddenly the calendar flew off the wall and Phil shot up into a sitting position with his arms up in the air."

"Too much energy!" Laticia exclaimed. "Try raising it off the bed and looping it back on to the hook."

"That's going to be even more difficult to achieve." Rachel relaxed for a few seconds and Phil dropped back on to the pillow.

"Don't give up. We need to practise." Laticia coaxed.

Rachel glared at the offending document and began to concentrate. The calendar began to rise off the bed but so did Phil. He remained in a sitting position with his eyes closed in sleep. As the calendar glided back to its original position, Phil's arms stretched towards it as if trying to grasp it.

"Steady now, ease off a bit." Laticia advised excitedly. "Nearly there."

At last the calendar hooked itself back into place. Rachel relaxed and Phil slumped back on the pillows.

We've cracked it!" Rachel exclaimed.

Laticia agreed. "We just need to practice a bit more to learn how to control our strength."

"If I could, I would give you a high five. Let's mimic it anyway." Rachel said gleefully.

"Done. Now let's see what happens tomorrow."

Chapter Seven

Phil Redwood (The Psychic)

It was seven o clock when Phil woke up. He drew back the curtains and opened a small window. Another bright and sunny day beckoned. He felt a bit light headed, as if he hadn't slept. Walking cautiously to the bathroom to see if it was free, he sensed something like a breeze on his arm. He turned towards the window. "Maybe there's a bit of wind outside." He muttered.

Pleased that the bathroom was free, he showered and returned to his room to get dressed. Last night Phil found Rachel's old room to be quite peaceful, but now he felt there was something strange about it. He had an uneasy feeling in his stomach. He dismissed the notion that it might be the effects of the red wine he had shared last night with Gavin and his father. They had got through two bottles between them. It had been a pleasant evening despite their obvious grief over first Rachel and then Anna.

It was four years since Phil was last in this house. On that occasion he had slept on a camp bed in Gavin's room. Though it was a large and spacious house, it offered just three bedrooms. Now, because of terrible circumstances he was staying in Rachel's old room. His expression turned to a grimace as he thought of what had happened to his friend's sister. He had been horrified when Gavin had told him the devastating news a year earlier.

Phil combed his shoulder length wavy hair still wet from the shower, then made his way downstairs to the kitchen. He needed a strong cup of tea to get him going in the mornings. Dan was already there. He was measuring ground coffee into a cafetiere.

"Good morning." Phil said cheerfully.

Dan reciprocated with an offer of coffee. Phil shook his head. "I'd rather tea if you don't mind."

"Tea bag in a mug or shall I make you a pot?"

Phil smiled apologetically. "A pot full would be great. I drink a lot of the stuff, especially in the mornings."

Dan refilled the kettle and told Phil to sit down in the dining room. "Help yourself to cereals." He called. "I'll make the toast when Gavin gets down. I heard him stir a few minutes ago, so he won't be long. He'll be needing this no doubt." Dan put the coffee pot on to the table. Phil poured himself some orange juice and then helped himself to some cornflakes just as Gavin sat down beside him. *Rachel and Laticia followed him in to the dining room.*

"OK mate? Sleep alright?"

Phil nodded. When Dan returned to the kitchen Phil whispered to Gavin that he had felt a strange presence in Rachel's room during the night.

"Well that's to be expected isn't it? Seeing as it's her old room. Some of her stuff is still in there, though a large proportion of her clothes and books went to the charity shops. Mum kept just a few of her treasured things. I always feel as if she is still in there when I go in to her room."

"Yes I get that." Phil replied patiently. "Everything appears normal and you want to convince yourself that she is still alive even though common sense tells you that she isn't. It's really like a memory distorting your sorrow. Part of the brain doesn't want to accept the reality. It's a natural reaction to grief. And I have to admit that when I first went into her bedroom I didn't want to believe she was gone. However, Thursday night I slept well and I felt relaxed the next day – yesterday - and the room seemed calm."

Phil fixed his eyes earnestly on to Gavin's drawn tired face. "Last night, just before I got into bed, again I felt a calm peaceful atmosphere in the room. "But during the night something changed."

Gavin frowned. Then he shivered as a cool breeze lightly touched his neck. He got up to close the window. However when he got to the window he realised that it wasn't open. Absently he rubbed his neck with his hand. *Meanwhile Rachel and Laticia wafted under the window and settled themselves on the chairs underneath it.*

"I think Gavin can sense us!" Rachel whispered. Laticia nodded. *"It must be our*

combined presence. We are stronger together."

Phil was about to elaborate on his experience, but held back when Dan returned from the kitchen with a pot of tea for Phil. Simultaneously the fire alarm started to go off. He put the teapot on the table and came back a few seconds later with a plate of partly burnt toast. "Sorry about that. I forgot about it. I don't think it's too bad. We've run out of bread so I can't make any more."

Before either man could say anything Leo began to bark.

"Right on cue. The dog always barks when I burn the toast." Dan shrugged apologetically to Phil and hurried back to the kitchen to turn off the alarm.

"I'll bring him in here that will reassure him." Gavin got up to open the door to allow Leo into the dining room. Dan followed him in and shut the kitchen door again. Instead of making a beeline for Gavin or Dan as he usually did, the dog headed towards Rachel and began to wag his tail making a pining noise at the same time. Eventually he sat down contentedly on what he thought was Rachel's knee. Though he couldn't feel any of her body he appeared to be comforted. The dog curled up with doleful eyes resting on Dan.

"Well he hasn't done that before." Dan said. He sat down and seized a piece of toast, scraped some of the burnt bits off then spread it with butter and strawberry jam.

Before he took a bite he glanced from Phil to Gavin.

"What makes me think you were in the middle of an important conversation?"

Before either man could respond, Dan continued. He turned to Phil. "I know why you are here, and whilst in the past I have been sceptical about your extra sensory powers or whatever you want to call them, I know Gavin has faith in you. If faith is the right word." He paused. "But I fervently desire to know who killed my daughter, and if you think you can help, then I'm in. So please don't try to whisper behind my back."

"Well done dad." Rachel muttered. She caught Laticia's delight and they exchanged a smile.

"Dad, Phil was just explaining to me that most people experience some kind of energy when they go into a room. It's like when you go into a crowded room or a pub and you can feel an atmosphere of some kind."

Dan nodded whilst he chewed his toast.

"The feeling can be accelerated when you are in a familiar place where you used to visit with someone you cared about, but is now deceased." Gavin explained. "Especially when you are still grieving."

Again Dan nodded.

This time Phil spoke. "When I arrived here two days ago, I felt your grief and Gavin's too here in this house, and for a little while I sensed some of it in Rachel's room. But during the night, that is – last night - I detected something even stronger. It was almost as if she was in the room with me."

Rachel and Laticia caught each other's eyes. They shone with glee.

"Are you sure it wasn't the effect of all that wine we drank last night?"

Phil looked put out and Dan instantly apologised.

"Please go on." Dan insisted.

"I'd been asleep for a while I know, then I kind of half woke up. You know, that kind of hypnopompic state of being between sleep and wakefulness?"

"I know what you mean, but I didn't know it was called that." Dan responded. "I suppose you mean dreamlike."

Phil nodded. "Yes but it wasn't that. It felt like a strange sensation creeping over my body. Almost as if something or somebody was telling me to get up. The feeling was overpowering and it was as if the room was filled with energy. I wasn't fully awake, I was in that heavy dreamlike state, you've just mentioned, yet I wasn't. I'm sure it wasn't a dream."

Dan wasn't convinced. He assumed Phil had slept heavily and had dreamed vividly as a consequence. But he didn't want to hurt Phil's feelings. He knew he meant well.

"I have once or twice felt like that after a bad dream." Gavin offered. He wanted to support his friend and wanted to believe him.

"That's because we lifted the month of April off the calendar." Rachel whispered to Laticia.

"Maybe it was the tiger in the picture." Laticia giggled. "It's nearly the end of April, what have you got for May girl?"

"I can't remember, but it's likely to be a rhino!"

"Ouch. Well let's hope we don't need to bring one into your bedroom!"

"So do you think Rachel is trying to get in touch with you through her bedroom?" Gavin asked his friend hopefully.

"Maybe. I don't know. There might be a clue in her room. I still haven't examined all her personal possessions yet. As you know yesterday was taken up with visiting my relatives, but today I want to concentrate on the case. I was thinking of walking down to the cemetery today."

"We'll come with you. Is that alright, Dad?"

"Yes. We need to take Leo for a walk, then we can call in the village for some bread."

When the time came to leave the house. Leo refused to get up.

"Come on Leo." Dan entreated. "This is unusual. Any chance to go for a walk and he's normally up and waiting by the door before me."

Rachel got up and wafted towards the kitchen and then the porch that led to the outside doorway. Immediately Leo began to bark and follow her.

"That's odd. He doesn't usually behave like this." Dan frowned.

"Maybe it's because Phil is here." Gavin suggested.

Phil agreed. "The dog is probably perplexed that Rachel and Anna have gone, and now I am here, a relative stranger. Though he did recognise me when I got here even after so many years."

As they walked along the garden path, Laticia hovered behind Phil, and suddenly Leo turned to bark at her. Phil assumed he was the reason for causing Leo's behaviour and he bent to pat the dog. Leo ignored him and ran around the back of him. Puzzled, Phil twisted around after the dog and felt a strange sensation assault his whole body, as Laticia's transparent form slipped through him to join Rachel at the front of the group. Instantly Leo leapt forward practically tripping Phil in the process. He stumbled into Dan who helped the man to right himself. Once he was sure Phil was stable he put the lead on the dog's collar and Leo settled down. Rachel hovered beside him and Leo wagged his tail in delight.

"That's a good boy." Dan said. He was just as puzzled about the dog's behaviour as Phil. "Are you ok? He asked him?"

"Yes. Fine. He's probably having a funny five minutes. Maybe it's the unusual weather we're having. It's quite warm already."

Inwardly Phil was not convinced. Neither was Gavin. Both felt that Leo was reacting to an unexplained phenomena that surrounded and lingered on Phil.

Chapter Eight

The Cemetery

Rachel guessed they would visit her mother's grave first, so she and Laticia lured Leo to Anna's graveside. He seemed content to stay there whilst Rachel and Laticia draped themselves a little distance away over Rachel's grave stone. They scanned the area looking for their fellow spirits.
"They are probably keeping cool in the crypt." Laticia gasped. The bright sunlight affects us just as much as humans. Strange that. Isn't it?"
"Yes, I can feel my energy dissipating."
"Dissipating! That's a good word girl, considering your power is scarcely strong!" Laticia said sarcastically. They giggled as they glided to a yew tree for shade.

Gavin and Phil watched Dan as he took his mobile phone out of his pocket. Phil frowned as Gavin explained.

"Mum wanted to be buried with her mobile so that dad could contact her and hear her voice. At least so she said. I think she had some wild idea that she would be able to communicate with him in her grave. Anyway, dad promised he would." Gavin shrugged, embarrassed that he had told his friend about this little idiosyncrasy of his mother's.

Incredulously Phil gazed at Dan. He realised how much he had loved his wife to indulge her in such an odd request, even though he had always been sceptical about anything that smacked of the supernatural.

Silently Phil and Gavin witnessed Dan punch in the mobile number and waited. There was no sound though Leo began to bark and jump on the half-dead flowers.

"As I suspected." Dan said. "The battery has gone. I would have been astonished if it lasted this long. Five days."

"Some mobiles last a few days if you don't use them too often." Gavin commented. "Leo's acting strange today. Do you think he knows mum is under here?"

Dan didn't answer. He was preoccupied with the grave. "I suppose we had better get rid of these dead flowers and tidy up the place."

Phil studied the dog's strange antics and wondered if Leo could sense something paranormal.

The three men spent half an hour clearing the grave. *By the time they had finished Anna came floating across the cemetery. She was accompanied by Margareta. They joined Rachel and Laticia under the yew tree.*

"A family reunion!" Anna exclaimed.

"Hardly." Rachel commented grinning. Half dead and half alive!"

"You know what I mean. Have you got anything to report?" Anna glanced casually

at her daughter, whilst devoting most of her attention to her husband and son.
"Not a lot, but something. Leo suspects something." Laticia teased.
"A fat lot of good that will be." Anna retorted. "It's nice to see Phil here."
Rachel explained what had happened so far.
"So Phil is aware of your presence. That's good."
"Yes, but how we can cash in on that is going to take some figuring out." Rachel replied. "Look, they've finished at your graveside, they are probably going to go to mine now."

From the yew tree Anna, Margareta and the two ghosts observed the three men walking towards Rachel's resting place. All three gazed at the headstone. They stood there silently.

"So young." Phil commented at last.

Rachel couldn't resist sashaying across to the site. Immediately Leo began to bark. Rachel turned her head so she could observe her mother's reaction to the dog's behaviour. Anna inclined her head as a signal that she had witnessed the scene.

"I would like to visit the place she was found." Phil spoke, breaking the silence. He sensed the grief of his companions. He was also bewildered by the dog's behaviour today. Leo wasn't like this yesterday. He considered the possibility that Rachel's spirit was guarding her grave and somehow Leo was picking it up.

Gavin nodded. He looked nervously at his father. He knew he hated to go there, but Dan agreed. "I have to do this."

The trio left Rachel's grave and made their way back towards the lych gate. *Anna and Margareta decided to accompany them as far as they were able within the confines of the graveyard. Rachel and Laticia with the excited dog led the procession.*

When they drew level with a newly wreathed grave that had encompassed just one leg of an unfortunate victim, they paused in sad respect.

"Poor old Stefan Kadinsky." Gavin said as he absently straightened one of the white lilies. It had worked loose from a bouquet and trailed down listlessly and as lifeless as the occupant in the coffin.

"Do you remember him Phil? He was on that computer course we both did a few years ago at Greenfield College."

"Hell yes. I do. He was a whiz kid with electronics and all that. Star student if I recall. What happened?"

"He had the misfortune of being in the wrong place at the wrong time. He was driving past a house on his way home from work when a gas explosion in that particular house ripped through his car. His leg was blown off but the rest of him was scattered into pieces along with the bits that were left of his car and the wall of the house."

Phil was shocked. "Poor bugger. He was a nice guy."

Gavin nodded. "He was studying to be a solicitor. He would have been a good one."

"So was this recently?" Phil asked. He picked up one of the cards on the wreaths and read out the message. "**To our wonderful son. We will never forget you.**"

"Actually it was several months ago." Gavin said thoughtfully. "This must be his second funeral."

"His what?" Phil frowned at Gavin then turned his head towards Dan hoping that one of them would give him an explanation.

"Stefan's parents were anxious to have a funeral and at the time, all the police and gas experts could find was his leg. Forensics took away what was left of the car along with bits of poor Stefan for analysis. It seems they have managed to separate enough metal from the debris to make their report. They also had the unsavoury task of separating bits of Stefan's body from the metal and the rubble from the house. Nobody else was injured. The various authorities involved, agreed that what was left of him could be buried alongside his leg. It was in the local paper."

Dan nodded his head. He was busy reading the messages of condolences. *Anna stood by his side. She tried hard to make him see her. He seemed to sense her presence and glanced up once or twice to turn his head towards the direction of Anna's grave.*

"Hence two funerals." Phil murmured.

"Yes." Gavin affirmed. "Come on let's get out of here before I get too maudlin." He continued his way towards the lych gate and Phil and Dan followed.

"So that explains why we haven't seen anything from that grave." Rachel confided in Laticia.

"I wonder how much of the rest of his body they managed to salvage. It would be nice if they could make him whole."

Anna and Margareta followed them to the boundary of the cemetery and watched the troupe make their way towards the lake. Rachel looked back over her shoulder to wave to her mother. In those few seconds she noticed that unobtrusively the spirit of Stefan Kadinsky had risen from his grave. She watched as his shape joined the side of her mother. She was pleased to see that his body was intact.

If Rachel had been standing closer to him she would have observed that two fingers on Stefan's left hand were missing and so was one eye. His face was a patchwork where the flesh had been pieced together. Rachel would also have seen her mother scrutinise Stefan with interest. It had amused her to call him the bionic spirit!

When they reached the spot where Rachel's body was found Gavin glanced protectively at his father. Dan was holding up well. He seemed to have changed over the last few days. A calm acceptance appeared to have swept over him. He himself felt different. He wasn't sure if it was Phil's presence or whether this was part of the grieving process.

"Apparently Rachel was still alive when those two young lads found her." Dan explained to Phil. "She was in the water lying on her back. Those evil bastards had left her there evidently unconcerned whether she survived or not. They probably hoped she'd drown but couldn't risk hanging around any longer to see it through, in case there were witnesses."

Dan breathed deeply before continuing. "This is such a lovely area I'm surprised that no-one else was in the vicinity." He sighed. "Still I suppose sometimes these occurrences happen – a natural interlude. I mean where suddenly it is quiet, before other people make a presence."

Phil nodded. "Yes, I know what you mean. Rachel was unlucky. Her assailants had the luck. It's like those odd occasions when you drive down a usually busy road, when for two or three minutes or so there's no traffic."

"At that time in the evening this part of the lake wouldn't have been busy. All the rowers and yachts would have returned to the boat house." Gavin gesticulated with his arm towards the opposite edge of the vast lake. Besides it would have been quite dark."

"Why do you think the assailants were hanging around Saint Winefride's well?" Phil asked. "That's where she was supposed to be, right?"

"They might have been using the new footpath that leads from the opposite end of the cathedral to get to town." Gavin suggested.

Phil frowned. "What path?"

Gavin explained. "Since you went away to Transylvania, a piece of land almost adjacent to the cathedral has been used to build more houses. When the builders finished, they created another access road that leads to the town. However, the town planners also felt it would be convenient for the new residents to have a footpath that gives people easy access to the famous landmarks. Some people have been using it as a short cut to get to the lake. I know that some locals use it to walk to the new pub that was also built near the new housing development. It's called *The Black Raven*. Gavin paused. He was struggling to feel calm.

"My theory is that the thugs had come from the direction of the pub and were walking down the path towards the old part of town when they saw Rachel. They made a nuisance of themselves, she tried to get away and they followed her here."

"Not a bad theory, but not quite right." Rachel commented.

"So you are sure there were two people who contributed to her murder?" Phil said.

Dan nodded. "The police are convinced there were two. The bruises on her body strongly suggested that they were rained on her by two brutes."

Phil cast his eyes around the local beauty spot. "Are there any surveillance cameras around here?"

Gavin shook his head. "There is CCTV closer to Winefride's well, and there is one over by the boat house. Neither of them reach this area. The authorities obviously felt there was no need for one over here. This bit including the area near the lych gate is out of range. Protecting the abbey and the well has priority."

Phil stood quietly surveying the land immediately surrounding him. It had been a few years since he had last visited Holywell. Memories began to flood back.

"Despite the local council giving planning permission to builders to develope, this section at least has been saved. I'm pleased about that. There are no houses around as far as the eye can see, yet I know within a mile from here there are plenty. My previous home being one of them." Phil sighed. "So we have no witnesses other than the last two young men to see Rachel alive."

"Not quite." Dan said quietly. "She was fading away when they found her in the lake. They pulled her out of the water, though not far from the edge. They could see she had a lot of injuries and they didn't want to make it worse. As one 'phoned for an ambulance two more young men arrived. They were from the boat house."

"I don't recall seeing them!" Rachel gasped.

"You were probably unconscious by then, or at least semi-conscious." Laticia suggested.

"You don't think the two men who found Rachel were the same two men who beat Rachel up, and they just pretended to help?" Phil asked gently.

"I think the police suspected that. I know they were both interviewed but were never detained. They also interviewed the other two men from the boat club. In fact no-one was detained, though I know the police made a lot of door to door inquiries." Dan said.

"Forensics?" Phil asked. He asked the question hesitantly. It was a delicate question knowing how Rachel had been raped before being left for dead.

Dan shook his head. "The water and the mud had contaminated everything. They found a large stone in the water, which they suspected may have been used to hit her but there was nothing on it to give them a clue."

"Due to the water and mud?" Phil suggested. He felt Dan was being remarkably brave.

"Yes."

"Whoever did this, covered their tracks, or they were very lucky that no trace was left on Rachel to lead the police back to them." Gavin said.

"Perhaps we could stroll down to the boat club and have a look around, and ask a few questions." Phil suggested.

"It can't do any harm." Gavin agreed. "I used to know a couple of people who work there."

"Can you remember the names of the two men from the boat club who helped the men who rescued her?" Phil asked.

"I'm afraid I've forgotten. But I think someone there might remember. What do you think dad?"

"It's a good place to start." Dan consented.

"If they find something we can follow it up." Laticia said.

Rachel agreed. "I think we should take a look at the boat club too."

Together they glided ahead of the three men. As they floated away Leo began to bark and chase after them.

"There is definitely something up with that dog today." Dan scratched his almost bald head absently as he watched the dog jump in the air as if he were catching flies.

"Perhaps he can sense Rachel's spirit here." Gavin suggested.

Phil agreed. "It's possible."

Chapter Nine

The Lakeside Sailing and Rowing Boat Club

Saturday mornings were always busy at the boat club during the spring and summer months. Some members moored their small yachts at a holding area at the side of the club. These were anchored and individually linked to a long length of chain. Most of the rowing boats for hire were stored in a shed usually referred to as the boat house. A few were left outside and secured on a chain similar to the security system used to fasten up the yachts. The keys and 'signing in and out' book for all these crafts were kept in the office. That morning in the reception area, several yacht owners maintained a steady pace of coming and going, whilst members of the public queued up at the reception desk to hire rowing boats for the day.
Gavin, Dan and Phil waited for the receptionist to become free. Dan kept a tight hold of Leo.
Rachel and Laticia took the opportunity to hover down a corridor, then the stairs that led to the staff locker room. They counted twenty one.
"That's a lot of staff even for a huge lake like this." Laticia commented.
"Some of them are volunteers who only work at weekends. There are also two engineers and an electrician as well as the secretary and chair of the club. The three

patrol wardens and the four guys who assist the public with the rowing boats make up the rest of the team." Rachel advised. *She was concentrating on trying to widen the opening of the door on one of the lockers. It hadn't been locked.*

"You seem to know a lot about this place already."

"I volunteered myself a couple of years ago. Jade and I wanted to get to know some of the workers here. So we both came on a Saturday morning."

"What you mean is you fancied some blokes!" Laticia smirked knowingly.

Rachel laughed. "Yep. It didn't work out though. The two blokes had girlfriends. They were older than us too, so after a few months, we gave up. It was the end of summer then, and we both went off to Uni."

Laticia joined Rachel's side and concentrated on trying to help her prise open the locker door. It didn't move.

"This isn't as easy as lifting paper on the calendar."

"No. I think we just have to keep testing our strength. There's nothing in there anyway, probably because you can't lock it. I've stuck my head through the door to have a look. I just wanted to try to get a door open. Let's go back to the reception area and see if the queue has lessened."

"Are those blokes that you and Jade fancied still here?" Laticia asked as they made their way down the corridor again.

"I don't know. I don't think so. They may have moved away, or got married, left the country. Who knows?"

"You don't think they are connected with your assault?"

"No. I'm pretty sure. Besides although they weren't interested romantically with Jade and me, they were kind to us and were friendly. If I had seen them in the street they would have stopped to talk to me, so I think we can rule them out."

"What were their names?"

"Derek Jones and Lester Price."

To Rachel's astonishment, they arrived at the reception desk to hear her brother utter those same names. The young receptionist to whom Gavin had directed the question shook her head.

"Derek doesn't work here anymore. He left well over a year ago. Lester is out on the patrol boat at the moment. He will be back here in about….ten minutes for his morning break." She glanced at her watch. "He usually swaps with Jamie or Maxwell round about now. Can I help at all?"

Dan started to explain that they wanted to talk to him about a personal matter, but Gavin interrupted. "Actually we want to talk to anyone here who knows anything about the murder that happened near the lake."

The receptionist's expression changed and she looked anxious. "Are you journalists?"

"We're not journalists. We're friends of the deceased." Phil started to explain.

The receptionist eyed Phil suspiciously.

Gavin took a deep breath. "She was my sister."

Something in Gavin and Dan's manner convinced the receptionist they were telling the truth.

"You need to speak to Jamie Weston and Maxwell Briggs. They are the ones who went to help. I believe it was too late though. I'm awfully sorry. It was terrible."

Extremely sympathetic now, the receptionist reached for the PA system. Young and slight though she appeared, her voice was strong and boomed out the words. "**Jamie Weston and Maxwell Briggs to reception please**."

Dan looked uncomfortable on hearing this message and went to stand near the doorway with Leo. Just outside the entrance door there was a wooden terrace with a seating area, Dan sat down to face the lake. Phil and Gavin joined him on the terrace though they remained standing. They stood facing the reception door expectantly waiting for the two men to arrive at the reception desk.

A few minutes later Jamie Weston and Maxwell Briggs arrived in the foyer. The receptionist intercepted the two men and pointed them to the terrace. They both went outside to introduce themselves.

Dan got up to greet them. "I never got the chance to thank you for helping the night of my daughter's murder." He said quietly.

Each man shook Dan's hand and murmured their condolences. They backed away slightly as there was little space on the terrace. Dan returned to his seat and allowed Gavin to conduct the conversation with the newcomers. Jamie placed himself next to Dan and faced Phil. Maxwell stood with one foot on the wooden terrace step and another on the path with his back to the lake and gave his attention to Gavin.

Laticia and Rachel hovered near the door to observe the interaction between the two men and Gavin and Phil.

"Do you recognise them?" Laticia asked.

Rachel was studying Jamie's face. "No. I can't sense any connection. Not with him anyway."

"Do you suppose you will feel a connection?"

Rachel shrugged. "I was assuming so. Now I am not so sure. Like you said I was probably unconscious when they arrived."

Laticia observed them thinking wildly. "You described your attackers as tall and of a heavy build. Do you think these could be them? You know. Like maybe, after they left you, they came back to finish you off, or something. I don't know, but when they got to you, those other two men found you first so they had to pretend to help?" She trailed off as she tried to imagine another possibility.

Rachel looked alarmed. "Do you think that's what happened?"

Laticia shrugged. "Just a theory. It might've been like that."

"They both fit my flimsy description of my attackers I suppose." Rachel said slowly, digesting this theory. *They are quite tall and both have broad shoulders."*

"Go a bit closer." Laticia suggested.

Rachel edged herself closer towards Jamie, but nothing about him seemed familiar.

Dan remained sitting down looking worn out and dejected.

Rachel shifted her attention to her father and hovered over to his side away from Jamie, wishing she could offer some comfort.

Leo wagged his tail and panted excitedly. Absently Dan patted the dog's head.

Rachel turned away again to give her attention to the conversation that Gavin was holding with the young men.

"You didn't pass anyone suspicious when you came across Rachel and the other two rescuers?" Gavin asked. He directed his question at Maxwell Briggs. For some reason Gavin took a dislike to him. He tried to shake off the feeling.

Maxwell answered. "No. The police asked us both that on the night it happened. We had just finished our shift. We stop hiring out boats after six o clock so we can get them all back to clean up. We close up the place at seven thirty. Jamie and I locked up and walked along the lake path." He flicked his thick blonde fringe out of his eyes as he spoke. The hair on his head reached over the back of his collar. Maxwell scratched at his neck with one of his hands as he leaned against the terrace framework.

"There's something about his voice." Rachel whispered. *"But if I was unconscious I wouldn't have heard him."* She frowned.

"Could he have been your killer and not your rescuer?" Laticia suggested.

"Neither of my killers said much, just expletives. It's hard to say, if it was him, but I don't like him."

Laticia shrugged. She was listening intently.

Jamie was agreeing with Max. "All the boat hirers had left by seven o clock, there were a few stragglers as usual. I saw the last of them walk up the steps at the side of the boathouse to go over the old railway bridge. There's a car park there. It's not far from there to walk to the *Angel's Wings* if you wanted to go for a drink or something."

Gavin nodded. "Yes I know where you mean."

"You used to be able to get a drink here at the club bar, but it closed down two years ago for renovations, work hasn't started on it yet! Most people go into town for a drink now. That part of the building was old anyway." Jamie added conversationally. He leaned against the club wall as he looked Gavin in the eye.

"So why were you walking in the direction of St. Winefride's cathedral? If you don't mind my asking." Gavin asked.

Maxwell shrugged. "The police asked us that too. We usually go that way along the lake side path towards the cathedral, to get to *The Raven*. We were meeting people there for something to eat. They do nice bar meals. It's a new pub."

"What about the night before?" Phil asked suddenly. He directed his question towards Jamie who was now fumbling in his jacket pocket for a cigarette. "Any shady looking characters hanging around?"

Both men shook their heads.

"Jamie's wearing a blue jacket." Laticia whispered to Rachel.

Just then a tall and slender built man joined them. His strawberry blonde hair was cut very short. He strode confidently towards Dan and Gavin and took off his sun glasses to reveal his blue eyes gleaming with recognition.

Rachel turned to Laticia who had been keenly studying Jamie and Maxwell's body language. "Here's Lester Price. The guy I used to fancy. He's wearing a blue jacket too."

Laticia groaned.

Lester shook hands with first Gavin then Dan's. "I'm sorry to interrupt, but I need someone to relieve me on the patrol boat. He turned to Maxwell. "Max, can you take over please?"

"Sure." Maxwell moved away from the terrace steps. He eyed Dan dispassionately and ignored Gavin and Phil. "Sorry I can't be of any help. Like I said I told the police everything I know."

"Unfortunately the police don't tell us everything." Gavin muttered as he watched Maxwell swagger away to the lake. Lester heard him and threw Gavin a sympathetic glance. He turned his attention towards Dan.

"So sorry to hear about Rachel and your wife." He began to say. He sat down next to Dan.

Rachel and Laticia moved further along the terrace. This caused Leo to whine. Dan stroked the dog's head again to calm him down.

"He's still good looking." Rachel observed as she studied Lester's face. Meanwhile Laticia was trying to assess Jamie who had stood up almost to attention when Lester had appeared.

"Is there anything I can do to help?" Lester levelled his question to Gavin. They both knew each other from their school days. "You've had a tough year."

"You could say that." Gavin agreed. "You probably know that the police are still looking for Rachel's killers. We came down here to see if we could gather any more information to help track them down."

"Them. Are you saying there was more than one?"

"The police seem to think so." Gavin returned. Phil stepped forward. "I don't suppose you remember me? Phil Redwood."

"Phil! Yes I do. I've just been racking my brains trying to think where I'd seen you before. Do you still live around here then?"

"No. I left about six years ago, but I keep in touch with Gavin."

"We were wondering if you were around the night Rachel was killed or if you noticed anyone hanging around who looked suspicious." Gavin asked.

Lester shook his head and glanced at Jamie who was still standing to attention. He looked uncomfortable.

"The police asked us that." Lester answered. "They interviewed everyone here you know. Not formally you understand, just a few general questions. Actually I wasn't here the night it happened, I was in London. I had tickets for a jazz concert at the Palladium with my partner Lily. She's a big jazz fan. No doubt the police checked."

He caught Jamie's eye who nodded his head. "Yes, I've just explained that the police came here and asked us all these questions. It sounded like the police were just making routine inquiries. I don't think they've got anything to go on." He turned to the group. "If you don't mind, I need to get on with some work."

"Thank you for your time." Dan said.

"I'm sorry for your loss!" Jamie responded. "Sorry I couldn't do anything to help."

Dan inclined his head. Gavin and Phil both muttered their thanks and watched Jamie walk towards the boathouse.

"I was devastated too when I heard the news." Lester said. He turned to face Dan, leaning his back against the side of the wooden frame of the seat as he spoke. "She was a good kid. Ever since I was told the news, I've agonised over it, trying to think who would do such a thing. I've even walked up and down that path looking for clues. No doubt so have the police. Nothing about that area stood out as odd. Obviously the night it happened, I wasn't here as I've said, but I don't recall anything suspicious during the days leading up to it." He paused. Phil and Gavin gazed at him intently, both of them mentally willing him to remember something that would give them a clue.

"The only other thing I can remember about that particular week, was that we'd had a robbery at the souvenir shop and a few items had been stolen." Lester confided. "Not a big robbery, if you know what I mean. I think there was an opportune moment for a thief to swipe a few certain items when the staff weren't looking."

"What kind of things?" Phil asked.

"Mostly clothing. It's good quality stuff that we sell here. Fortunately it's all locked away in various cupboards and drawers. We just have a few things on display and it was the display things that were stolen. Two jackets and two sweatshirts were taken off the counter. We usually have four of each on the glass display counter. Whoever took them was careful not to take the lot, because it was not until the end of the day before we realised that they had been nicked."

Laticia and Rachel exchanged glances.

"What kind of jackets?" Gavin asked. He was unsure if it had any significance but he wanted something to think about.

"They are like this one I am wearing. Blue. We have two shades of blue. On one of the sleeves there is the logo of the club. 'St. Winefride's lake sailing and rowing club' in yellow print." Lester turned to his side to demonstrate one of the sleeves on his own jacket.

"Did you tell the police?" Dan asked.

"The manager of the shop informed the police, but I'm not sure it came to anything. Anyone could have taken them. We get a lot of visitors to the shop. They could even have been taken by members of the club. Many of them are wealthy but you would be surprised how mean one or two of them are and would try to get away with not paying if they could."

Lester got up. "Look I'm glad to see you again, but I have to get back to work in fifteen minutes. I've just got chance to grab a quick coffee and a snack."

They watched him go.

"What do you think?" Phil asked.

"Well I don't think Lester killed her." Dan said.

"I agree." Gavin said.

Phil nodded. "He's got an alibi. Do you think the other two were telling the truth?" He asked.

"Hard to tell, but I think so. What do you think dad?"

Dan sighed. "I really don't know what to believe." He glanced at his watch. "Why don't we walk over to the *Black Raven* and get an early lunch? We could ask some questions there. It sounds like it's a popular pub with these boat people. Maybe someone at the pub saw something that would give us a clue. I think I heard Rachel say that she had been there once with that boy she was seeing - Josh. Apparently they have live bands every now and again. Not my type of music."

"Fine by me dad. We might pick up some interesting gossip. That reminds me, I wanted to have a chat with Josh again. I haven't seen him since Rachel's funeral." Gavin replied.

"It would be nice to see this new pub that's been built in my old home town. I can take a look at the new housing development on those fields that the council saw fit to sell off. Have you been there before?" Phil asked as they strolled towards the cathedral. "I'm assuming we're going to take the new pathway behind Saint Winefride's well route?"

"No I haven't been to the pub. Yes we will take that route, though actually I have never been along that before, either. Have you dad?"

"No. There's never been any reason for me to go that way. I usually go to *The 'Winking Frog'* if I fancy a pint. It's closer to home."
Rachel and Laticia led the way back to a now very familiar place for all of them including the dog.

Chapter Ten

The Black Raven

On their way to the Black Raven the group were tagged as they passed through the graveyard. *Anna sidled along Rachel eagerly. "Any news?" Meanwhile the dog tried to circle Anna's legs. This confused Dan who was holding on to the lead. Momentarily distracted, Anna looked down at the dog.*
"Can Leo see me?"
"We're not positive, but we think so. He's been following us around and getting excited." Rachel replied.
"How wonderful. I wish I could pat him on his head." Anna replied. "Laticia are you still here? I thought you would have been on your way to Barbados by now. If the Assessors see you here they may withdraw your pass."
Laticia grimaced. "I hadn't thought of that. Perhaps I had better not come here again. I will keep outside the boundaries."
"Very wise. Now quick tell us what you have been doing!" Anna persisted. Several spirits known and not so well known to Rachel clustered around her. Graciously, more for her mother's sake, she gave them a hurried update on what had happened at the boat club. Glancing anxiously towards the back of the cathedral, she saw the receding outlines of her father, Gavin and Phil. She attempted to detach herself from

the group of spirits, though Anna followed her. One or two others lingered behind Anna as if waiting for instructions. She indicated that they should keep their distance. Rachel marvelled how her mother, within a few days, had managed to take charge of them all. Anna had lost no time in utilising her skills as a deputy head teacher.

"I'd better go with the rest of them now. They are on the way to the Black Raven.*" She said hastily.*

"Oh yes. The new development. I have heard of it." Anna said.

Hovering behind her was a new addition to the group. He beamed at Rachel.

"This is Stefan Kadinsky. He wants to help." Her mother said as she moved aside for Stefan to get closer to Rachel. Despite her impatient desire to leave, Rachel remained a little longer to gaze at Stefan's patchwork body. The stitches that sewed up one empty eye socket were just visible above a black plastic eyepatch. She would have liked to stay to talk to him, but was anxious to catch up with her father and brother and Phil.

"That's great. Pleased to meet you. We need all the help we can get. Sorry I must go. I will catch up with you later when they are back at home. Dad wants a pub lunch."

"Good for him." Anna said cheerfully.

Anna's little troupe of spirits followed Rachel and Laticia as far as they could. Soon the two ghosts caught up with the living trio. As the entire company progressed down the pathway through a housing estate, they eventually became out of the spirits' vision. Anna and her allies remained hovering on the cathedral's inside boundary wall.

"All that building work that's going on will transform the town beyond recognition Margareta complained. "At least I have my memories of what it used to be like before I died ten years ago."

Desmond and Tom agreed with her. "New developments aren't always a good thing."

"I wouldn't mind having a look at this new pub." Big Steve said.

"Actually it's very nice. Very modern if you like that kind of thing." Stefan offered. "They have a good choice of beers and wines. The food is good too."

At that moment Dan was surveying the menu in the *Black Raven* whilst Gavin and Phil went to the bar to get drinks.

Rachel and Laticia lingered around the bar whilst their eyes scanned the room. It was obviously a well-supported place. Saturday lunch time seemed to be popular.

"Considering a lot of pubs are closing down, it's nice that this pub which is new seems to be doing alright." Gavin commented as he sipped his pint of beer.

Phil sighed. "Yes the traditional pubs seem to have gone, and meanwhile we get places like this lined with television screens everywhere you look. This one isn't too bad. They have got the right idea to put screens in one big room for those who want to watch sport, whilst they have kept this room for people who want to chat. My wife Clare can't bear going to a pub with TV screens." He laughed. "We walk miles to avoid them. Cheers."

Gavin thanked and paid the barman then picked up his pint, whilst Phil carried his own and Dan's to the table.

Dan put down the menu. "I think I will have the cod goujon pieces with chips."

After studying the menu for a few minutes, Phil went to the bar to order their food. After he had done that, he decided to buy more drinks, but had to wait to be served again. As he waited, he noticed that just to the right of the bar there were two young girls eating their meal. They had both discarded their jackets and bags and had put them on a spare chair at the side of their table.

Rachel pointed to the wooden chair where the garments lay. "Can you see those jackets over there?"

"Yeah. What of them? We are looking for men's jackets."

Before Rachel could retort that very often couples wore similar jackets, or that girls nicked their boyfriends' clothes, a tall, thick set man appeared through the door and sat beside the girls. His appearance sparked a peculiar sensation within Rachel.

"That man seems familiar." She confided. Laticia glanced around her and scrutinised the man Rachel had pointed out to her.

"Do you know where you've seen him before?"

Rachel shook her head. "No, not really." She frowned trying to think where she might have seen him, then allowed herself to be distracted by the jackets. She gave her attention to her companion.

"I've got an idea." Laticia said. "Why don't we try to make those jackets slip on to the floor? Then we can try to see the logo. That's if there is one. At least it will give us something to do."

"Hmm. Great. Can we do it? It might be easier than that flamin' metal locker in the boat club." Rachel commented. She was as anxious as Laticia to test her strength.

"Combined effort could work. Keep an eye out for Phil's arm though. We might raise that too! I wouldn't like him to spill his pint!"

Giggling they drifted across to the table. They positioned themselves each side of the wooden chair and concentrated on trying to move the jackets. For a few seconds nothing happened, then to their delight one began to slip down the side of the chair. Both ghosts took time to rest. They congratulated themselves on their efforts.

"At least they are engaged in conversation so they won't see what is happening." Rachel commented.

Together they tried again. This time one of the jackets slid completely to the floor. The other garment had been pulled along with the first one, though half of it stayed on the chair. It stayed in place because a section of it was captured by the weight of the girls' shoulder bags.

As Phil waited for his drinks, he experienced an extraordinary sensation in his stomach. Simultaneously he turned towards the girls and saw the jackets slide off the chair. Meanwhile, Leo who had been sitting contentedly next to Dan at a good distance from the bar, leapt up and began to bark. The dog strained against the firm hold Dan had on his lead. Leo was causing quite a disturbance and several patrons turned their heads in the direction of the dog. Despite Dan's efforts to quieten the dog, Leo began to howl piteously.

The owners of the jackets distracted by Leo's unexplained howling, provided Phil the time to inspect the first jacket unobserved. Later, he explained, he felt as if he was inexplicably being guided towards them. Unable to stop himself he examined the front and sleeves of one of the garments before positioning it around the back of the chair. He had just managed to dislodge the second item of clothing, trapped by the weight of the bags, when the man who had sat by the girls challenged him. "Hey mate what are you doing?"

Phil apologised. "I'm sorry, they fell on to the floor. I thought I would put them back for you. They're safer like this. I wasn't after those bags."

One of the girls thanked him and smiled. She had a pleasant disposition, Phil thought, as he noted her blonde hair fastened up with a purple ribbon. Waves of escaping hair trickled down the sides of her face giving her an angelic appearance. Her companion was also blonde, her hair cut short into a spiky style. She managed a vague smile and glanced guiltily at the man beside her. The spiky haired girl picked up one of the bags from the chair then took the remaining jacket from Phil who was still holding it.

"They are nice jackets." Phil offered. His arms remained outstretched as if the jackets were still in his possession. Both men stared at each other. Phil was experiencing a medley of sensations, as if someone was controlling his actions and speech. His stomach was behaving oddly too.

"Are they from the sailing club?" Phil was astonished he had asked the question.

"Mine isn't. I can't afford their prices." The first blonde laughed. She seemed very friendly. "But it is similar. Nicky's one is the sailing club one though isn't it?" She pointed to the garment in her companion's hands. The girl called Nicky had rolled it up and was holding it to her chest.

"She's lucky Ryan here bought it for her." The first blonde said.

"Well it's his really. He just lets me wear it." Nicky said. She stole another glance at Ryan who was glaring at Phil. He grabbed the jacket from Nicky.

"I guessed it was his." Rachel muttered. Laticia grinned triumphantly.

"Thank you." Ryan said begrudgingly. His glare was now turned towards Nicky. "Don't tell everybody our business!"

Rachel and Laticia backed away, and Phil felt released from the turmoil that had gripped him. He returned to the bar to buy his drinks. Gavin strode across to help him.

"What was all that about?"

"I'll tell you when we are sitting down out of earshot." Phil replied. He looked pale and his friend was worried.

"Are you alright mate? I hate to say this but you look as if you have seen a ghost."

Phil managed a grin. When they sat down again their food arrived. Phil took a long glug of his pint before talking.

"I think a spirit or a ghost or something is trying to communicate with me. When those garments fell off the chair, I felt as if I was being manipulated. I could hear a voice in my ear telling me to examine the jackets. Some kind of presence seemed to motivate me and I think that's what started the dog off."

Gavin looked excited. Dan said nothing. He wanted to believe Phil but it was going to take more than that to convince him.

"Can you feel it now?" Gavin asked.

Phil shook his head. "Not so powerfully, but something is lingering. I think Leo can sense something too. His eyes are very watchful, but he's quiet now isn't he? Whatever it is, it isn't far away."

Rachel and Laticia exchanged smug smiles. They were draped across the bench at the side of the dog.

Dan patted the dog's head and Leo made a contented whimpering sound. Gavin cut a piece of his sausage and put it at the side of his plate to cool down before giving it to the dog.

Once Phil had eaten his meal and drank half of his second pint he began to tell Dan and Gavin how aggressive the man with the two blonde girls had been with him, when Phil had picked up the jackets from the floor.

"Do you remember Lester told us about some jackets having been stolen from the sailing club? I was curious to see if those jackets had the club logo. It seems that the bloke's girlfriend was wearing such a garment that had once belonged to him. He was very possessive of it and was pissed off with his girlfriend too, it seems to me. She appeared to be a bit scared of him."

"Do you think he may have something to do with the stolen clothes from the club?" Gavin asked.

"I've no idea. I suppose it was on my mind, after what Lester told us. Maybe I'm too suspicious, especially after that strange sensation I just experienced. I can't explain it. It's probably just a coincidence. That bloke looked shifty though."

"Are you suggesting that the person or persons who stole the clothing from the club, killed Rachel too?" Dan asked. "It doesn't seem likely to me that a petty thief or thieves would murder." He dipped a goujon into some garlic mayonnaise.

"I'm keeping an open mind. We don't know what Rachel's attackers were wearing. Didn't you say the police couldn't find any witnesses, and forensics had nothing to offer?" Phil said.

Dan nodded. "How can you prove that a man who stole a jacket is responsible for murder? How do you prove a man has stolen a jacket? We can't just assume that every jacket we see is a stolen one."

The questions hung in the air because none of them could think of what to say.

"Still it's a line of inquiry." Gavin offered. "What else have we got? Nothing."

"Your face was scratched and bruised in the assault. Wasn't it?" Laticia asked Rachel.
"Yes."

"You told us before that you thought there might be blood stains on the jackets? Possibly the sleeves?"

Rachel nodded. "Yes, and there's something about that man that makes me feel odd."

"Maybe he's one of the men we're looking for? You might have glimpsed him when, you know, you were pulled to the ground." Laticia suggested.

Rachel shrugged. "Possibly. Let's follow him home, we can have a look at the jacket when he gets in. At least we know Nicky's jacket is from the sailing club." She reflected.

"OK. If they separate when they leave the pub, I think we should too. I can tag Nicky and you tag Ryan."
"Deal."

The three men finished their meals in silence. Dan bent to give Leo a piece of his goujon which he had left to cool. Likewise the dog ate the sausage from Phil and heartily munched on the piece of chicken that Phil gave him.

"He isn't very discerning when he comes to food. Is he?" Phil laughed as he patted the dog's head.

Dan and Gavin smiled. Both of hem indulged the dog more than usual. It was as if they both took comfort from the animal to compensate for the loss of two loved members of their family.

Gavin contemplated his father as he fondled the dog's head. He knew how keenly he felt about the death of his wife who they had buried only five days ago. Gavin missed his mother too, but whilst he knew there was nothing he could do to bring her or Rachel back, he vowed he would try his damned hardest to find his sister's killer.

When the door at the side of the pub opened again, two young men entered. They scanned the room for a place to sit. When they noticed Dan and Gavin they remained quietly just inside the doorway, contemplating each other as if trying to read each other's thoughts. Presently, by mutual agreement, based on facial gestures they walked across to the little group and introduced themselves.

"Hello Mr. Bellis, Gavin. Sorry to hear about your wife."

Immediately Gavin stood up. He recognised the young men as those who had pulled Rachel out of the lake the night she was murdered.

"It's Jason and you are Stuart?" He shook their hands.

Dan got up also to shake their hands. "Thank you."

The two young men moved to walk away, but Gavin invited them to sit down. "Can I get you a drink?"

"No. It's alright. We just wanted to say hello that's all."

"Please sit and have a pint with us. Actually we were hoping to come and see you, but unfortunately we don't know where you live. I had intended on asking the police for your addresses."

The two young men both looked confused.

"Why has something come to light?" Stuart asked. "Have the police found the murderers? There were two weren't there?"

Gavin sighed. "I wish I could say yes."

Phil was curious. "How do you know there were two?" He asked.

"We were asked to go to the inquest, weren't we Stu?"

Stuart nodded. "Yeah. It wasn't very nice. The police read out their statements and said they thought Rachel was the victim of a

vicious attack from two unknown males. It was horrible."
"What did you want to ask us?" Jason posed his question to Gavin. He glanced at Phil as he spoke and Gavin introduced him.
"Are you a cop?" Stuart asked.
Phil grinned. "No. Just a friend of the family. We're doing our own investigation and starting from scratch. So I hope you don't mind us asking you questions, probably the same ones the police asked."
Both men shook their heads. "But first, please let me buy you a drink." Phil offered. This time they agreed and Phil went to the bar. He chose to stand a distance away from Ryan, Nicky and her friend. They were in deep conversation as he passed, though Ryan looked up at Phil and gave him an unpleasant stare. Phil felt uncomfortable and was glad that he was served quickly with the drinks. He carried the tray back to their table with the glasses of beer. He handed half pints to Dan and Gavin, then another half for himself. Stuart looked confused when he saw that he and Jason had been given pints.
Gavin saw their perplexed glances and explained. "We've already had two pints each. The beer here is very strong."
Jason took a sip appreciatively. "What do you want to ask us?"
"The night you found Rachel, where were you coming from?" Gavin asked.
"We'd been to *The Winking Frog* for a pint, but it was deserted, so we were going to

walk through the cemetery to come here. As you can see it's livelier in here." Jason gesticulated with a wave of his hand around the room.

"Did you see anyone, or pass anyone?"

Jason glanced at his friend before answering. "Yes, we saw a few people near the town square, not far from the *Winking Frog.*

"Which direction were they coming from?" Phil asked.

Stuart shrugged. "Hard to say really, because they were hanging around talking. There's no knowing where they had come from or where they were going."

"Can you describe them?" Phil persisted.

"A couple of young girls. They were Rachel's friends Jade and Emma. I didn't know them then, but I noticed them at the police station afterwards when I was giving my statement. I saw them a few days after the murder too. We had a bit of a chat."

He took a deep breath whilst Jason broke in. "It was horrible in that police station you know."

The little group became quiet as they acknowledged that the gruesome experience of finding Rachel and then being questioned by the police must have been harrowing.

Jason continued his story. "Emma told me that she was on her way to meet Rachel but she was already running late before she'd even called for Jade. To make things worse, Jade wasn't ready and in any case she had decided to go out with someone else. Emma had waited for her anyway so they could walk together part of the way and chat. Jade had left Emma at the town square. That's where we saw them, at about five past or ten past seven. Then we went to the *Winking Frog.*"

"Probably true." Rachel affirmed.

"There were also three elderly women. Probably on their way to the women's Institute, because we noticed that the door to their meeting place was open. Maybe you know it? The hall is just across the way from The *Winking Frog*?"

"Yes. I know it. My wife used to go there." Dan said.

The two young men nodded sympathetically at the mention of Anna.

"Who else? Can you remember? Gavin asked.

"I told the police that after we left the pub I thought I saw three men and two girls hanging around not far from the kissing gate."

"What time was that?" Phil asked.

"About twenty to eight maybe a bit later." Stuart said. He glanced at Jason. "We told the police we weren't sure exactly." Jason agreed.

"So after you left the pub you came straight here?" Gavin stated.

Stuart frowned and exchanged a worried expression with Jason. He chose his next words with care. "Umm, well, as you know we didn't get here."

Gavin's face slumped as he realised what they were trying to delicately tell him. Phil sensed the uncomfortable atmosphere and took up the questioning again.

"So did you see anyone else after you left the *Winking Frog?*"

"Once we'd got through the gate we didn't see anyone. It was dark anyway. We were on the lane that goes from the pub to the gateway that takes you to the lakeside path and eventually the back of the cathedral to come here."

Gavin and Phil nodded. Dan inclined his head. They knew the paths very well.

"Then I needed a pee, so we made a bit of a diversion to the bushes near the lake....." Jason finished quietly.

"So other than that group of people when you first left the pub, you saw no-one else." Phil stated.

Both Stuart and Jason affirmed that statement.

"But we didn't know any of them. Whoever they were they seemed to be having a good time." Stuart rubbed his neck and stretched his head from side to side. "Sorry, I've been playing football and hurt my neck yesterday." He turned to Jason. "Actually I think one of the men I saw is sitting over there. What do you think Jase?"

Jason turned his head towards Ryan and the two girls and lazily watched them getting ready to leave. "I don't know, I'm not sure. Maybe."

Stuart wheeled round again to face Gavin and shrugged. "I might be wrong. I only saw him for a few seconds. Perhaps you already know him anyway?"

Gavin shook his head. "No, we don't know him."

Ryan and the two girls passed them on their way to the exit door. Jason and Stuart took the opportunity to scrutinise Ryan's face. The friendlier of the two girls turned towards Phil and smiled. Her glance lingered on Gavin before she said goodbye. "Thanks for looking after our jackets." She called.

Ryan growled and turned his head to glare at her. "Come on Abi."

"Too late to ask him any questions now!" Phil said. "So you don't recognise him?

Both men shook their heads.

"Sorry. I can't be sure it was him I saw." Stuart admitted.

"I definitely don't know him either." Jason confirmed. "Though I wouldn't mind knowing the girls. They're hot!" He grinned. Mind you one of them seems to have her eye on you Gavin."

"What do you mean? I don't know her." Gavin protested. He took a swig of his beer to hide his confusion.

The others chuckled. "I think you're in there." Jason agreed.

Phil came to Gavin's rescue. He wanted to stay focused.

"Alright. We've established that you didn't know them. But there's a possibility that one of the men you saw may have been that man who has just left the pub. It's a shame he's gone I could have asked him if he'd seen Rachel that night. I should have stopped him." Phil cursed himself for not acting quicker.

"I'm not sure you would have got anything out of that surly young man." Dan said.

Stuart and Jason adopted serious faces again.

"Stu and I thought that your sister's blood might be on the murderer's clothes. The police must have thought the same thing. They asked to examine ours because we found her." Jason informed them.

"Did they ask to examine the clothes of the other two men who helped?" Phil asked.

"I don't know." Both young men shrugged. "The police didn't tell us. Maybe they checked them later."

"The police would want to keep that information to themselves." Dan suggested.

"And they have no other suspects." Gavin grimaced.

"Did you tell the police that you had seen all those people you told us about?" Phil asked.

"Yeah, but because we didn't know their names and we weren't able to describe them I don't think it was much help. You see we didn't really take much notice of them. I don't know if the police followed it up." Jason said.

Meanwhile Rachel and Laticia had followed the trio outside. "Now what do we do? Rachel asked. If I follow Ryan and you

shadow Nicky, how can we get more info from Stuart and Jason?"
"Leave it to your brother and Phil."
"But we need to know where they live and what else they know."
"I don't think they know much more. We will catch up with Gavin and your dad later. They're bound to discuss it with Phil when they get home. We will soon pick it up. I think it's more important that we find out where Ryan lives and if he leads us to that other chap."
"I suppose you are right." Rachel relented. "I know those two - Jason and Stuart didn't kill me. Besides, we don't know if there is a connection with me and the jackets."
"I'm not so sure about that." Laticia returned. "I think Phil is suspicious about Ryan. I think that Nicky knows something too."
As planned the ghosts trailed behind their targets. When they reached the new housing development Abi said goodbye to her companions. They saw her walk to a house which she shared with her parents and two sisters. Nicky and Ryan continued walking down the new road to the older part of town. Eventually outside the guildhall Ryan embraced Nicky roughly and kissed her before she boarded a bus heading for Chester. *Laticia boarded the bus too.*
Ryan adjusted his sun glasses and walked down 'Chester Road.' He turned left down Watery Avenue. Eventually he entered number sixteen.

Rachel followed him in.

Chapter Eleven

Dissemination

After Rachel and Laticia left the pub, Phil felt the agitated state of his body dissipate and he felt more like himself. He noticed Leo was more relaxed too. He looked around the crowded room, everything seemed normal.

During the last few years, he had conducted many séances and each time he had experienced similar sensations to those he had experienced just now. That tight uncomfortable grip like hold in his stomach was a familiar feeling to him. The prickly caress at the back of his neck was a regular occurrence too. Absently he rubbed his neck. He wondered if Rachel had been trying to contact him.

For the moment he wouldn't say anything to Gavin and Dan. When they returned to their house he would start to investigate Rachel's personal items. Both father and son had given him permission. After staying in their house these last two days he felt he could proceed. He had tried to be sensitive to their feelings and hadn't waded into Rachel's bedroom as soon as he had arrived in Holywell. In any case, as he had explained to Gavin, he had felt obliged to visit his sister Emily and her young family who still lived in the vicinity. He'd also managed a quick visit to see his parents who had moved from Holywell to Mold many years previously.

Gavin was checking his watch. "Two o clock dad. I think we've missed the beginning of the Monte Carlo tennis semi-final. They might have it on in the other room if you want to watch it in there. I believe Nadal is playing. I've recorded the game so I can watch it later. Phil and I can walk on to the town and get some bread from the bakery before they run out."

Dan was a keen tennis fan. He liked his son's suggestion and all three men made their way into the next room. There was a large plasma screen on two of the walls. The width of the screens created a life like effect in the room and this brought a smile to Dan's face. He sat down, immediately captured by the game. "This is good. Thanks son. I'll see you at home later."

"If you like I'll take Leo just in case he gets bored watching that tennis ball going back and to." Gavin grinned as he took the lead. Dan's attention was already on the tennis.

Outside Phil and Gavin set off for the town centre. They decided to avoid the graveyard route and followed the rough road through the new housing development down to the town.

"This road hasn't been adopted by the council yet, that's why we are walking on rubble." Gavin commented.

"Looks like they still have plans for building more houses." Phil returned. He kicked a few grey stones into a pothole. Eventually the access road joined up with the Chester Road. This was the main route in and out of Holywell. The pair made their way to a pedestrianised square at the centre of the town where there was the bakery aptly named 'Winefride's Bakes.' It was also a café.

"Do you fancy a coffee and a custard tart?" Gavin suggested. "That beer was quite strong. I think it was about six percent!"

"Good idea. And I never say no to a custard tart. Do they have any of those Portuguese ones that seem to be popular?"

They both peered through the wide glass door of the bakery to see the display of cakes and pastries.

"Yes they do." Gavin replied. He ordered the food and coffees and went outside to find a table whilst Phil who had insisted on paying, searched in his pocket for his wallet. Outside, sitting at a somewhat rickety wooden table on the wide pavement, Gavin stirred his coffee thoughtfully. "Do you think those two lads we've just been talking to in the *Black Raven*, Jason and Stuart are telling the truth?"

Phil took a bite of his custard tart and nodded his head. Taking advantage of his friend's temporary incapacity to talk Gavin asked him another question.

"What about that guy who was sitting in the corner with the two girls? The blonde and the not so blonde?"

Phil swallowed and took a sip of his coffee before answering. "I didn't say anything earlier because I didn't want to alarm your father, but I really think there is a connection with those three and Rachel. That guy, Ryan, I think they called him was very protective of one of the jackets."

"Did it have the sailing club logo on it?" Gavin interrupted.

"Yes. Not that I saw it properly. One of those girls actually told me it was from the sailing club. But more importantly when I was trying to examine the jackets, I felt as if I was being manipulated. It was like as if I was getting a message from the other side. I've experienced it before." He took another sip of his coffee before continuing. "Gavin I am convinced that Rachel is trying to communicate with me."

"Are you sure?" Gavin said excitedly. He cradled his pastry in his hand. He still hadn't sampled it yet.

"I feel certain. At least if it isn't Rachel, some kind of spirit is trying to tell me something. I think it is connected in some way to those jackets."

Gavin looked confused. "So are you still thinking there is a link with what Lester told us this morning about the stolen clothing? Some kind of link with Rachel?"

Phil sighed. "It's a long shot, but we have nothing else. There may be a connection with those stolen items or, there may not, but why did I get that supernatural pull in my gut when we were in *The Raven?*"

"Well I think we need a bit more to go on before we risk asking that aggressive man any questions. He looks like a moody person to me. Anyway we don't know where he lives." Gavin said gloomily. Absently he bit into his pastry.

"Well there is someone who might know." Phil said. He was gazing over Gavin's head at a blonde girl who had just walked into the bakery.

Still chewing his food, Gavin whirled around to follow Phil's stare. His eyes fell on the friendly blonde girl from the pub.

Phil struggled to remember the name he had heard the surly young man call her. "Abi, yes yes, that's it .. Abi. Probably Abigail!" He pronounced loudly.

Upon hearing her name, the girl turned around in the shop. She was handing over some money to pay for her bread.

Gavin swallowed his food quickly. "I think she heard you."

Phil nodded. The girl stepped out of the shop and approached them amused.

"Hello you two again. Are you still trying to steal my jacket?"

They all laughed. At least the girl has a sense of humour Phil thought.

"Sorry about that. I genuinely wanted to pick them up off the floor for you."

Abigail laughed. A slight breeze blew strands of blonde hair into her eyes and she tossed it back with the tips of her immaculately manicured nails. "I guessed that. I would have done the same if the situation was reversed. It's just that Ryan gets edgy when someone touches that

jacket, even though he actually gave it to Nicky. I think he might have got a bit more aggressive if your dog hadn't started to bark. He seems alright now doesn't he?"
Abigail bent down to fondle Leo's head.
"Was it a gift?" Gavin asked. "The jacket I mean." He observed the girl intently. He was captivated by the glitter in her hair which made her hair sparkle as the sunlight caught it. Her hair was in his opinion a work of art.
"No, not really. He used to wear it, but then he said Nicky could wear it. She is rather attached to it, because it's posh. Ryan's bought another one, he can afford it. The boat club clothes are good quality you know, but expensive. Ryan gets agitated if people comment about it and then he takes it out on Nicky. He's possessive of her too. I don't know why she bothers with him. But still that's her business. Sorry, I do rabbit on sometimes. I'm talking too much."
Abigail turned to go. "Nice to see you again."
Phil made a desperate attempt to detain her. "So do you live around here?" He couldn't think of what else to say.
The girl eyed him suspiciously. "Yeah. Do you?"
"I used to." Phil returned. "I used to live in Cathedral Road, until a few years ago. My sister and her husband still live here - in Bell Street actually. Gavin lives the other side of the lake in Fairhaven."

Abigail smiled but was careful not to give anything away about where she lived. "I know Bell Street. I don't know anybody in Fairhaven. Too posh for me. See ya." She turned away quickly and walked off.

"Bugger." Phil said and shoved the last piece of his custard tart into his mouth.

"Well you tried." Gavin smirked. "She seems a bright kid. And good for her that she didn't tell us where she lives. Remember there is a murderer at large. She is probably too aware of the dangers of speaking to strange men."

"Phil's mobile rang. He glanced at the screen and answered it eagerly.

"Hi Em. Are you ok?"

Gavin finished his coffee whilst his friend spoke to his sister Emily. She was a few years older than Phil. She married young and now she had two children under the age of five. Her husband was a bus driver for a local firm.

"Em wants to know if we'd like to go for Sunday lunch tomorrow. Your dad's invited." Phil held the mobile away from his body and whispered. "Say no if you'd rather not. The kids will be running wild making themselves a nuisance."

Gavin shrugged. "I don't mind. It might do my dad good."

"Sure?"

"Yes. Why not?"

Phil confirmed a time with his sister and closed his mobile.

Gavin stroked the dog thoughtfully. "Leo seems to have calmed down now. He's not as excitable as he was this morning."

Phil agreed. He too had noticed the change in Leo ever since they left the pub. He couldn't help feeling that there was a connection with Leo's behaviour and the weird impulses he had experienced in the *Black Raven.*

"I suppose we'd better get back. Do you want to catch a bus or shall we walk the two miles home?" Gavin stood up as he spoke and untied Leo's lead from the chair where he had been tethered.

"Let's walk. It's a pleasant route. Most of the trail is within view of the lake. You're lucky to live in such a scenic place. I miss it sometimes."

"I'm the first to admit I'm lucky. Mum and dad worked hard to buy that house. Some people don't think that teachers and civil servants work hard at all, but believe me, they were both dedicated to their work. That's what inspired me to do something similar. Though I often get scorned for what I do."

"Your mum was head teacher wasn't she?"

"Deputy Head. She enjoyed her work, but was glad to retire when she did. Not that she had many years to enjoy it."

Phil squeezed his arm to try to comfort him. He knew there was nothing he could say to console him.

Meanwhile Gavin had been turning their previous conversation over in his head. He stopped walking and frowned as the futility of their talk slapped into his consciousness.

"You know something. Even if we did know where that man, what's his name, Ryan lives, we can't just go knocking on his door and ask him questions about the night of Rachel's murder. He'll probably tell us to 'fuck off', and I wouldn't blame him. We've got no right to ask him any questions.

We'd get the same reaction from his girlfriend too, if we asked her if she knew where Ryan was that night. We can't even ask who Ryan hangs out with. It's all conjecture Phil. We know nothing. We are just clutching on to the possibility that, boat club jackets were worn by the two murderers on the night Rachel was killed. All this just because Lester told us two jackets had been stolen from the boat club. It's hopeless."

"Don't despair. I really think we have something to go on. Suppose whoever killed Rachel had blood stains on their clothing, they would want to get rid of the garments. But if those garments were expensive and relatively new, their vanity would stop them. Besides, where would you dispose of them without attracting attention? The general public would have been alerted of Rachel's murder and would know that the police were searching for evidence. You can't be too careful, not if you have blood stained clothes to get rid of. The police would have been scouring the place. They would also be asking people for information. You'd be surprised to know how many people I've seen going through rubbish bins in the hope of finding something valuable." Phil paused. Gavin didn't look convinced.

"Just supposing, I'm not saying he is, but, say Ryan is guilty and he panicked; where best to hide it but give the jacket to Nicky?" Phil suggested.

"If Ryan really was involved maybe he would." Gavin conceded. He bent his head down in despair. Together they walked for a few minutes in silence.

"Would your father take part in a séance?" Phil asked the question abruptly.

Gavin heaved a sigh. "I don't know. You know he's sceptical about these things, but he has said he would suspend his scepticism if we thought he could help us in some way."

"How about we have a séance tonight?"

Gavin was getting interested again. "I'll ask him."

When they got back to the house Dan was dozing in an armchair. He roused himself when the dog licked his face.

"Enjoy the tennis dad?"

"Excellent match. Nadal is through to the next round."

"If you don't mind I think I will go and have a shower and a quick nap." Phil winked at Gavin.

"Sure you go ahead. Cup of tea dad?"

Phil raced to the bathroom and quickly showered. It had been another hot day and he was feeling drained of energy, and hot and sticky. He wanted to get his wits together. He realised that the extra half pint at lunch time had had a potent effect on him. Still, chatting to Stuart and Jason in the *Black Raven* had been worth consuming the extra drink. Feeling refreshed he entered the bedroom to get dressed. He stood still for a moment warily checking the atmosphere for a ghostly presence. He couldn't perceive one and so continued with his task of getting dressed. He'd just finished buttoning his short sleeved shirt and was pulling on his trousers when an all too familiar ache in his gut swept through him. He sat down on the bed to try to contain his stomach muscles as unrelenting spasms of pain ripped through them.

Chapter Twelve

16 Watery Avenue

Ryan swaggered into the house and into the kitchen where his mother was peeling potatoes.
"Hello love. I'm making shepherd's pie for tea. What time are you going out?"
"Dunno yet." Ryan strutted out of the kitchen again and slumped into an armchair. He grabbed the television controls and then the pre-recorded button looking for an alternative from the tennis match. He selected a film he had recorded earlier and settled himself down to watch it. But he couldn't concentrate. Something was gnawing at him.
For a few minutes Rachel observed him. Was this her rapist and murderer? She couldn't be sure. He certainly had the manner and the build of one of her attackers. If she could see both of her assailants together, it might help her remember. That night was so terrible she had scarcely been able to believe what was happening to her.
Ryan switched the TV off and got up. He pulled out his mobile phone and keyed in a number. *Rachel tried to see who it was on his contact list but he was too fast. However when the number came up momentarily before it began to ring she was able to see the first three letters.*

"Max. We need to talk. Something's come up."

Rachel was startled when she heard Ryan utter the name Max. She glided over Ryan's shoulder and leaned towards the mouthpiece so that she could hear the conversation.

"What do ya mean?"

"I can't talk here. I'll meet you in *The Sacred Heart* at seven thirty."

"Make it eight. I can't get there before then."

"Alright."

Ryan returned to the kitchen. "Mum what time is that pie gonna be ready?"

"About six o clock. Is that ok?"

"Yeah. I'm going upstairs for a bit."

"Playing games on your computer are you?"

"Yeah."

In his bedroom Ryan switched on his computer. Whilst he waited for it to fire up, he got his mobile out again. *This time Rachel was quick to look at the contact that he aggressively punched with his thumb. She was able to see that he was sending a text to Nicky.*

The text read: "**Can't make 8 tnight. C ya 9.30.**"

Within a few minutes Nicky responded. "**Not worth it so late. Come tmw.**

A vindictive frown curled over Ryan's face and he sent another message. "**cant do tmw will come tnite.**"

The return message read: **Fine**.

Rachel got the impression that Ryan was in a bad mood and needed to see Nicky. She also surmised that he was used to getting his own way and that was why Nicky had agreed on the later time for them to meet. She decided to return home to compare notes with Laticia. Then they could go together to listen to the conversation between Ryan and Max at the Sacred Heart.
Laticia had followed Nicky from the bus stop to the flat she shared with her two friends Amy and Jessica.

Nicky's flat was on the top floor of a large, converted house called Broom Manor, a two mile bus ride from Holywell to the village of Five Bells. The name inspired by the church with the five bells that stood in the village square.

"Nice place." Laticia enthused. She glided across to the window and looked out across the village square. A sweetshop a chemist and a bookshop met her eyes first of all. On the corner next to the bookshop, a pavement café offered snacks and afternoon teas. Nearby a queue was forming in front of a kiosk for home-made ice-creams. 'A bit of sunshine and everybody is out enjoying themselves.' Laticia observed. For a moment her thoughts flitted to her native Barbados and she felt a pang of guilt that she hadn't yet started her journey. But solving the mystery surrounding Rachel's death was compelling her to stay a bit longer in the UK.

Nicky flung her jacket and shoulder bag over an armchair and sauntered into the tiny kitchen to get herself a glass of water. She drank thirstily and refilled her glass then carried it out of the kitchen into the small passageway that led from the kitchen to three bedrooms. She knocked on the first of the bedroom doors. No answer. Amy must have gone out she surmised. She was rarely home early from work. Nicky didn't bother knocking on the other door because she knew Jess had gone away for the week end.

Sighing, Nicky went into her own bedroom and sank on her bed. She was getting worried about her relationship with Ryan. He seemed nice when she started dating him over eighteen months ago, but as time went on she noticed that he seemed to have a lot of mood swings. They varied from sweet possessiveness to aggressive controlling. She was beginning to have the same feelings of fear she had when she had lived in Frodsham with her parents. She had managed to bury those memories when she left home four years ago. Her father who was the cause of her fear was dead now. His drunken lifestyle had got the better of him. Her mother had a new lease of life and had re-married - to a much nicer man.

The burring sound from her mobile in her bag, raised Nicky from her reclining position on the bed. She got up to retrieve her bag from the living room and picked up her mobile. She noted a text from Ryan wanting a later time for their date that night. She tried to put him off. What was the point of coming at nine thirty? They would probably end up in the pub again. Then no doubt he would demand sex whether she wanted it or not. She had hoped they would go to the Odeon. Not that Ryan liked the films that she liked, but she would rather watch something he liked, than sit in a pub drinking all night.

Laticia bent over Nicky's shoulder to read the text message, then studied Nicky's face as she returned the text with an alternative suggestion. When Ryan sent another text to insist he would see her at nine thirty, Laticia realised that Nicky was not happy with the text but resignedly sent a message back: **"Fine".**

Unable to relax Nicky picked up a couple of magazines and text books from a small bookshelf near the window and put them on the sofa. Her intention was to read a text book on beauty therapy. First though, she picked up her bag and jacket then took them back to her bedroom to hang them up in her wardrobe. She smoothed down the collar on the hanger taking time to pick at a stain on the inside of the collar with her finger. *Laticia glided closer to watch.*

Nicky sighed, she had never been able to get rid of that stain, nor the one on the cuff of the right sleeve. She twisted it over to examine that too. All along the stitching on the under seam of the sleeve as well as the cuff was a trailing dark stain. The fabric of the sleeve was gathered at the wrist into the cuff. The stain was scarcely noticeable, when she was wearing the jacket, but it bothered Nicky. She liked things to be neat and clean.

Before Nicky closed the wardrobe door, Laticia swooped herself into it so she could examine the spots that Nicky was scratching at. "I wonder if that is Rachel's blood!" She exclaimed.

Nicky returned to the living room, she settled down on to the sofa, picked up her text book and began to study. She was interested in specialising in electrology when she had finished her training as a Beauty Therapist. She and Abigail planned to go in to business together. Abi was more interested in the hair, make-up and nail technology side of the beauty industry. Very soon Nicky became engrossed in her reading.

Laticia decided to return to Rachel's house. She left Broom Manor and arrived just when Phil was putting on a fresh pair of trousers.

He was a careful dresser. This was something his wife Clare admired about him. Though Phil liked slim fitting jeans and casual slacks for the day time he disliked wearing T shirts. He always wore a shirt, though rarely a tie. If he was going out somewhere special, he always wore tailored trousers.

Laticia saw Phil's body tense up as soon as she entered the room. He finished zipping up his chinos and whirled around to face the spot where she had swathed herself on his bed. He then sat down clutching his ribs.

"He knows I'm here." She told herself.

"Hello? Rachel?"

"No. I'm Laticia. She smiled even though she knew he couldn't see or hear her. She decided to play with him. Concentrating hard she managed to lift the calendar sheet displaying April. She let it flutter a few times before releasing it. She congratulated herself that she could do it without Rachel.

Unsure whether it was a freak rustle of wind coming from the open window or whether a ghost was causing the calendar to shake, Phil took it down off the wall and laid it on the bed. "OK if you are really in this room, now move the calendar again."

"Anything to oblige." Laticia smiled. A good exercise for me. This time it was easier. She could feel more strength in her powers of levitation. Instead of raising the month of April, she raised the whole calendar into the air. "Wow that feels good." Experimenting, she guided the document across the room and laid it to rest on the dressing table. She was impressed with her own ability and silently observed Phil's reaction.

Phil was ecstatic, though he seemed to be experiencing intense pain.

"Hello Rachel. This is Phil. I hope you remember me. We met about four years ago. I'm a friend of your brother, and I am here to help him and your dad find the bastard who killed you."

Rachel entered the room and the charged atmosphere intensified.

Phil felt his stomach clench. He fell against the open door which slammed beneath his weight.

"What's going on? Rachel asked. She looked in dismay at Phil's profile lying on the floor. He seemed to be choking.

"Our powers are increasing." Laticia replied gleefully. "I was just experimenting to see what I could do without you, and it seemed to be working well. Then when you arrived I got extra charged. We need to learn how to control our power."

"What can we do? Phil's choking!"

"I don't know. I'm not used to this."

"Well neither am I. We must do something." Rachel said. "My own power seems to be out of control too." She had felt a new strength when she was in Ryan's place. She recognised it was sparked by her emotions. Her dislike of Ryan had intensified and with it her powers. Yet she wasn't sure why she disliked Ryan. She wondered if the Max he had contacted was the same Maxwell at the boat club. It was confusing. Surely too much of a coincidence. Max was a common name.

Seeing Phil's obvious agony, Rachel realised what was happening to him and that she and Laticia should stay calm.

"Perhaps if I go into another room it might relieve him a bit." Laticia suggested.

Without waiting for an answer, Laticia wafted over Phil's head, then slipped through the door on to the landing. She glided down the stairs passing through Gavin as he climbed up them. He didn't flinch.

Immediately Phil began to breathe evenly, though he still clutched his stomach.

Rachel concentrated hard, willing herself some control over her increasing strength. The sound of Phil's choking forced Rachel to stop thinking about Ryan. It took a few seconds to reign in some of her power. She watched as Phil managed to get off the floor.

Phil lurched towards the chair at the side of the bed. Then a hard knocking on the door startled him again.

"Phil! Are you ok?"

"It's ok. Gavin. Come in. I've got something to tell you."

"Hell. You look awful. Are you sure you're ok? I heard a bang."

"Now the awful pain in my stomach has gone and I'm not choking yes."

Gavin was startled to hear those words from Phil. Choking and having stomach pains didn't sound good to him. He pulled at his ear nervously as he sat on the edge of the bed to scrutinise his friend. His long dark hair wet from a recent shower dripped down his neck. In contrast to Phil he was casually dressed in an old pair of jeans and a sweatshirt with a hood. He wore jeans and T shirts most of the time and if he felt he could get away without formal dressing he would.

Gavin considered himself lucky that the relaxed dress code at the college where he worked made it easy to wear the clothes in which he felt more comfortable. The college principal seemed to favour casual clothes too. He frequently turned up in shorts and T shirt during the summer months. The rest of the lecturers in the Art block followed the college principal's example. Gavin sometimes sensed that two of his five female colleagues liked to compete with each other. Both of them regularly turned up for work in flamboyant if not outrageous outfits. He liked them all, nevertheless, he had never formed a special bond with any of his colleagues. They all met up occasionally for a drink after work but nothing more.

Phil still looked pale and Gavin scrutinised his face.

"That sounds bad to me. Do you think I should take you to hospital?"

Phil shook his head and managed a grin.

"I'm not ill. Gavin, I've had the oddest supernatural episode yet. Rachel is definitely trying to make contact. In fact, I will demonstrate though I warn you I might end up on the floor feeling like death, but I'm willing to risk it."

"Risk death?" Gavin looked alarmed.

"No. Not really. I mean the pain and the choking. Maybe she doesn't know her own strength."

Gavin frowned. He was feeling alarmed. Yet Phil seemed pleased about something. He decided to indulge his friend.

"Demonstrate? How?"

"Rachel, if you are there, can you please do what you did before?" Phil asked. He put a finger to his mouth to gesture to Gavin to be quiet.

Rachel was perplexed. Whilst she would be delighted to communicate, she had no idea what Phil was talking about. She guessed that Laticia had done something to make him think it was her. After all he didn't know about Laticia.

As nothing happened, Gavin got up off the bed. "Never mind. Perhaps after scaring you she's gone."

"No, no. She's still here. I can feel a presence. She removed the calendar from the wall. Look it isn't there any more. It wafted in the air and settled over here. Look! Phil struggled out of his chair to pick up the calendar from the dressing table.

"Yeah right. Now I know you're having me on."

"It's true. Look I will put it on the bed and I'll ask again. Maybe she doesn't like your scepticism. I thought you believed in the supernatural."

"Well I do up to a point, but I can't believe you can tell a ghost to move things around a room for god's sake. And now you said you were bloody choking!"

So, that's what she did, Rachel thought. She concentrated hard.

"Rachel, please move the calendar." Phil beseeched. He was desperate to prove to Gavin that he wasn't a fraud.

After a few seconds, Rachel managed to raise the calendar gently from the bed and let it rise above Gavin's head. She allowed it to hover for a few seconds before willing it back to its original position on the wall. This was the tricky bit because the loop at the top of the calendar was supposed to hang on the hook. Remembering how her efforts the previous night had caused Phil to wave his arms around, she tried to control her energy so that he wasn't affected. She had to find a way to channel just enough of her energy without harming Phil. Despite several initial attempts Rachel couldn't muster up the skill to manoeuvre the loop. The calendar swayed from side to side. Meanwhile Phil and Gavin gawked, both of them also willing the calendar back on to the hook. With one last effort Rachel centred her thoughts on to the hook, and to her glee the calendar returned neatly to its place.

Rachel felt a glow of satisfaction.

Phil was triumphant.

Gavin was gob smacked.

Neither of them spoke.

Rachel glided to the top of the wardrobe and looked down at them smugly. She was temporarily exhausted.

Eventually Gavin spoke. He was lying outstretched on the bed now. Though he was unaware of her perch, he was actually looking straight at her. "Rache, if you are there and you are listening, that was bloody spectacular. I miss you Rache, and Phil and I are going to find your killer. Perhaps you can help us."

"Yes. Thank you Rachel for demonstrating to your brother that I wasn't imagining things. Tonight perhaps we can have a constructive conversation with you. We hope to have a séance with your father."

"Bugger! Thought Rachel. I wonder what time. I have to get to the pub to listen to Ryan and his mate.

Just then Laticia returned to the room. Immediately Phil began to choke again and clutch his stomach.

"Phil. What's happening? Are you alright?" Gavin jumped off the bed to help his friend.

In the same instance Rachel remonstrated with Laticia.

"Control your power Laticia. You're choking him. You have to learn to control it. Quick."

Laticia glided towards Phil. He seemed to be staring into her eyes as he struggled for breath. Memories of her violent death flooded to her and she understood now where her energy was coming from. She wanted revenge. But she didn't want to harm Phil. She made a valiant effort to distil her energy and eventually Phil's breathing returned to normal. He let go his stomach and relaxed.

Gavin let out a big sigh of relief. "You had me worried then mate."

"Glad to take one for the team." Phil breathed. "That was worse than before. It was almost double the strength. Do you think she may have someone helping her on the other side?"

"My mum!" Gavin cried. "She would be a powerful force to reckon with." He managed a grin.

"Of course. Well I hope they realise soon that their combined power is nearly killing me."

"Come on downstairs. I'll make you a cup of tea. Dad's awake now. We can tell him about our plans to hold a séance tonight. What time do you think is best?

"You nearly killed Phil!" Rachel reproached Laticia. "You will have to try to control your power."

"I'm sorry. It seems to have increased dramatically since last night. I didn't think we would get so much energy so soon. But I think I have worked it out. When I saw Phil choking - and incidentally for the record, I don't believe I have the ability nor the desire to kill anyone - it reminded me of my death. I realised the power was coming from rage. I think I am harbouring anger over my murder and have been feeling the need for retribution. It started when I was at Nicky's house. Rachel, I think Ryan is our killer. Or at least one of them. Nicky is unhappy. I can see it in her face. She is being controlled by violence just like I was. Being in her house has reprised everything for me. I felt my power growing stronger, so

when I got here, I let it flow to see how far it would go. Sorry. I don't want to hurt Phil."

Rachel nodded. She realised that Laticia who was ten years older, had more experience of life. She also recognised that she too had been the victim of a gruesome murder.

"Alright. I understand. I'm sorry too. I think it's resentment and anger from where I am getting my own power. Anger that I was raped and murdered. But it seems to temper down when I am surrounded by family members and friends, dead or alive!" She managed a grin. "Tell me what happened at Nicky's and then I will tell you what happened at Ryan's. At least we know their addresses now."

When each had finished giving an account of their activities, Rachel pointed out that they now had another problem.

"It seems Gavin, Phil and dad are going to hold a séance tonight expecting me to be there, but I need to be at the Sacred Heart *at eight o clock tonight. And you need to be at Nicky's for nine thirty. To be quite honest, I would prefer that both of us were at each venue together."*

"I don't know what to suggest." Laticia confessed. "Let's go downstairs to listen to them and try to distract them somehow. Gently, I promise." She added, catching Rachel's warning glance.

Chapter Thirteen

Atmospheres

Gavin made a pot of tea and handed a mug of it to Dan before he broached the subject of a séance. He waited for Phil to sit down with his own mug of tea and then taking a deep breath made the suggestion to his father.
Dan sipped his tea thoughtfully mulling over their proposition. He had been expecting something like this.
Phil observed him anxiously. He was wondering if Dan refused to participate, whether he could ask Emily to take part. She'd done it before, and it was always better if there were at least three people around the table. As he would be the medium, it would only be fair for Gavin to have at least one other sitting beside him. It could hardly be called a séance if it was just him and Gavin.
"I suppose you want to do it at midnight. Isn't that the traditional way?" Dan asked.
Yes. Yes. That would be perfect. Go for midnight." Rachel said excitedly. Her eyes scanned the room, desperately trying to find something to attract Phil's attention and make him agree. She found nothing to help her.
"It doesn't have to be midnight." Phil said. "In the movies they tend to do it like that to have a dramatic effect. You could do it any

time really as long as everyone who needs to participate is actually present."

"Do you intend to invite someone else?" Dan asked.

"I hadn't intended to, but we could ask someone you know, if you want to?" Phil cast a quizzical glance at Gavin. His friend inclined his head in a gesture of assent and shrugged.

"Well if it doesn't have to be midnight, that's a relief. How long would it last?"

"It varies Dan. It could be five minutes, it could take an hour. It depends if we make contact and if we can get some answers. I'm pretty certain we will make contact."

"How do you know that?" Dan looked perplexed. Gavin smothered a smile with his hand.

"I'm getting strong vibes." Phil answered. He didn't want to elaborate on what he had just experienced in case it alarmed Dan.

"I see. Well how about ten o clock then. The programme I want to watch on TV starts at eight o clock and finishes at ten. I could record it, but I would prefer to watch it if I can."

"Perfect." Phil said.

"Well now that's settled, I'll make something for our tea?" Gavin said. "Sandwiches with that nice bread we bought earlier?" Without waiting for an answer, he got up and went into the kitchen.

"The time is not so perfect for us. But it will have to do." Rachel said. *"We can both go to the* Sacred Heart, *and then we'll have to*

split up. You could follow Ryan to Nicky's and I will come back here. I'm not sure you will learn much more at Nicky's though."

"I think you're right. But I would like to keep an eye on them anyway."

At quarter to eight that evening the two ghosts drifted their way towards the Sacred Heart *pub. There they settled in a corner close to the entrance door and waited.*

"The last time I was here, was the night before I died." Rachel commented uneasily.

"Do you feel anything?" Laticia asked excitedly.

Rachel shook her head. "Not really."

Just after eight o clock Ryan entered followed by another man that both ghosts recognised immediately.

"Bloody hell. It's that Maxwell Briggs from the Sailing club." Rachel exclaimed.

Laticia nodded her eyes glimmered with contained rage and malice.

"Now don't try anything." Rachel warned her. "We mustn't jump to conclusions. Let's get closer so that we can hear what they are saying."

Laticia nodded. "It's alright. I'm in control."

Despite warning Laticia to keep calm, Rachel was struggling with her own rage. These two men could be her attackers. Instinctively she disliked them.

Both men were at the bar buying pints of beer. After they had been served their eyes roved around the lounge looking for somewhere to sit where they wouldn't be disturbed. Around the walls of the room there were leather bound seats set within stalls similar to those often found in restaurants. Wooden lattice work at the side of each stall provided a small amount of privacy. Both suspects settled themselves in to one of these compartments in a quiet corner.

Laticia and Rachel suspended themselves over one side of the stall. The pub was busy. It was a Saturday night, and a special live music event had enticed many more punters than usual. The opposite corner from Ryan and Maxwell was occupied by a band setting up equipment to perform a gig.

"Let's make it quick." Ryan said. He glanced around him furtively to make sure no-one was listening. "We could get drowned out by the music very soon. I don't want to have to shout out what I need to say."

"What's the problem?" Maxwell looked perplexed.

"It's about that girl Rachel Bellis."

Maxwell's jaw dropped. "Shit. Have they been asking you questions too?"

Ryan was wrong footed. He hadn't expected Maxwell to be ahead of him. Mixed emotions ran through him. Why hadn't Maxwell given him a heads up?

"What? What do ya mean '*they*'?" Who are '*they*'? What the hell are ya talking about?"

Ryan was beginning to panic even more now. Guilt and fear were running through him in waves. He felt no remorse for Rachel, only fear for himself.

Max turned to Ryan and faced him squarely with a nonchalant expression on his face. "The brother and father of the dead girl. Another guy was with them. They came asking questions at the boat club. I'll tell you a bit more in a minute. You carry on with what you were saying. Don't panic. Nothing to worry about."

Ryan breathed heavily. He didn't entirely trust Max.

"No! *They* haven't asked me anything. But, I think those three men you are on about were in the *Black Raven* earlier and I saw them. They were looking at me. I recognised *them* from the papers. Two of them anyway. I didn't know the other guy."

"Are you sure they were looking at you? Or is it just because you are feeling guilty? They have no idea who you are. Neither do the police. You weren't even a suspect. They didn't even ask you any questions."

This time Rachel's eyes glittered with anger. Laticia was livid. "There I knew it."

"Let's keep calm." Rachel warned. Yet she was having difficulty to keep calm. To think her father shook hands with this man only this morning at the boat club.

Ryan tried also to remain calm. "One of them, probably the man you described was trying to get information out of Abi and Nicky earlier on. Just before I got here."

"Did he ask about the dead girl?"

Ryan shook his head.

"Well what are you worrying about then? The chances are he was chatting up one of the girls."

"He kept asking about the jacket that Nicky was wearing. The one that I gave her."

"Well so what? They are good jackets. The cops don't know about the blood on the jackets. They didn't even ask me for mine, nor Jamie's. It was those two guys that found her, the cops were interested in, not me and Jamie." He took a swig of his pint.

Ryan sat silently, re-assessing what Max had said. He wanted to believe him.

Max laughed callously. "Calm down. Chill. Those jackets are like gold and that bloke probably used them as a chat up line. Nice one. I might try that line myself. The girls are hot too. He probably fancied his chances. Shame that Abi is such a fucking stuck up bitch. I wouldn't mind shagging her."

Maxwell took another swig of his drink. "Come on. You're losing it! It's cool mate. Don't worry! If anything, I'm the one who should be worrying. I was interviewed almost straight away by the police. Me and Jamie. You were out of it. I keep telling you, nobody knows you were involved. The cops haven't a clue!"

Ryan visibly relaxed. "Does Jamie know or suspect anything?" He asked. He was still worried.

"Not a bloody thing." Maxwell bragged. He took another gulp of his drink, drained his glass and got up. "I have to go. Got a hot date at a party."

"Wait Max. Tell me what happened at the boat club this morning."

Max sat down again. "Like I said those three came asking questions. They wanted to talk to me and Jamie about that night. They asked if we had seen anyone walking towards the boat club along the lakeside. We told them no, just like we told the police. They'll never know now mate. The only ones who know are you and me. It's been a year. It's a good job we rolled that bitch into the water, they haven't got a clue."

"And they didn't ask about your clothes?"

"No. I told you what happened. I keep telling you. How could they ask about the jackets? No-one saw us so there would be no description of witnesses. Those two lads who pulled her out of the lake assumed that me and Jamie had just come from the boat house. No-one saw me leave you at the end of the railway track. Like I've told you over and over again, I ran down that old disused rail track at the back of the boat club and got back in through the window. I knew Jamie would be outside scrubbing the boats with the rest of the gang.

It took longer than usual because bloody Lester had gone to London and Steve was off sick. If either Jamie, or Lester had come to look for me when I was with you, they would have assumed I'd climbed to the railway bridge for a smoke, which I sometimes do. All I had to do was grab a mop and make out I was cleaning the floor in the locker room. Something we leave until the last minute.

Anyway with Lester not there it was dead easy. After we got that bitch, I shoved my jacket into a bin bag and stuffed it in my locker. Then I put on a fresh new one." He winked at Ryan. By that time, all the staff were leaving and walking to the car park. It was just me and Jamie left. He had the keys. He locked up and we walked the long way back on the lakeside path and then towards the *Black Raven*. He didn't know a thing. Just another day at the sailing club. Except we didn't get to the pub and ended up in the cop shop."

Max grinned and got up again. "Just as well I had nicked those two jackets a few days earlier. Mine was still in my locker. We're clean mate." He glanced at his watch. "I've got to go. See ya."

The music started to play and Max swaggered confidently out of the pub. Ryan still had half a pint in his glass. He picked it up moodily and took a long swig, his free hand ran nervously through his short dark hair. His long fringe which offered minimum appeal to his banal face, drooped into one of his eyes changing his already surly expression to something more sinister. Glancing at his watch he noted it was eight thirty. He sent a text to Nicky to say he would see her earlier than planned. Probably just after nine. He decided to catch a bus. Originally he had planned to drive there, but he'd had a lot to drink that day. The last thing he wanted to do was to risk getting picked up by the police for drunk driving. They might start asking awkward questions. He finished his beer and walked out of the pub towards the bus stop. Whilst he waited for the bus he smoothed down his pilfered blue sailing club jacket. It was in pristine condition. Maxwell was still in the car park talking to someone he knew. Ryan inclined his head towards him but didn't speak. Max acknowledged the gesture with a confident wave of his hand.

Outside the pub, Laticia and Rachel were consumed with rage. They tried to contain their anger to concentrate on their discovery.

"Do you think those two lying murderous bastards were here when you came for that interview?" Laticia asked.

"I can't say for certain, but it's more than likely." Rachel replied slowly. She was livid. Her fury made it difficult for her to think rationally.

"They may have recognised you when you were hanging around waiting for Emma."

Rachel nodded. "It's possible. I ignored all the men staring at me, in the pub. I wanted to get out of the place as quickly as possible. I didn't really bother to look at any of their faces properly. Anyway, the night they killed me they were wearing shades and their jacket hoods."

"Men like that don't like being ignored by pretty women. They probably wanted

revenge." Laticia said. "Believe me, I know." She was seething too. Memories of the violence she suffered from her ex-husband flooded back. Both ghosts were silent for a few seconds reflecting on their discovery.

"So let's stick to the plan. I will go to Nicky's with Ryan to see what happens." Laticia said when she managed to control herself.

Rachel nodded. "Right. I will follow that monster Maxwell then I'll see you at my place. With a bit of luck we will get there for ten. He's getting into his car. I'd better go."

Seated on the bus *with Laticia beside him*, Ryan mulled over his conversation with Max. His friend had seemed relaxed and confident about the whole thing. It had been his idea in the first place to rape that fucking girl. He hadn't realised how aggressive Max could be and when he saw him thump her into unconsciousness he had half thought of backing away. Not that he hadn't used violence himself with girls, but never until that night to the extent Max had.

Ryan admitted to himself later that he had actually enjoyed it. Watching Max shag her had aroused him, and so when Max said "Come on. Your turn," he hadn't wavered. She was still alive when they dumped her in the lake. He stupidly thought the water would revive her and she would swim back. He'd been confident that she hadn't seen their faces. Of that fact Ryan was certain. They'd been wearing hoods and shades and she was barely conscious. Plus the fact he'd kept his arm over her eyes holding her head down. They'd no time to hang around, they had to get away fast before anyone saw them. He didn't think she would die. His thoughts drifted back to that fateful night and for the first time he started to feel uneasy. *Sitting next to him Laticia sensed his anxiety. She also felt her powers increase as the fury at what he had done intensified.*

When Ryan got off the bus he managed to calm himself, then a thought struck him about Max's jacket. The one he was wearing that bloody night. Did he get rid of it or is it still in his locker? Outside Nicky's place, Ryan punched in Maxwell's number on his mobile. Laticia peered over his shoulder. No response. Getting angry again Ryan sent Max a text. "**wot did u do wiv the jacket**?"

A response came back. **"Forget it!"**

Ryan wasn't satisfied with that answer from Max. He started to worry again. It would be just like Max to have the bloody jacket still in his locker stuffed in a bin bag. His only consolation was that the police were unaware of his own existence. In frustration he kicked the main door to the mansion house that contained Nicola Parry's flat, then rang the bell on her intercom service. When the buzzer opened the door he ran up the stairs to Nicky's flat his mood changing from second to second.

Though Laticia felt their work was done, she wanted to make sure that Nicky was safe.

Ryan was in such a bad mood, she feared for Nicky's safety. She knew all too well what it was like to be the butt for someone else's anger. The time on Ryan's mobile had displayed 21.14. There was still time to get to the séance. She slid through the flat whilst Ryan grabbed Nicky roughly to give her an aggressive kiss.

"Are we going to a pub?" Nicky asked. She smoothed down her dress. She had decided to make herself look nice even though they weren't going anywhere special. Saturday night at the pub again she sighed. It would have been nicer to go somewhere different for a change, perhaps a nightclub. There weren't any nightclubs in Holywell. The nearest and the best was in Chester sixteen miles away. Both Nicky's flat mates Amy and Jessica went there regularly. They had gone there that very night and had invited Nicky to go with them but she'd reluctantly refused. She knew Ryan would get jealous if she went to a night club without him. It was rare that Nicky could persuade Ryan to take her there himself. He begrudged paying to go in and then complained about the price of drinks. They used to go to the Tivoli in Buckley but Ryan lost his temper one night and got in a brawl with someone he knew. Consequently he was banned. The Tiv manager warned him that if he turned up again he would call the police. So that was the end of that.

"If you want." Ryan said.

"We may as well since I got myself ready to go out." Nicky managed a smile. "There's a live band on at the *Angel Wings* tonight."

"I've just left one live band at the *Sacred Heart*."

"What were you doing there? Is that why you are late?" Nicky felt put out.

"I had some business to attend to with Max."

"Max? Is he the guy who works at the lake?"

Suddenly Ryan got tense again. He pulled Nicky roughly to the door. "Stop asking stupid questions. Come on if we're going to the *Angel*, let's go." Nicky winced as he gripped her arm. She wrenched it free to get her bag from off the sofa. Ryan thought she was refusing to go and pulled her arm back again.

"Ryan stop it you're hurting me. I want to get my bag."

He released her quickly. "Sorry. Come on." He stormed out of the flat and Nicky having collected her bag and keys followed him out. She wasn't looking forward to going out at all now. All Ryan could think of doing for their dates was to take her to pubs. If someone looked at her he would get jealous, just like he did today when a kind man picked up her jacket from off the floor. She didn't know who he was. Most of the people in the *Black Raven* were regulars and she recognised a lot of them. But that man and the two he was with were strangers to her. They both looked sad, sitting there with the barking dog. She rubbed her arm and sighed. Maybe it was time to end her relationship with Ryan. The trouble is she doubted he would let her go.

Laticia followed them to the local pub The Angel Wings, *watched them buy drinks and sit down then she decided to leave. There seemed no point in hanging around. Ryan wasn't going to confide in Nicky his worries and it seemed that Max was with someone else that night and didn't want to be disturbed. She drifted her way back to Fairhaven and Rachel's previous home. Hopefully she would be able to participate in the séance. She wondered what extra information Rachel had gleaned.*

After Ryan left the *Sacred Heart,* Maxwell got into his sleek sports car to drive out of town.

Rachel followed him and got into the car beside him. She was seething, thinking how she hated the idea of being in such close proximity to a man who had violated her body. She watched him get his sunglasses out of the glove compartment and check himself in the mirror. She reeled with shock when suddenly she recognised the horrible man who had abused her so violently.

She tried to control her rage and concentrated on how she could communicate with her father and brother later at the séance.

Maxwell drove for five miles to the small hamlet of Birchgrove. He parked his car outside a house where it seemed obvious to any passer-by that a party was in full swing. Loud music boomed from the window whilst drinkers hung around in the portal of the open front door. Other revellers spilled on to the step below or sat outside on the lawn. Taking advantage of the unseasonal warm weather, several guests, clutching glasses of various drinks sat at a garden table. Even as Maxwell left his car, other party goers tumbled out of more parked vehicles, laughing and chattering. Maxwell sauntered to the open front door and was greeted by his friends. He made his way into the kitchen where visitors were helping themselves to drinks. Someone offered him a can of beer and he accepted it with a wide grin.

Rachel surmised that this was not Maxwell's home. She was disappointed because she wanted to know where he lived, so that somehow or other she could get Gavin to inform the police. She hadn't yet worked out how she was going to convey this information to Gavin, but that had been her ultimate, though as yet unformulated plan. She weaved herself through the guests looking for someone she might know, then returned to the kitchen. There was no-one she recognised. Evidently this was Maxwell's circle of friends. It didn't seem to include Ryan. She wondered how Maxwell and Ryan came to be together when they murdered her. Anger overtook her and without realising the potency of her rage, she momentarily lost control. Her passion supercharged her powers and she vented this energy on Maxwell. Unexpectedly a huge dent appeared in the can of beer from which he was drinking. The thin aluminium tin that contained his beverage suddenly collapsed under his grip forcing the beer to gush out over his shirt. It also splattered some of the people standing close to him.

"Hey Max what are you doing? You're not supposed to hold the can that tight!" The two men standing next to Max wiped the beer splatters off their shirts good naturedly. Max apologised.

Rachel grinned. She felt as if she had won a little victory. So much so that when he was handed a fresh can of beer, she did it again.

This time the small group of guests standing near him were not so sympathetic and moved away. They mumbled amongst themselves that Max was too aggressive. Two of that same group were annoyed that their clothes were damp. Max's shirt was soaked and he wasn't happy either.

Gleefully, Rachel turned to leave, but was distracted when she saw more newcomers arriving at the party. One was her old boyfriend Josh. He was holding hands with her friend Emma. 'Oh, so that's how it is. I wonder if they were seeing each other behind my back. And how does Josh know Maxwell's friends?' She decided to stay a little longer. She felt she could spare a few more minutes and still be in time for the séance. She might learn a bit more about Max.

Josh sidled up to Maxwell and introduced him to Emma. His eyes openly roved her body and Emma frowned. She wasn't used to being treated like an inanimate object. Her hand tightened on Josh but he seemed to enjoy the attention his girlfriend was getting from his friend. He was like a schoolboy displaying his new toys in the playground.

'What did I see in him?' Rachel muttered. *This is a side of his character I hadn't noticed before.* She hoped Emma would dump him soon. Emma seemed to be occupied with her mobile. Rachel wondered if she was pretending to get a call. She could tell that Emma wasn't impressed with the way Josh was treating her, nor with Max.

Leaning over her old friend, Rachel found it useful to check the time on the mobile. Nine forty. 'I'd better scarper, or I'll never get back in time. Sorry Emma I can't help you.' She drifted away from the party to the main road, where she hovered next to the traffic lights. When they turned red she got into a waiting car that seemed to be heading in the right direction for Holywell. When they got to the town square, she floated out towards Winefride's well and the lakeside. As she hurriedly glided along the path towards Fairhaven she had a pang of guilt for not contacting her mother. She had no time now to give her an update. It would *have to wait until the next day. She was still fuming with anger over the information she had gleaned, and she worried whether her old boyfriend Josh knew that Max was a rapist and murderer. Had he informed Max where she would be on that fateful night? And would her friend Emma be in danger? She tried to take hold of her fury as she entered the home of her father and brother. She was ten minutes late.*

Chapter Fourteen

The Séance

After their evening meal of soup and sandwiches, Phil spent an hour in Rachel's room looking for clues. He examined her jewellery box, meticulously inspecting the few pieces that it contained. He even scrutinised an opal ring wondering if there was a secret opening under the stone. However he put that aside, not wanting to break anything. When he finally picked up the silver locket he gently prised out the photographs and tried to work out the letters and numbers written in pencil at the back of each picture.

'She must have devised some code for herself.' He supposed. The letters and numbers made no sense to him. His attention wandered and his eyes fell on to the calendar. A small grin of satisfaction curved his face as he remembered his recent encounter with the tiger on the calendar. Phil got up off the bed and walked towards it to look more closely at the tiger. Bending down he noticed some delicately etched letters in the ears of the tiger. Well, not so much as letters but something more like a collection of initials and numbers making up a type of code. It was similar to those annotations he had found on the reverse of the photographs in the locket. On the back of one such photograph she'd drawn a heart around another mysterious series of letters and numbers SH06.jJ7.Mm3.   He sighed. He couldn't fathom what they meant. 'Were they of any significance to her death?' Did J signify Josh her old boyfriend? Or is this just something she devised to amuse herself. He knew she was a good mathematician. Perhaps it was just an exercise she had invented for no-one's pleasure other than her own.

Gavin had given Phil carte blanche to look anywhere he liked in Rachel's room. However he had been hesitant about opening her wardrobe. Stealing himself to open the door again after seizing the jewellery box, he noticed her old school satchel. It was lying at the bottom next to the box of other possessions the police had returned. A few clothes still hung as if waiting for her. It seemed to him like an intrusion. However, he reminded himself he was here to try to find out who killed Rachel. He picked up the box of oddments and closed the wardrobe door. He spent over an hour flicking through various pages of notes, in her diary and notebooks. He couldn't find any mention of new relationships with either male or female since leaving school two years ago. He found that odd. Rachel had been a sociable person. It was hard to believe that she hadn't made friends during her first year in university. So why no names and phone numbers in her diary? Then he realised she had probably stored them in her mobile. Yet something nagged him. At the back of her last diary was the same pattern of initials and numbers that were on the photo in the locket.

Out of curiosity, Phil picked up Rachel's diary from the year before she had started university. This was full of her encounters with old female friends. A few initials, numbers and exclamation marks at the side of each entry, convinced Phil it was a secret language. After all he had done something similar in his youth to confuse his sister and his parents. He knew they went snooping amongst his things. Phil grinned.

The last entry under addresses in her latest diary was Josh's name but there was nothing at the side of his name. From what Gavin had told him, Rachel had met Josh during the Christmas holidays before she had been killed and so it hadn't been a long term affair. His name was there for all to see at the bottom of a list. The remaining entries on the list made no sense to him. They were just a jumble of letters and numbers. Phil deduced that as there was no exclamation mark or other symbol such as a heart after Josh's name that she wasn't serious about him.

He looked at her old address book and compared the entries with her latest address book. In the new one, there was just a list of more letters and numbers. Phil was now convinced that as Rachel had matured and become a university student she had probably wanted a bit of privacy when she returned home for the vacations. He realised that there were certain things going on in her life that she wanted to hide from her parents. Maybe she had come up with a way of recording names and mobile numbers in a code. Phil grinned. 'Clever girl.' He got a fresh piece of paper and began to copy out some of the letters and numbers starting with the photographs from the locket. Maybe the heart shape at the back of the photo signified something, perhaps someone's mobile number or name in code. Phil had no idea if anything he found, would lead them to Rachel's murderer, but he was curious about Rachel's attempts to conceal personal things from her parents. He worked for a while until he was conscious of a cool breeze caressing his neck.

"Rachel?" He called.

It was Laticia. In reply she gently scattered the photographs on the bed. Not content with that she forced the pages of the opened address books and diaries to flutter. She had no idea if there was anything of significance in these documents. Laticia just wanted to play. Within seconds Rachel floated into the room and hovered by her side. "Those photos have secret codes. I think Phil might be able to figure out I went to the Sacred Heart the night before my murder."

"Oops. Sorry. What about the notebooks and stuff. Anything in them?"

Rachel shook her head. "Nah. But I bet Phil will crack my code if he spends time on it. Not that it will be of any use."

"Well we can save him time if we can give him the information we've gathered." Laticia replied.

"Hopefully." Rachel agreed.

"Is there something significant here Rachel?" Phil asked.

Carefully, Rachel caused the photo from her locket to flutter before Phil's eyes.

"What's that? Laticia asked.

"It's the phone number for the Sacred Heart. It might be worth them going there to have a look around. We know Ryan and Maxwell go to that pub so Phil and Gavin might see them together and perhaps put two and two together. It's a long shot." She sighed. "I don't know. After seeing those bastards there together, and hearing what they said, I just want them to be discovered as soon as possible."

"I agree. They're mean, horrible, despicable, repulsive, terrible I can't think of enough adjectives to describe them, thugs."

Phil reached out for the photo and studied it for a few seconds. "Is this a clue? Rachel?"

"What are you going to do now?" Laticia asked.

"I don't know." Rachel looked at her friend helplessly. "He'll have to work it out."

"I wonder if the heart symbolises something other than love." Phil muttered. He glanced at his watch and realised that it had gone past ten o clock. He began to tidy up the documents on his bed and scooped up two sheets of blank paper that had drifted on to the floor.

The two ghosts both hovered over the bed to watch him. The results of their investigations had excited them, and their elation was stimulated as they eagerly anticipated the séance. Both felt a new surge of energy flowing through them. It started to affect Phil. He felt a heavy presence. He dreaded getting a pain in his stomach again but was prepared to suffer for a while.

"Phil are you ready?" Gavin called from downstairs. It was ten past ten and Phil realised that he hadn't prepared properly for the séance. Carefully he replaced the photo in the locket and then returned it to the box along with the documents. Grabbing a handful of blank sheets of paper and a pen he went downstairs. *The two ghosts followed him.*

The credits on Dan's Swedish noir programme on TV had finished, and he was flicking channels as Phil entered the room. Gavin had made a fresh pot of tea. He put it in front of Dan on a small coffee table where he had already laid out milk, sugar and some biscuits.

Gavin fired nervous questions at Phil
"Do you want to do it around the table?"
"Do you want the lights out?"
"Would you prefer candles?"
"Where shall we sit?"

Dan switched the television off and poured some milk into a cup. He added to the list of questions.

"Do you want a cup of tea before we start Phil? Help us relax a bit. I think Gavin is getting a bit tense."

Phil grinned. "I'd love a cup of tea." He sat down opposite Dan and helped himself to the tea. Then he turned to Gavin.

"I don't mind how we do it. We can sit around the dining table if you like. Actually it might be better because we need to lay down some letters for our contact to help us. And we don't need candles, though if you could dim the lights it would make it a bit more comforting. Less harsh I suppose I mean."

"Nice one. Rachel approved. At least we will be able to see as well."

"What do you mean – letters?" Dan asked. He bit into a ginger biscuit.

Phil brandished the blank sheets of paper. "The letters of the alphabet. Sorry I meant to get this sorted before we started. I got a bit distracted. He caught Gavin's glance but neither made a further comment on his excuse. Phil got a pen and began to write in large capitals the letters of the alphabet. "We need about three maybe four copies of each so that our contact can use them to communicate with us."

Dan was amused despite his scepticism. "So have you done this before Phil?"

Phil nodded. "Lots of times."

"And does it work?"

Again Phil inclined his head.

Gavin felt he should support his friend with a verbal reference. "Yes dad I've seen it work before. Though I've never been in one where there was just three of us and we wanted to ask specific questions." He took a sheet of paper from Phil and began to help write down the alphabet. Dan finished his biscuit and took another sheet of paper. He thought he may as well help them. He was beginning to enjoy himself despite his anxiety of participating in a séance. He had no faith in what they were doing, but it helped pass the time away. He might get a decent night's sleep afterwards. Having Phil in the house helped to take his mind off his grief.

When they had four sets of the alphabet, Phil began to cut them in to individual pieces. Gavin piled each corresponding letter on top of one another so that the alphabet was replicated four times.

Laticia and Rachel were draped over the back of the sofa watching them.

"We'll have to try not to use too much energy or all those bits of paper are going to go all over the place. It's a shame Phil didn't get something like thin cardboard." Rachel commented.

"This will test our skills." Laticia said. "I just hope they ask the right questions. They don't know what we know."

"Hmm. Maybe we can force them to ask us the questions." Rachel replied.

"Oh yeah, and how do you propose to do that?"

"It will depend on how things go. Play it by ear." She said vaguely.

Phil drained his tea, and Gavin took the tray of tea things out to the kitchen.

"Ready?" He asked on his return to the living room.

The three men walked slowly to the dining room. They each displayed a sudden feeling of self-consciousness. Dan moved stealthily as if expecting danger. He was the first to sit down around the large rectangular table. Gavin warily sat opposite him. Phil carefully carried the alphabet letters to the table and laid them out in a large circle. Satisfied that each pile of four letters were as tidy as he could get them, he sat down.

"Should we link hands?" Gareth asked.

Phil shook his head. "That's not necessary, though I think we should put our hands flat on the table and concentrate on calling a spirit to help us get some answers."

Dan turned towards him in surprise. "I thought you were going to try to contact Rachel or Anna."

"Ideally yes. It would be good to get one of them, but there is no guarantee they will hear us call. Though I have a strong feeling that they are actually with us now."

Phil eyed the dog. He noticed that his eyes were roving the room as if he was watching something move about.

Dan blinked. Gavin looked impressed.

"Right." Gavin said. "Let's do it."

"Get ready. Its show time." Rachel said.

"Why do they think they should link hands?" Laticia said casually. "Do they think they are getting extra strength from each other?"

Rachel grinned despite herself. She wanted to concentrate on what was happening. "Maybe they've been watching too many films on television. That's what they do in a séance – link hands. Or, perhaps it's a comfort thing. You know, a way of telling the person that's sitting next to you that everything is fine. Now remember try not to use too much force."

"Don't worry. I will try my best, but if you ask me that paper that Phil has used for the alphabet is so flimsy I can't see it working very well."

"Yes I know it is a bit thin and the fact that he has got piles of four for every letter of the alphabet on top of each other is going to make it difficult to extricate them one by one."

Laticia draped herself around Gavin's chair. Rachel positioned herself behind her father.

Phil closed his eyes. Dan raised his eyebrows and glanced at his son, as if to check with Gavin that he should do the same. Gavin nodded his head. They seemed to have a tacit agreement that they shouldn't speak until Phil said something.

"Is there anyone there?" Phil asked.

"Of course there bloody well is. You know we are here." Laticia groaned.

"I think we are supposed to answer?" Rachel suggested. Laticia consented with a nod of her head. "How?"

Carefully Rachel lifted a 'Y' from the pile and laid it in the centre of the circle of letters. Next she selected an 'E' and then an 'S'.

"Who is it?" Phil asked.

Again Rachel selected the letters to spell her name. She heard a gasp from her father and brother after she had laid out the letters. RACHEL. Dan's face was tense and his eyes glittered with unshed tears.

"Are you with someone?" Phil asked

"YES." The letters fluttered across the table and settled on top of the previous YES.

"Nice one." Laticia said admiring Rachel's skill.

"So far, so good." Rachel said smugly.

"Is it Anna?" Phil asked again.

Laticia caught Rachel's eye as if asking a question. Rachel guessed she wanted to reply and introduce herself, so she inclined her head to agree.

The letters fluttered in the air and though they all laid themselves out flat on top of Rachel's name the T and the C were upside down. Some letters overlapped forming strange symbols rather than letters.

Phil stared at the letters and tried to pronounce the name NO LAIJATA, LATOBIA.

Laticia quickly selected the T and C again to re-arrange them. The line of letters were slightly uneven but Phil managed to read it.

LATICIA! Not Anna." He was excited and enjoying himself immensely. So much so that he was slow getting to the real reason for the séance. Gavin and Dan stared wordlessly in wonder. They were dazzled by what was being played out in front of them.

Phil caught their eyes and asked another question excitedly.

"Rachel. Have you seen your mother?"

"YES." Rachel raised the letters so they fluttered in the air.

The three men exchanged glances. Dan and Gavin hiding their grief, sighed heavily.

"Rachel we want to try to catch your killers. On the night you died, were you able to see your attackers?" Phil asked. He was suddenly worried that they would run out of time, so decided not to ask questions about Anna.

Rachel obligingly raised another NO.

The three men looked disappointed. Dan was very sad as he was forced to recall that dreadful night. But Phil persisted.

"Can you give us any clue who might have done it?"

At last they are asking the right questions." Laticia drawled.

"I think I should just give them the names and let them figure it out. Rachel said.

Laticia shook her head. No he's asked for a clue. They need evidence not names. If you give him a name now it will confuse him. Tell him about the jackets.

Rachel was doubtful. Phil was an intelligent man he would work it out. Her father and brother would analyse the names from all angles. But she could see the sense of what Laticia was saying. She began to lift the letters.

"I'm short of another E. I will have to use an 'I'. Carefully she managed to spell JACKITS. Some of the letters fluttered across the table and got mixed up. Rachel concentrated hard to get them together again. In the end she got them to stay in a haphazard muddle though some of them, as had happened previously, were overlapping and crooked as they lay on top of each other.

Phil strained his eyes to make them out. He was afraid of leaning too far forward in case it broke the séance. "I can make out some of the letters. He concentrated then realised what the word would be. Jackets." He announced.

"Brilliant. Laticia said. He's got it.

"Anything else? Phil asked. He exchanged an excited look with Gavin and his father. Dan was holding on to the table tightly now. Phil could sense he was getting emotional. Gavin's grip was even more intense. His knuckles were white with the exertion.

The letters for B.L.O.O.D. were raised in the air. This time Rachel's fury got the better of her, and her power got too strong for her to control. The letters scattered on the floor. Phil bent down to read them.

"So there is blood on the jackets." Phil said. "Are these the blue jackets from the sailing club?"

Laticia took over. She tried to re-use the letters from the previous three yeses. She exercised too much energy and dislodged the whole pile of those specific letters. They fluttered separately across the table.

The three men gasped in shock. Simultaneously, they interpreted that mishmash of letters to signify YES.

Gavin couldn't hold back any longer. He burst out with a question.

Rachel do you suspect someone from the sailing club?" He glanced at Phil.

Phil held his breath hoping that their contact wasn't broken. He was experiencing harsh discomfort in his stomach. The flow of energy in the room was stifling. Even Leo was beginning to whimper.

"Damn I can't do another yes". Rachel said. Quickly she pulled up some of the unused letters from the muddled heap on the table. They fluttered in the air. Two of them landed on the floor. The three men watched mesmerised. Rachel eventually laid out some letters in front of Gavin.

"Not Lester. Please don't say it is Lester." Gavin said with anguish as they waited for the letters to settle. "I really liked the guy. Besides he had an alibi. Didn't he say he was in London with his girlfriend on that terrible night? Surely the police would have checked?"

With mounting anticipation they watched as the letters unevenly spelt the name M.A.X.

"Max. Max who?" Gavin asked. He frowned.

"There was a Maxwell at the boat club, when we went there earlier today." Dan burst out. He was unable to contain himself any longer.

Phil nodded. He stared at all the letters on the table. There was quite a mess there but he was exultant that they had something more to go on. Dan hadn't finished speaking though. He was getting excited.

"When we spoke, or rather when you two spoke this morning to those two men at the sailing club, there was someone with Maxwell. His name was Jamie something. He could have been the other man. The police said there were two." The words poured out of Dan in a torrent. "Those two who allegedly went to help, are they really the thugs we are looking for? Oh my god. I shook hands with Maxwell. Is he a murderer? Sorry Phil. I couldn't help talking." Dan stopped speaking.

"Don't apologise. I remember those two. I felt they were a bit shifty. One of them anyway."

"Nice one dad." Rachel said.

"Rachel do you suspect the other man Jamie?" Gavin asked. He had no worry that the séance would break now as all three of them had asked questions.

Dam. I need another O for NO. Rachel said. At the mention of Maxwell's name

Rachel felt her fury return and with it her power increased. This unexpected rush of energy caused her difficulty to maintain control. The letters on the table went haywire, rising up and down in a mini tornado of paper. The alphabet settled into another muddle of letters out of sequence. Laticia looked on half in admiration half in despair.

"You get the N and I will get the O from the floor Laticia said helpfully. An N still on the table sailed dramatically up into the air before falling again to the table to face Gavin. Then Laticia exerted more power than was needed and got the O from the floor to circle too high before falling down again on top of the N.

The men sighed. "No, not Jamie. But who?" Phil asked.

"We need to spell out Ryan but the A's and Y's are all over the place." Rachel said frantically.

Laticia was determined that Ryan should be implicated. "We'll have to rearrange the letters from under that pile." Unfortunately the mention of Ryan had made Laticia's anger rise and the letters went soaring up in the air then spiralled down again to the floor."

To make things worse her combined power with Rachel's had intensified as both ghosts were becoming agitated. Phil was given a severe jolt of pain in his stomach. It came so suddenly he felt he had to let go of the table. "I'm sorry, I can't stand the pain." He clutched his stomach. Leo sensed the highly charged atmosphere and began to bark. He jumped up and tried to paw the letters soaring above his head.

Phil was doubled up with pain. Sweat poured down his face. He closed his eyes trying to blank out the pain and so didn't see the capital letter R fly above his head. *In a desperate attempt to save the séance, Rachel forced the R to land on the table in front of him, where it settled upon a shuffled heap of paper. Unfortunately, her eagerness triggered another clump of unrelated characters to immediately tumble down on top of it.* Meanwhile, the excited dog chased floating bits of paper as they wafted off the table in front of his eyes. Dan restrained Leo whilst he and Gavin cast concerned expressions towards Phil.

"Laticia we're losing control." Rachel admonished. *"Phil's in pain."* Laticia still in a rage apologised then fled the room.

Laticia's departure had an immediate effect on the pain in Phil's stomach. It began to subside though he still folded his arms across his stomach. He began to breathe evenly. Believing the séance was no longer viable he apologised.

In a last attempt to keep the momentum, Rachel moved another R to make it fall from the table on to Phil's foot.

Still doubled up in pain with his eyes half closed, Phil didn't see the letter R float down towards him. *In any case Rachel's unbridled energy caused another panoply of letters to cascade. They settled to cover the top of Phil's shoe, upon which Leo took the opportunity to pounce and nip Phil's ankle.* Phil's reaction was to shout then move his foot away from the dog.

In the resultant confusion, more characters fluttered to the floor, though the men took no notice. They believed the séance was over.

"Phil are you ok?" Dan and Gavin regarded him helplessly.

Rachel left the room with mixed emotions. She was elated that she had managed to convey to her family and Phil some important information, but slightly disappointed that she had been unable to divulge Ryan's involvement in her murder. Still she told herself we can remedy that soon I'm sure. She went in search of Laticia and found her upstairs in Phil's bedroom. She was hovering near the window.

"I'm sorry I let rage over take me again." Laticia apologised as soon as Rachel entered the room. I so wanted them to know about Ryan that I got carried away and made Phil sick again. I'm sorry, sorry, sorry."

She glided across to the recliner chair and made herself comfortable to talk to Rachel.

Rachel regarded her friend with a rueful smile. "Don't worry. I was out of control myself. I felt the same rage and fury about Maxwell. And when I started thinking about that beast Ryan as well, my emotions got the better of me. I'm sure there will be another opportunity to get through to Phil and Gavin and my poor father. Meanwhile I think we should let them mull over things. It's a good start. We can try to communicate again tomorrow. It's nearly midnight, they will be going to bed soon."

Chapter Fifteen

Analysis

Downstairs, the three men were in various stages of astonishment. The thought of going to bed was furthest from their minds. Gavin went to the kitchen to make more tea. Silently Dan followed him to get a bottle of brandy. He poured three generous amounts. With a trembling hand he handed one glass to Phil, then sat down in an armchair nursing his own.

Though Phil still had a few queasy tremors in his stomach he felt much better now the séance was over. He was experiencing mixed feelings of amazement and achievement. Mentally he reviewed everything that had just occurred whilst surreptitiously observing Dan.

When Gavin returned with the tea tray Dan broke the silence that had engulfed the three of them.

"I have to say I would never have believed that what I have just witnessed would be possible. It's incredible that you made contact with Rachel and were able to extract so much information. Well done Phil."

"Yes. I'm dazed too." Gavin said. "This is the craziest séance I have attended. Who do you think Laticia is? And why did the letters suddenly fly all over the place?"

Phil had been pondering quietly over those two questions Gavin had raised. He put his thoughts into words.

"I think I under estimated the amount of characters in the alphabet that we needed. Also, the ghosts may have difficulty lifting them to spell. That's probably why at the end of our session the last few letters went haywire." He sipped his tea then his brandy. Both beverages were restoring his composure. He tipped a small amount of brandy into his tea and decided he would drink that whilst it was hot. "With regards to Laticia, I can only assume she is another ghost who is helping Rachel.

At first I thought we had called up two ghosts separately and neither of them were aware of the other, if that's possible. But I think they are working together. It could be their combined energy is more powerful and makes it easier for Rachel to communicate with us. But this is just a guess. I don't know for sure." He took another sip of his tea. He felt completely revived and elated. "I have heard that it could happen, though it's never happened to me. Two separate ghosts unconnected, I mean.

"Do you think the combined power is what gives you a kick in the stomach? That's what it looked like the way you reacted earlier today." Gavin asked. He caught his father's puzzled glance, and turned to his father to explain. "Dad, Phil had a similar reaction this afternoon. I thought he was ill, and when he told me that a ghost was trying to contact him, I didn't believe him."

"So has it happened before at other séances?" Dan asked.

Phil nodded. Not so violently though. I'm wondering if there is a special reason for me to feel such a forceful energy. It was working fine until we asked if Rachel knew the names of her attackers. Perhaps it was rage fuelling the energy."

Gavin frowned as he said slowly, almost half to himself, "Do you think it's because you knew Rachel and the sensations you are getting is the result of that?"

A ripple of shock ran through Phil as he digested Gavin's words. "You know, I hadn't looked at it that way, but you could be right."

Concern shaded Dan's face. "Are you alright now Phil? Twice in one day is hard on you."

"Oh don't worry about me. I'm delighted that we have made contact." He drained his tea and then reached for his brandy. "We need to discuss the clues that Rachel has given us."

"Yes. I've been thinking about that." Gavin agreed. "When we discussed the matter with those men at the boat club, what were their names, that Maxwell and…." He shook his head, disgust wearing his face as he tried to recall the name of the other person at the sailing club.

"Jamie." Dan supplied the name.

"Yes Maxwell and Jamie. Thanks dad. I thought they looked a bit shifty. Both insisted they came upon Rachel when they saw those other two guys who had rescued her, as they were leaving the boat club. The police have interviewed them and not detained them by their own admission. Even the two lads who found her said that Maxwell and Jamie had arrived from the direction of the boat house. So why does Rachel accuse Maxwell and not Jamie? And how come they both arrived after Stuart and Jason had found her?" Gavin got up to put his empty mug on the tray and then lifted up his glass of brandy before sitting on the sofa. Dan and Phil faced him from the two arm chairs.

"She mentioned blood and jackets." Dan reminded them.

"So she must know that there was blood on their jackets. Her face was bleeding and she must have felt the contact of the jackets." Gavin said. He grimaced as he thought of what his sister had suffered and he took another swig of his brandy.

"I'm as perplexed as you Gavin. I don't understand how she can say that one of the attackers is Maxwell, yet she started off by saying that she didn't know her attackers." Phil frowned.

Dan put his glass down and got up. "Well maybe she didn't know them before or during the attack, but she now knows who they are. Is it possible she has done some sleuthing herself?"

Phil paused. "Well yes, I suppose so. I hadn't thought of that." He managed a grin.
"But who is the other guy if it isn't Jamie?" Gavin said.
"I think she was on the point of telling us when I couldn't stand the pain any more. Sorry." Phil said. He was annoyed with himself, even though he acknowledged the pain had been agonising.
"You did well. You must be tired. I'm tired anyway. It's been an emotional day." Dan said. "I'm going to bed. Thanks for your efforts Phil. We can discuss this again in the morning. Gavin are you playing football in the morning?"
Gavin shook his head. "No we've called it off. We're short of players. Two players are going to the same wedding. One is the groom the other is best man. Two others have booked holidays. Anyway the weather forecast says it's going to be very hot. Something like 27 degrees. So I'm not complaining. Come on, let's get to bed. As you said, we can discuss things again in the morning before we go to Emily's for lunch."
Despite being exhilarated, Phil fell asleep almost as soon as he lay down in his bed. He was totally oblivious that Rachel and Laticia were in quiet repose at the corner of the bedroom.
Laticia couldn't resist the temptation to float over to Phil's bedside and gaze for a few minutes at his peaceful countenance.
"He looks serene."

*"Let's make sure he stays that way."
Rachel warned. She was conscious that Laticia was enjoying her new found skills of being a ghost. Both of them had calmed down again after the séance.
Laticia re-joined Rachel's side. "Just curious."
Phil began to snore lightly. Both ghosts giggled.*

The aroma of toast and scrambled eggs filled the whole house when both Gavin and Phil arrived at the breakfast table the following morning. Dan called from the kitchen that he had just made a pot of tea and that Gavin should take it to the table.

As they sat eating, Rachel and Laticia glided into the dining room and draped themselves around two chairs near the window. The room was bright with dazzling sunlight forcing both ghosts to move their positions. Each took up a corner in the opposite ends of the room.

The dog bounced excitedly towards Rachel and lay contentedly at her feet. Phil glanced at him suspiciously then sipped his tea.

"Another warm day as forecasted. I'm glad we cancelled the game this morning." Gavin commented.

"Do you regularly play football on a Sunday?" Phil asked.

"Yes. Even through the summer if we can." But as I said last night, we're a few men down. Besides, today it's very hot even for April, we could risk sunstroke. He examined his white skin under his T shirt. Some of those players are too macho to wear sun cream!" Gavin grinned wryly.

"The seasons are all over the place. Climate change." Dan said. He poured himself another cup of coffee. "I'll take the dog out for a walk later then we can go to your sister's house in the car." He offered. "I don't intend to drink alcohol today if you two want a drink. I think I had too much yesterday."

Gavin grinned. "We probably did too, but you know what they say, 'the hair of the dog.' That reminds me. We'd better take some wine for Emily."

"Yes. I'll get it. I know the one she prefers."

"Right I'll take you to the supermarket when dad takes Leo out." Gavin offered.

"But first, I think we should go over the events of last night." Dan said.

Phil nodded. "From what I can recall, Rachel and her friend Laticia, who ever she is, suspect Maxwell Briggs as one of the attackers. She is suggesting he has a blood stained jacket somewhere. Is that correct?"

Dan agreed. "She also suspects someone else who supposedly also has her blood on his jacket. But we don't know who the second person is."

"I think she knows, but we either ran out of time or we didn't give her enough help to guide us. That is, I mean to say that we didn't provide enough of the alphabet letters. That's my fault. I should have been more prepared."

You can say that again. Laticia agreed.

Rachel chuckled. "There was a bit more to it than that. Poor Phil suffered because of us."

"Don't forget you were doubled up with pain." Gavin echoed Rachel's observation. "Do you think that our questions had provoked some anger and fury? I felt there was a strong element of viciousness bordering on violence as soon as we asked about the second attacker. The manner in which those bits of papers scattered was frightening. Then Leo had his pennyworth." Gavin grinned as he recalled the dog's behaviour. His companions shared wry smiles. "It was almost as if that Laticia or Rachel was enraged." Gavin continued.

"I think both ghosts were enraged. The blasts of energy were coming from two sides of the room. That's why the letters fluttered in all directions." Phil replied.

"The thing is, what are we going to do with the information?" Gavin asked no-one in particular. It was a rhetorical question, though he hoped his companions had a plan, because he didn't have one. He inclined his head towards first his friend and then his father, hoping for ideas.

"We can't go to the police without evidence. And we can't interrogate that Maxwell and Jamie again either without raising suspicion." Dan commented. "In fact if we did, it would be tantamount to harassment.

Anyway, I'm not sure I would be able to control my temper."

Gavin agreed. "I feel the same."

"I hate to suggest this, but do you think we should try again? Have another séance?" Phil inquired. He studied Dan's face. Surprisingly he seemed cheerful considering the events of the previous night. Before replying Dan glanced at his son. They spoke with their eyes, giving consent.

"Alright." Dan said. "But not tonight. I'd like to sleep on it for a day or two. "Maybe tomorrow night."

Gavin agreed. "Yes. It will give us time to think over what we know now and then consider what we can ask Rachel and her friend."

"It's funny Anna wasn't with her." Dan mused.

"Perhaps mum hasn't developed her powers yet." Gavin suggested. He smiled at his father. "Are you becoming a convert dad?"

"I've certainly had my eyes opened." Dan ventured a rueful grin.

"Yep dad. You certainly have. And as for mum. I am going to go and see her right now." Rachel said.

"I s'pose I'd better stay here." Laticia muttered. "If I am seen at the cemetery by the Assessors they may take away my permission to leave."

"Great. You can keep an eye on these two whilst my dad takes the dog for a walk. I'll join you all at Phil's sister's house."

Laticia watched Rachel go and settled herself down to shadow Phil and Gavin. She was enjoying herself.

Meanwhile Rachel floated purposefully towards the cemetery to seek out her mother.

Anna had just risen from her grave when Rachel arrived. She arranged herself at the edge of the newly dug plot. A few withered petals had blown together to form a small mound at the foot of the grave and this decaying heap provided Rachel's perch.

"Rachel! At last. I've been wondering when you would come back. Where's Laticia?" Anna peered over Rachel's shoulder expecting Laticia to float before her eyes.

"She's checking on Gavin and Phil. Dad's going to go for a walk with Leo. I wouldn't be surprised if he shows up here soon."

Anna smiled. "How is he?"

"After last night he is surprisingly perky."

"Why? What happened? What have you discovered?

Rachel related the events of the previous day and then the séance.

"So you know who your killers are?" Anna asked delightedly. "Good work. So what are they going to do? Will they go to the police?"

"That's the problem. They don't know what to do. They don't think the police will take any notice of what they say. Besides they only have the name of one of the killers. Things went a bit awry when we tried to convey to them Ryan's name."

"I wish I could have been there." Anna sighed.

"They're going to have another séance tomorrow night. With a bit of luck I can suggest to them the name of the other killer."

"Do you think they will go to the police when you've done that?" Anna pondered half to herself.

Rachel shrugged. Absently she blew away some shrivelled leaves. She watched them soar in the air. For her own amusement she made them circle high above Anna's grave then let them drop.

Anna watched. "I can't do that - yet."

"It takes a lot of concentration. I'm still getting the hang of it. Mum, if dad goes to the police, do you really think they will take him seriously? He has to provide some kind of evidence."

"Probably they won't believe him. But if Gavin and Phil support him they might. It would depend how they presented the case. If they mention the séance they will be laughed out of the police station unless of course they find a psychic police officer. Not much chance of that, I suppose."

"What if they suggest they search Maxwell's locker at the boat club for a stained jacket?" Rachel pondered half to herself.

Anna frowned. "If they could that would be good. But they would need a good reason for doing so, and they would probably need a warrant. Don't forget that Maxwell and Jamie were interviewed just like everyone else at the boat club. It was just routine. I don't think they suspected anyone. How could the police obtain a warrant on such a flimsy suspicion? Their prime suspects were the two young men who found you, and they were cleared. After that it was Josh and he was cleared too."

At the mention of Josh's name Rachel felt angry, but chose not to tell her mother that she'd seen him with Emma. She sighed again and listened to Anna.

"Besides. You don't know for certain there is anything incriminating in Maxwell's locker. Hopefully there is. Come on, let's go and find the others to see if they have any ideas. You should talk to Stefan Kadinsky he's been working on some ideas on how to communicate with the living. He's a bit of a computer geek, amongst other things. Apparently he knew your brother."

Despite herself, Rachel laughed. "Let me guess. You've been talking about mobile phones."

"You may laugh." Anna admonished. "But you never know. Oh look, here comes your dad with Leo."

The dog bounded up to Anna and began to wag his tail. Dan looked around to see what had excited Leo. He couldn't see anything that would have distracted him. He began to wonder if the dog could see ghosts. After the séance last night, and the dog's behaviour, Dan had become less sceptical about dead spirits and such like. He half expected to see Anna rise from her grave. Checking that he was alone, he stood very close to Anna's grave, took out his mobile and dialled her number. Nothing. It was, he knew, completely dead. Sheepishly he looked around once more to check no one was eavesdropping then bent down to speak in a whispered voice to the grave.

"Anna, I don't know if you are there, or if you can hear me. Last night a strange thing happened. I was present at a séance with Gavin and Phil. We made contact with Rachel and she has told us the name of one of her killers. Maybe you are in contact with her. I was hoping you might have been with her last night. I miss you very much. I'm trying to do all those things you asked me to do. It's very hard without you. Rest in peace love."

"Anna was moved. "Poor thing. I wish I could let him know I am fine. Did they ask about me in the séance?"

"Yes, kind of. I think they expected you to be with me. They seemed surprised that Laticia was there. I think they thought they had limited time with us so rushed their questions. It isn't the time that they should worry about. They don't realise the effort it takes to control what energy we get to be able to do what they want us to do. Maybe tomorrow night will be better."

They wafted their way to the crypt where they found Margareta, Desmond and Stefan Kadinsky.

All three were eager for news from Rachel and she recited everything to them just as she had to her mother.

Stefan was the first to speak. "We didn't get much chance to introduce ourselves last time you were here. I just want to let you know that I am willing to help in any way I can. I remember reading about your murder in the papers. I'm so sorry for your ordeal."

"Thanks. I'm sorry to hear of your terrible accident. It must have been awful."

Rachel took some time to study his form more closely. His face bore an earnest countenance, detected even through the patchwork re-construction of his body. Whoever had painstakingly put him together, presumably for the sake of his family, had done a good job considering what they had to work with. The rest of his body was more of a mishmash construction. When the spirit moved, his limbs, loosely attached, trailed behind his body giving him a scarecrow appearance.

Stefan shrugged. "It was. But worse for my grieving family, just as it is for yours. That's why I want to help."

Rachel sighed and thanked Stefan again. "I don't know how you can help me, seeing as you are here and the suspects are on the other side." She replied.

"Stefan knows a lot about electronics and computers and mobile phones." Anna announced excitedly.

Rachel groaned. "Oh no. not mobile phones. Stefan are you going to tell my mum that it's impossible to use that mobile to communicate with the other world?"

Stefan grinned. His eyes twinkled in his stitched up face which stretched into a grotesque aspect as his smile widened. Rachel studied it fascinated by the façade.

"I'm not ruling it out. We are on sacred ground, where Saint Winefride performed miracles. I could at least try." Stefan reasoned.

Anna gloated as if she had found a treasure trove.

"Actually it was her uncle Bueno who put Winefride's head on again and he used the water from the font to do it. So I wouldn't count on Winefride's help." Rachel said flatly. "If anybody could help it would be St. Bueno but he's buried in Wrexham!"

"Besides she can't understand a word any of us speaks." Margareta interjected.

Rachel noticed that Margareta and Desmond looked as animated as Anna and Stefan at the prospect of communicating with the living.

"Aha, that is where you are wrong." Big Steve said. He had sauntered up as Margareta made her last statement. He was accompanied by Tomtit. "It seems that Stefan can speak in a similar language to our Saint Winnie."

Rachel whirled round. "What kind of language? I thought it was an old French or Welsh type of language that doesn't exist anymore."

"Actually you aren't far wrong. It's an old Indo European language that also has Celtic influences including an old Welsh dialect." Stefan said. "My family are from a long line of old Wallachians. I'm a descendant of a big clan of travellers and adventurers who loved roaming across Europe. Most of my ancestors married and multiplied learning various languages as they travelled. Travelling, it seems, was in their blood. Anyway the point of my rambling is, they settled in Romania. One of the old languages that has survived, in a very small way; in the area where my family live in Transylvania; is the same one that Winefride speaks."

"Bloody hell." Rachel breathed.

"Exciting. Isn't it?" Anna's eyes gleamed.

"But have you spoken to her? Has she agreed to help?" Rachel asked. She was getting excited too. She still maintained her belief that Stefan's ability in electronics was of no consequence, but if he could communicate with Saint Winefride, then Rachel was ready to concede that the saint may be able to assist in her quest for justice for her murder."

"Yes. She has." Stefan's eyes twinkled again. "She seems to spend her time in the older part of the cemetery. Apparently a few ancient spirits who speak medieval languages are buried there. They are a few centuries apart from each other, but they seem to have concocted a way of communicating amongst themselves. They

are very wary of us. But I have managed to gain her trust. I'm not fluent by any means, but I know enough to make them realise I am asking for help."

"Bloody hell." Rachel said again.

"We need to have a meeting to decide what to do next." Margareta suggested. Everyone agreed.

"Alright. But can we do it later? I have to get to Phil's sister's house. Dad, and Gavin and Phil are having lunch there. I want to listen to their conversation. Emily might know something."

"I know Emily and Phil." Stefan said suddenly. Phil used to like my stories about Transylvania. We used to chat at his sister's house."

Rachel grinned. "You are probably the reason Phil is living there now. He's a psychic, amongst other things."

"I had a feeling he had a sixth sense." Stefan smiled awkwardly, his patchwork face stretched in various directions. Through the sutured framework Rachel detected a bemused expression. One thing puzzled her. Why was he wearing an eye patch? She decided to ask him.

Stefan grinned. "I think it was for the benefit of my mother. When they finally got the rest of my bits and sewed me up, they probably thought an eye patch might make me look a bit more human."

The spirits murmured their agreement. Rachel shrugged.

"I must go. Let's meet here at half past ten tonight. I'll see you all later." Rachel drifted away.

Chapter Sixteen

Sunday lunch at Willow cottage. (Emily's place)

Gavin and Phil were in the wine aisle of a supermarket just half a mile away from Emily's house.
"Does Emily prefer red or white? Gavin asked. He picked up a bottle of Portuguese rosé.   Or maybe she would prefer something in between?"
Phil was looking through the reds. "She's just discovered white Sicilian wines and has been talking about Grillo. We may not find it, but in the meantime we could take this nice red one for us." He held up a bottle of Malbec.
"Fine. I think I've found a Grillo. There's only one to choose from with that variety of grape. Shall we take it?"
"Yes. She'll try anything once."
"What about Jack? Does he like wine?"
"He doesn't drink wine. Anyway he won't be there, he's working. Let's get that white and this red."
At the checkout they both recognised the blonde haired cashier.
 "You two again." Abigail said as she scanned the bottles. A faint blush tinged her face.
"So this is where you work." Gavin said. He was extraordinarily pleased to see her.

There was something about her that attracted him.

"Only on Sundays if you must know." Despite her sarcastic comment she managed a smile. Phil wasn't sure if that smile was because the supermarket manager was watching the transaction or if it was because she liked Gavin. He knew that the store's policy was to get the cashiers to engage in polite conversation with the customers.

"We should stop meeting like this." Gavin managed to say. He felt a bit embarrassed. Phil cast his friend an amused glance. He was surprised at Gavin's sudden bashfulness. He felt there was a spark of interest between the two of them.

"What a pathetic line!" Laticia thought contemptuously. She had followed the two men into the store.

"I haven't seen you here before." Abigail said. She took the twenty pound note from Gavin and handed him his change. Phil noted that the colour of Abigail's cheeks had deepened. A dark pink streaked her immaculate makeup.

"That's because I usually play football on Sundays." Gavin felt as if he had to explain. He could see that the line of customers were getting impatient behind him and so he and Phil moved swiftly out of the store, but not before Gavin had said "see ya." The response was another smile as she picked up an item to scan for the next customer.

"So what was all that about?" Phil asked as they walked to the car.
Gavin smiled sheepishly. "I really don't know. There's something about her. It must be that dazzling hair."
"She's certainly dazzled you."
"You can say that again." Laticia remarked.
Emily lived in a stone house that had been constructed from two very old and small stone cottages. She and her husband Jack had done most of the transformation themselves and it had taken several years. Built on Bell Lane just half a mile away from the cathedral, the sound of the cathedral bells were just audible. She and her neighbours assumed that the sound of the bells gave the lane its name. She and her friends, liked to joke about the bells. Emily enjoyed listening to the bell ringers on Tuesday evenings and again on Sunday mornings.
The smell of a traditional Sunday roast dinner greeted them as they walked through the door. As predicted, Emily was pleased with the wine choice. She made a fuss of Dan who said he didn't want to drink alcohol that day. She offered him some elderflower and lemon fizz. "I made it myself." She said proudly. "Don't worry it isn't alcoholic."
After Emily had served up generous portions of homemade blackcurrant cheesecake for their dessert, they sat outside in the shade of a gazebo to drink the rest of the wine. The children were happily playing with their toys on the patio.

Unable to contain her curiosity any longer, Emily asked if they had managed to glean anything from their séance. She sat back and relaxed in a plastic garden chair, smoothing down her denim skirt as she listened to her brother's account of the previous night. *Observing them, Laticia commented that Emily and Phil were very alike.* "You can tell they are brother and sister."

Rachel agreed. *"Yes, same straight nose, and wide chin, dark eyes. People used to say that Gavin and I were alike."*

"Yes I can see that too."

When Phil finished telling her all they had gleaned, Emily was astonished that they had discovered so much.

"So you think the other guy is Jamie?" Emily said. She poured herself another glass of wine.

Phil breathed heavily. "We're not sure. Jamie was with Maxwell when they allegedly went to offer assistance to the other two blokes helping Rachel. But we think Rachel is trying to tell us that Maxwell is guilty yet Jamie isn't. The letters in the séance started to get a bit muddled. So it *could* be someone else."

"They're on the right lines. Rachel said. Laticia agreed.

"Have you ever seen this Maxwell and Jamie before?" Emily asked.

All three men shook their heads.

"The only other connection is their clothing. Rachel hinted that there was blood on the jackets. But we don't know how to investigate that theory. Actually it isn't a theory, Rachel believes it to be true." Gavin said. He spoke slowly as if for the first time realising the significance of the clues that Rachel and Laticia had given him.

Emily looked stunned. "You talk as if you really were in conversation with Rachel. Almost as if she was real."

Gavin nodded. "She seemed very real last night."

Dan agreed. "I couldn't believe it myself that we were communicating with my daughter. It was uncanny."

"Anyway there is a coincidence about the clothing though." Phil said. "When we were in the pub yesterday we saw two young girls with kagoule type things that looked like sailing club jackets. I managed to get a look at them, and one at least had the sailing club logo on the sleeve. The girls were accompanied by an aggressive young man. He seemed to be very possessive of the girls and in particular their jackets."

"That is to say, he was possessive of one of the girls." Gavin corrected. "The darker blonde haired girl."

Phil smirked and looked pointedly at Gavin. "Ah yes. Not the blonde blonde!"

Dan looked confused. "Have I missed something?"

Emily laughed. She guessed that Gavin had a crush on one of the girls.

Rachel laughed too. "My poor brother." Laticia smiled.

"Tell me about the girls and the bloke. I might know them." Emily sipped her wine as she spoke.

Phil explained what had happened to him in the *Black Raven*, then the chance meeting later on with Abigail outside the bakery. "We saw her again at the supermarket this morning working as a cashier. She has distinctive blonde hair which is covered in some kind of pink glitter."

"Unmistakable." Gavin agreed.

"Yes I remember the glittery blonde in the pub." Dan said.

"She's obviously made an impression on you guys." Emily laughed. She bent down to pick up one of her children who was now bored with playing and wanted to sit on her mother's knee.

"Actually I think I know who you mean. I don't know her name, but very often I see her in *Walsh's* on the other side of town. I walk past it most days on my way to work at the bank. Her hair is distinctive."

Emily's statement was met by three blank faces. "'*Walsh's Hair, Beauty and Complementary Therapy Salon*' to give it the full title." Emily explained. "That will explain the glittery hairdo I shouldn't wonder. She's probably a student there and works at the supermarket to supplement her income."

She took another sip of her wine. "I'm glad you went to that supermarket by the way, because I like this wine. I will have to shop there myself to buy some more, then I can see for myself if it is the girl I am thinking of. Though from your description I think I am right."

"She only works at the supermarket on Sundays." Gavin said. "She must be the one you described. Her hair is a giveaway."

"We ought to give Gavin a clue about Abigail and Nicky." Rachel confided in Laticia. *"They will lead them to Ryan and to Maxwell."*

Laticia nodded. *"We can do that tomorrow at the séance, but I think we should go to the boat house and see if we can find a bloodstained jacket in Maxwell's locker."*

"Yes. You're right. I hope Maxwell hasn't put it somewhere else."

"I doubt it. He's too lazy and too cocky. He's convinced he's got away with it."

"So far he has." Rachel grimaced.

"What's the other girl like? You mentioned Abigail's friend." Emily asked.

"She was pretty too." Phil offered. "Or at least she would be if she smiled. She scowled at me when I picked up the jackets from the floor. They'd slipped off the chair you see. Her whole sullen countenance seemed to be connected to her boyfriend's attitude somehow. He practically dragged her out of the pub. Abigail followed." Phil stopped as he recalled the conversation the previous day with Abigail outside the bakery.

"Do you remember what Abigail said yesterday Gavin? She said that she didn't know what her friend Nicky saw in him – her boyfriend." Phil said.

Gavin sighed. "Yes. You had a strong inkling that he is the other attacker along with Maxwell and not Jamie?"

"Yes, I was convinced he had some connection with Rachel. The sensations I experienced in the pub were strong. But I don't know why? I just had the urge to pick up and examine those jackets. It doesn't make sense." Phil said.

"What was his name?" Emily asked.

"Ryan." Dan said.

"Nice one dad." Rachel said.

Emily frowned. "I don't know anyone of the name Ryan."

"There might not be a connection." Gavin reminded them. "We were desperate for clues and we didn't like the man. He was very obnoxious, so we tried to make him our prime suspect. Still it's odd that Phil had such a weird experience."

"I think it's because Lester had told us earlier that clothing had gone missing at the boat club. So it preyed on Phil's mind. I think that's why he decided to look at those jackets in the *Black Raven*." Dan suggested.

"No. Dad. You're wrong. Rachel frowned and shared Laticia's worried expression.

"Phil wasn't convinced with Dan's explanation but said nothing.

"So what are you going to do with the information you have?" Emily asked. "Are you going to go to the police?"

"We'll have to try." Dan said. But I think we'll wait until Tuesday. We are going to have another séance tomorrow night."

"Why wait?" Emily asked.

"I wanted to mull over a few things first. Besides I wanted a clear head. I was feeling groggy this morning, I don't mind admitting, though after that lovely meal I feel a lot better thank you. And I enjoyed the home-made elderflower fizz."

Emily nodded sympathetically. "I understand how you feel and I'm glad you enjoyed your meal."

She turned her gaze from Dan to Gavin and then back again to Dan. "Can I ask you, if it isn't too painful a question, what time Rachel died? And do you know if forensics managed to find out the exact time of the attack?"

Gavin breathed heavily. "When the two guys, Stuart and Jason found her, it was five minutes past eight. She was barely conscious and died before the ambulance could get to her. We know it's that time because Jason had a mobile phone call, and though he didn't bother answering it, out of respect for Rachel's condition, he'd glanced at his mobile and noticed the time." Gavin paused and his father continued.

"We don't know what time the incident occurred, but we know she was supposed to meet her friends at quarter to seven. It is estimated that she was possibly in the water for about twenty to thirty minutes, maybe more before she was found." So we can assume she was attacked sometime between quarter to seven ish and approximately twenty past seven." Dan reported this automatically. He had had to relate this information so many times to family members. He looked down at his shoes as he recalled the event, just like he went over and over it again in his head each day. He found a welcome release to talk about it to Emily, even though he hardly knew her.

"Do you think that's relevant?" Phil asked. "The time I mean."

Emily nodded before answering.

"Have you considered that this Maxwell could have done the murder earlier, then double backed to the club to pretend he was always there? Jamie would not necessarily be the other assailant."

"She's good. Rachel breathed excitedly. Laticia agreed.

Phil and Gavin exchanged glances then directed their eyes towards Dan. He too sat up in surprise. They hadn't considered that angle.

"But that would make it a planned attack rather than a random one, as the police surmised." Dan said.

Phil analysed the possibility. The theory was something he had considered earlier but couldn't conceive how it could be accomplished.

"It still could be a random attack, if the person he was with was the instigator. He may have agreed to meet someone, sneaked off from work, randomly attacked Rachel and then panicking ran back to the boat club." Phil suggested slowly.

"No that's not quite true. But he's on the right track." Laticia threw a sidelong questioning look at Rachel. Her companion nodded her agreement.

"Much though I detest them both, and that it was Maxwell who started the attack, I hate Ryan the most because of the way he treats Nicky." Laticia said.

"The mention of him certainly strengthens your power." Rachel acknowledged.

"If Maxwell was supposed to be working his shift at the boat club why would he arrange to meet someone before his shift was finished. And how would he sneak out without Jamie or anyone else noticing, and then return?" Gavin threw the question to everyone around the garden table before continuing. "Obviously it would have to be a man he was meeting. But why meet? Surely not to rape any random girl who happened to be there? It isn't as if Rachel was in that area every night, so that they could plan to attack her. If Maxwell was meeting someone, there must have been a good reason. It would take two very confident, heartless persons to carry out that despicable act, and then turn up an hour or so later at Rachel's body some time later. Pleading innocent mind you!" Gavin drew breath.

"Yep Rachel said bitterly. That's what Max did!"

Gavin asked another question. "And how did he leave and return without anyone noticing?"

"I can answer the last question." Emily said. She leaned forward, her eyes gleaming as she went over her theory. "There's a path that used to run almost level with the old railway line. It's not used because the local council don't maintain the path and it is covered in overgrown branches and all kinds of wild vegetation. It's very narrow but someone who knows it could easily get on to the path, well it's not so much a path really, but more like a goat track. It passes the rear of the boat club. I think it was used by the railway maintenance crew when there used to be a railway along there. The actual old railway line used to pass where both the boat club and the boat sheds are now standing. Those buildings as you know are new ones, only a few years old."

Emily paused as she recalled how things in the town had changed over recent years.

"If you follow the goat track from the sailing club and boat sheds towards town, it will bring you out near the kissing gate. As you know the gate is set into the boundary wall of the town. From there you can walk into Holywell town centre, if you follow the pathway. Or," Emily paused for breath, then Gavin finished the sentence for her. "You can get access to St. Winefride's well, the abbey and the cemetery!"

Emily nodded. "From any of those places you have the option of using the new pathway to the *Black Raven* or you can walk down the slope to the lake. It's much quicker than the usual route along the lakeside." Emily continued. "So if someone had a secret liaison, as it were, at the well or within the vicinity of the well, they could easily get back to the boat club within five maybe ten minutes."

"Bloody hell! Rachel exclaimed.

Emily's small audience listened intently then quietly mulled over Emily's words. Phil was the first to speak. "The kissing gate is about a hundred yards away from the town square. There wouldn't be many people around much after seven o clock because there isn't anywhere open at that time. The *Winking Frog* is concealed from the lake by the town wall. The only people you are likely to see are dog walkers or one or two couples going for a stroll."

"Jason and Stuart said they saw some women go to the women's institute opposite the '*Winking Frog*; but scarcely anyone else." Gavin commented. "Except a group of men and women he didn't know, outside the pub."

"It was also cold and the light was fading. It had been sunny most of that day." Dan said. He recalled the day vividly in his mind, as he often did. He had grown animated listening to Emily's observations. "So it seems that the only people about were Rachel, her friends, a few women and some early drinkers at the pub." Dan stated quietly. "Rachel was in the wrong place."

"They were meeting to go to see a film and then plan a week end away, so I recall." Gavin said.

Is that true?" Laticia asked. Rachel nodded. Yes we were going to stay in Emma's cousin's house in London. We would have had to sleep on the floor though. It's not a big house. It was a cheap way of getting to stay in London for a couple of days."

"So why would this Maxwell want to meet someone for half an hour before he finished work, and sneak off to do it." Dan asked.

"Actually I think I know that path Emily. It used to be well used until the council gave planning permission to build the sailing and rowing boat club. I suppose most people have forgotten its existence."

"Well I think someone knew about that path and has used it for their own evil ends. Someone local." Emily suggested. "Someone called Maxwell." She added.

"That path will have been so overgrown that anyone wanting to use it would have to be prepared to hack a way through, yet make sure no-one else could see and use it." Phil commented thoughtfully. "I agree with you Emily. It would have to be someone local to know about that path. Maxwell is the obvious person. But who else?"

"Someone able to sneak out from the sailing club un-noticed." Gavin answered Phil's rhetorical question. His face was grim as he allowed himself to imagine the fear his sister would have known. "I think Maxwell and someone else is engaged in an illegal practise. Not only that, but they are a pair of thugs prepared to randomly and viciously assault a young woman."

"But if the other man isn't Jamie who is the other brute? This other person you were talking about, Ryan, what if he works at the boat club." Dan suggested.

Phil shook his head. "If Ryan is the other man we are looking for, I don't think he would be working at the sailing club. There would be no reason for Maxwell to skive off to meet him."

"That Maxwell seemed very arrogant when we spoke to him." Gavin commented. He was thinking hard. "It may have been a way of covering up his guilt."

"But you can't go accusing a man of murder just because he is over confident." Emily said.

"Maybe Rachel had stumbled on to something. You know, saw them doing something and they had to silence her. In the most brutal way." Emily continued. She made this last comment in a quiet voice. She could see that Dan and Gavin were upset. Both displayed their emotions in different ways. She sensed that father and son were trying to be strong for each other. She hesitated before continuing.

"Two possibilities come to mind to explain why Maxwell was there on that fateful evening.

One: He needed to meet someone at a particular time to plan a future robbery and

Rachel overheard their plans. Though I don't recall any burglaries that night nor days later.

Two: Perhaps he is dealing with drugs and needed to pick up or drop off supplies and Rachel stumbled on to them. In my opinion something drugs related is more feasible." Emily sat back and drained her wine glass.

"Or maybe he was blackmailing someone, or collecting a debt, a gambling debt maybe?" Dan suggested.

"None of these theories are impossible, if you try to put yourself into the mind of an evil person." Emily agreed. She turned on her brother. "Phil when are you going back to Romania?"

"Wednesday."

"I was thinking, that you should have another séance tonight." She turned to Dan, "I know you said you would prefer to wait until tomorrow, but time is getting short. If Phil is to utilise his time to the best advantage, I don't think you should wait. If you could get more information from Rachel and her friend, then you will have more ammunition to present to the police. At the moment you have no evidence, only information."

There was an awkward pause after these words and Emily tactfully got up to gather the empty glasses on to a tray. "I'll make some coffee." Leaving the others to contemplate her observations, she walked to the kitchen followed by her two young children.

Rachel gasped at Emily's statement. She turned to Laticia. "What she suggests is good in one way, but bad in another. I've arranged to meet up with my mum and the others at half past ten in the crypt. If my dad agrees to hold another séance tonight, I hope it will be early."

"Do ya have to meet your mum and the others?" Laticia asked. "Surely another séance is more important. Of course I could stand in for ya."

"Thanks, that's very good of you. But you're right, the séance is more important."

"What do you think dad?" Gavin asked tentatively.

Dan sighed deeply. "I suppose it makes sense to continue where we left off." He turned to Phil. "How about starting earlier than last night though. Say about eight o clock? I would like an early night, if that's ok with you two."

Phil was excited. "Yes. That's fine with me. Gavin, what do you reckon?"

"Yes. Eight o clock is a good time."

"Perfect!" Rachel enthused. That means I can help with the séance then go and see mum and the rest of the gang. Meanwhile we can go and see if we can find something incriminating in Maxwell's locker."

Chapter Seventeen

Searching for Evidence

Once Dan had agreed to hold another séance the conversation turned to other matters mostly concerning Emily's house alterations and her children.
Rachel and Laticia left the little group chatting and made their way down to the boat club.
The time was almost six o clock and several members of the public were still testing their skills at rowing boats on the lake. Sunday afternoons were usually busy especially when the weather was warm. Families were enjoying themselves on the water and keeping the wardens busy. In the distance the two ghosts could see that Jamie and Lester plus two other boat club employees were engaged in surveying the lake for any sign of danger. Closer to the club building, Maxwell was giving advice to would be boat hirers.
"That's a bit of a contradiction - Maxwell being some kind of a body guard when he savaged me to death!" Rachel said bitterly.
"Well, never mind him! Let's go and see if we can check out his locker." Laticia suggested. "We must be careful. If we have to use all our energy to find what we are looking for, things may start jumping out of all of the lockers! If Maxwell or anyone else for that matter, sees items of clothing airborne it could ruin things for us. There

could be a mighty big clean up forcing Maxwell to hide the evidence elsewhere." Laticia draped herself over the doorway and grinned. *"On the other hand it could be funny. They might call in a poltergeist or something, and get the lot of 'em to remove their belongings."*

Rachel rolled her eyes at such a thought. "I doubt it." She commented. "Let's hope the evidence is still in Maxwell's locker."

There was no-one in the staff changing room fortunately. However, Rachel realised forlornly that they didn't know the number of Maxwell's locker.

"Dam it. How are we going to find that out?" Laticia asked. "I s'pose we could try the office to see if there's a register?"

Rachel nodded. "Yes there is, but I don't think we have the power to get it out of the drawer and then open the pages in the book. I remember seeing the book when I used to work here as a volunteer. They may have transferred everything to a computer now, and that's even less helpful for us."

Together they glided out of the staff changing room and made their way towards the main office. The receptionist was on the 'phone. Rachel showed Laticia the locked drawer where she thought the register was kept. "I haven't got the energy to open the drawer. Besides the receptionist will get alarmed if I did."

"Her back is turned away from the drawer. Let's combine our sources. It's worth a try."

Laticia suggested. "After three. One, two three."

Nothing happened. They tried several times and then gave up.

"The drawer is probably full of stuff. It's too heavy. We'll just have to wait until Maxwell comes back." Rachel sighed. She noted the time on the wall clock above her. "It's ten past six. We've got about twenty minutes before they call the boats off the lake."

"And probably another hour after that for them to clean up everything." Laticia observed. "In that time we could have a look through the door of all the lockers to see if we can see a black bin bag lurking around and hopefully something with his name on it."

"I suppose so, but lots of people use black bin bags. And unless all the employees make a point of putting their name on the inside door of the lockers we have no way of knowing which one is Maxwell's. It's also possible that he might have transferred the jacket to a carrier bag."

Laticia shook her head. "Nah. He's not gonna use a carrier. More likely he would just shove it away and forget it."

During the next five minutes they pushed their heads through the doors of several lockers without success.

"I'm losing energy." Rachel said. "I need to rest or I won't be able to help with the séance later."

"Me too. Let's wait a while." Laticia agreed. "We've done most of them."

They settled themselves near the door and were startled twenty minutes later to see Maxwell enter the room with Jamie and Lester and two other employees. They dumped a box of cleaning equipment on the floor along with a brush and a mop. Lester turned to give instructions to the men. "Dave, Steve these are the lockers where you can keep your things. I will arrange for you to have a key each tomorrow."
"They must be new members of staff." Rachel said.
Laticia agreed. "Getting ready for the summer I suppose."
"Jamie as soon as the last boat is in, you start cleaning up in here, and Max and the rest of us will scrub the boats."
Jamie grinned. For once he was getting the easier task. His grin soon disappeared, when Max said, "Actually, If it's alright with you I'd rather clean up in here, my back is giving me gyp again."
Lester looked faintly perplexed. "I thought your back problems were sorted now."
Max put on a pained expression. "It comes and goes."
Lester scrutinised Max's face. He hadn't noticed Max displaying pain during the day. He sighed. "Right. You clean up in here and Jamie can help with the boats. Perhaps we should re-arrange your shift patterns Max." Lester offered.
This time Max looked worried. "No, it's OK. I'm sure it will be fine soon. I'll go back to

the doctor and get some stronger pain killers."

"Alright. Suit yourself. But we need to sort this out." Lester turned to the two newcomers to include them as he spoke to Max. "The club policy here is that everyone gets a turn at doing everything on a rota. This is the fourth time this week that Jamie is on boat scrub. He's had to cover for Simon. I really think we should consider changing your timetable completely and take you off the evening shift."

Max appeared worried at Lester's suggestion. "I'll sort it out." Max reiterated. He held Lester's gaze.

Lester shrugged. "Well if you're sure." He turned to apologise to Jamie. "Sorry."

Jamie smiled good-naturedly. "It's o.k."

The five men left the room and Laticia and Rachel exchanged glances.

"Hmm. That sounds suspicious to me." Rachel said. "I think Lester is suspicious too."

"I think you're right. Max is a skiver, amongst other worse things. He didn't want a change in shifts. That was obvious. Whatever he is up to a change of shifts would spoil things for him. But let's see what that horrible man gets up to when Lester is out of sight."

Half an hour later, when all the boats were in, Maxwell returned alone to the locker room. He opened his locker and pulled out his jacket and boots. Taking off his wet wellingtons he then shoved them back into the locker and put on his boots and jacket. After a furtive look over his shoulder to make sure he was alone, he lifted a small brown padded envelope from the shelf and put it in his breast pocket on the inside of his jacket. He then closed the locker door and turned the key to secure it.

"Hmm I wonder what that could be." Laticia said. "Are you thinking what I am thinking?" Rachel nodded.

In the corner of the room there was a large sink where Max filled up a bucket with water and poured in some detergent. He then seized the mop.

Deliberately he poured a large quantity of water from the bucket over the floor, and swished it with the mop to spread it across the floor. The water covered a large section of the floor, but Max was careful not to let it become too saturated. Without bothering to clean the floor properly he dumped the mop in the bucket then left the room. *Laticia and Rachel followed him.*

In the reception area there was no-one about, and Max stealthily strode across the wide foyer, then down a short corridor to a small back room. This was used for keeping cleaning equipment. The window, just like all the windows at the back of the building was a metre and half above the floor. They were quite narrow in height approximately half a metre, yet they stretched widely across the walls including the reception and foyer area. Whilst they afforded no pleasing view other than a high overgrown embankment, the windows provided a lot of light.

With the aid of a chair to stand on Max easily slipped through the window of the cleaning equipment room. He then jumped on to a narrow dirt track that ran all along the rear of the building. The width of the pathway, wide enough perhaps for a gardener to cut back some brambles each year, bordered the steep embankment. Max was faced with a thick mass of wild vegetation which at first glance appeared to present an impenetrable undergrowth. He confidently strode to a thick wedge of green ferns that curtained a small opening. Taking care not to break the branches as he sidled through the ferns, Max eased himself under a canopy of dense greenery on to an old goat track. Within seconds he was out of sight.

"So Emily was right. That's the old railway embankment track used by railway workmen. This is where he skives off. It's probably where he went the night he killed me." Rachel said. *"Look at that old log propped against the wall over there. I bet he uses that to climb back through the window."*

"But where is he going?" Laticia mused.

They decided to follow him. Max moved quickly up the embankment with no sign of a bad back. In some places he had to bend to avoid the sprawling brambles. This presented no problem for the two ghosts.

At the top of the old railway embankment he jogged along to where the path met with the adjoining paths that gave walkers options for either trails to the town; the lake or the cathedral and well. Max chose the cathedral. Laticia and Rachel were not surprised to see Ryan standing near the lych gate of the cathedral. They saw Max hand over the package to Ryan and in turn he handed Max a small brown envelope.

"I bet that's money for drugs or something like that." Rachel said.

Laticia nodded. "You bet. This is probably what they were doing when they saw you a year ago. Perhaps they thought you were spying on them."

"The irony of that is, that I wasn't spying then, but I am now. It would be comical if I didn't feel so outraged."

The transaction was made with barely a word said. Both men looked furtive. Maxwell hurried back to the boat club with Rachel and Laticia close on his heels. In the locker room, he cautiously looked around him to see if anyone was watching. He put the brown envelope next to a small box on the top shelf of his locker, and carefully pushed the door too but not completely shut. Whilst Rachel pushed her head through the locker door to peer inside, Max set about cleaning up the floor with his mop.

"There's definitely a black bin bag at the bottom of his cabinet. It's crammed against the locker wall and he's piled his boots and

a pair of shoes on top. There's a couple of tiny rips in the bag, probably punctured from constant dumping of his heavy boots, shoes and wellingtons on it. I can see something blue in it, but I haven't the strength to lift the things on top to check if it is a jacket. It might be a blue towel or a jumper." Rachel said.

"Let's try together. First of all we need to remove the shoes." Laticia said. *After a great effort they managed to loosen one shoe which fell out of the locker on to the wet floor. Maxwell cursed, picked up the shoe and rammed it back inside closing the locker door hard.*

"Don't give up. We might be able to move them if we try again." Laticia said.

Together they concentrated, but whilst they managed to move one shoe it merely turned on its side dragging the other with it. The pair of shoes became pinned to the wall of the locker whilst half balancing on the boots.

"They're wedged too far down on top of his boots." Rachel replied. *"Those are going to be too heavy."*

They tried anyway but without success. Their efforts resulted in causing the shoes to slip further down the side of the bin bag and lie embedded against the locker wall. The movement forced the heavy boots to rock sideways pinning the shoes down and crushing the bin bag even more. Despite their continued labours they couldn't shift the boots.

"That's that then. We'll just have to depend on Dad and Gavin to sort it out." Rachel said resignedly. "At least we now know we can move things heavier than paper!"

Sadly they watched the thug mop up the floor.

"And we know the number of his locker is fourteen and that there is a bin bag in there." Laticia said. "I reckon it's the same bag with the jacket in it."

"I hope so." Rachel replied.

Laticia sensed Rachel's disbelief and tried to cheer her up. "Of course it is girl. He's too damned cocky to have thought of dumping it somewhere. He thinks he's got away with your murder."

Rachel felt a little buoyed up at Laticia's encouragement and she allowed herself to feel optimistic again. They hovered around observing Maxwell with loathing.

Max took the bucket to the sink to empty it and rinse out the mop. He then changed his wellingtons for his boots, pushing them down hard on to the bin bag. He seized his shoes and re-positioned them on top of the wellies.

Rachel and Laticia exchanged glances of resignation.

After securing his locker door he carried the cleaning equipment through the reception entrance to the storeroom. In there he shoved all the stuff and closed the door. At that point Lester and Jamie returned. With them was the receptionist who had been outside helping with the boats, and the two new young men.

Lester locked up the building and together all the staff left the building. The clock on the wall struck eight o clock.

"We're going to be late." Rachel said.

Laticia laughed. "They can't start without us."

At that precise moment, Phil was writing out another round of the alphabet. He'd rescued the remains from the previous session and had already added another complete set. This meant, when he'd finished writing another round there would be six copies of each letter. Gavin watched him anxiously as he laid them out in a circle as he had before.

Dan was standing by the window looking out at the changing scenes in the evening sky. Smudges of grey clouds edged with gold from the setting sun formed a streaky trail above. He watched as the splodges gathered then broke into small pieces that scudded away into nothing. Dan wondered if that was how it was to be a ghost. To scud away into vapour. He turned towards his son and then gazed at Phil still busy with the slips of paper at the table.

"Ready?" Phil asked. Signalling to Gavin with a nod of his head Dan sat down. This time Dan was more hopeful than he had felt before. Phil noticed a change in him for the better. Even though he was tired, he seemed to have enjoyed the afternoon at Emily's and now looked relaxed. Gavin seemed twitchy. Ever since Emily had mentioned the railway track at the back of the sailing club, his behaviour had been noticeably jumpy. He was anxious for results. Phil was sympathetic. Quietly he spoke into the silence.

"Is there anyone there? Rachel can you hear me?"

Nothing. Phil tried again. This time he thought he would call Laticia. Still no response.

They waited pensively. The atmosphere was charged with pent up emotions. Phil could feel their longing, but he felt nothing else in the room. Disappointed he spoke to his two companions. "There doesn't seem to be a connection."

"Maybe it's too early in the evening." Gavin said lamely.

Phil shook his head. "I don't think the time of day matters."

"We can try later?" Dan suggested. He looked at his watch. It was ten past eight.

Phil shrugged. "If you like. Ow." He gasped as Laticia passed through him to hover near the table.

"Are you ok?" Gavin asked hopefully. He recognised the symptoms Phil was experiencing and even before Phil assured him he was fine, he knew that a ghost or two had arrived.

"I think we're in business." Phil nodded. He took a deep breath.

Rachel admonished Laticia for hurtling herself at Phil.

"Sorry. I was anxious to get here as you know. I miss directed myself. Still it's good to know he can feel the energy." She grinned and Rachel felt she could only agree. They had used a lot of energy to get to the séance. In fact they had used a lot of their power during the last few hours. Rachel felt they hadn't achieved an awful lot for their efforts. She wanted to establish if the bin bag at the bottom of Maxwell's locker did indeed hold the evidence they were hoping for.

No matter what Phil asks us we need to make sure that they pick up a lead to Maxwell and Ryan." Rachel said to Laticia.

"Yes. And also tell them about Abigail and Nicky. They could be key to all of this."

Rachel was doubtful. "Possibly, but only in an indirect way."

Laticia surveyed the alphabet letters laid on the table. "Well at least Phil has provided us with more letters."

Rachel nodded. "I just hope we can manage to lift them one by one and not scatter them."

"Rachel are you there?" Phil asked.

Obligingly Rachel raised the letters Y.E.S.

"So far so good." Laticia said as she admired the precision the letters were raised. They both witnessed the animated faces of the three men.

All three men gasped with mixed feelings. Phil was relieved, Gavin became more excited, and Dan displayed astonishment that he was actually involved in a séance once again.

Phil plunged in quickly afraid that he may lose contact. "Rachel, if you remember, last time you were going to tell us the name of the second person who attacked you. Do you know his name?"

"Don't waste time saying YES. Laticia advised. Just spell out RYAN."

"I'm going to do just that." Rachel said. Carefully she lifted the letters to spell R.Y.A.N. The pile of letters signifying Y seemed to be compressed tightly on top of each other and so Rachel inadvertently removed two of that same digit. They lay awkwardly on top of each other though this didn't affect the message she wanted to convey.

All three men seized on the name RYAN.

"It's the name Ryan! Maybe you were right Phil?" Gavin asked excitedly.

Phil nodded. He shared Gavin's excitement. "But Ryan who?"

Rachel and Laticia exchanged shrugs. Neither of them knew Ryan's surname.

"Tell them to search Maxwell Briggs's locker." Laticia said.

Rachel shook her head. "He should ask Nicky about Ryan's jacket."

"He doesn't know Nicky."

"She must mean that guy in the pub with those two girls. His name was Ryan." Dan said.

Phil acknowledged Dan's remark with a nod of his head. "Yes, I told Gavin that I had a strong feeling that Ryan was connected in some way. But just to make sure we have the right man, let's ask Rachel if we are right."

"Rachel do you mean Ryan the boyfriend of Nicky?"

"Y.E.S."

"Where will we find him?" Gavin asked.

"MAXWELL LOCKER." Rachel replied. She was running out of ideas to communicate with limited letters. It took a lot of effort to get the letters together.

"Tell them about the bin bag." Laticia said. She hovered over Rachel getting exasperated. She badly wanted to participate.

Rachel looked at her friend for inspiration. How could she communicate with such small letters? Already they were becoming jumbled, the paper was so flimsy. She was also limited in her reserve of power to be able to move the pieces of paper. She gave Laticia a warning look as she saw her getting ready to use her own capacity. Quickly Rachel hovered closer to the table and with some effort tried to raise the letters to spell evidence.

Phil shivered as he felt Rachel's closeness.

The characters of the word she wanted required three E's. She laid them out haphazardly and despite being a character short the participants seized on the word E.V.I.D.E.N.C.

"So there is evidence in Max's locker?" Gavin said excitedly. "What kind of evidence. His mind worked fast, mentally listing the kind of proof that would be useful in a murder case. "Do you mean a blood stained jacket?"

In the absence of E's. Rachel laid the letter Y over the first e in evidence and then added S underneath as if she was forming a crossword.

Using some stray letters she gave them another clue. B.I.N. B.A.G.

"Surely this is enough to go to the police." Gavin asked excitedly. He aimed the question at his father.

"But will they believe us? They have no reason to believe Maxwell is a suspect and we don't know who Ryan is." Dan reasoned. "But I'm willing to give it a try."

Rachel wanted to tell them to ask Lester for help, but the medley of words on the table now made it difficult to spell out the name. She was also feeling rising rage as she called up the letters needed to spell her assailants names. Inevitably slips of paper began to go haywire and cause another jumble of letters. Attempting to take control of her new surge of energy Rachel concentrated on the jumbled mishmash that contained the necessary characters that she needed. She longed to tell her brother that making contact with Lester as well as the two girls Abigail and Nicky would lead him to Ryan.

"Let's rearrange everything a bit." Laticia said. Excitedly she began to move the debris on the table. Unfortunately, her *stored up energy combined with her over enthusiasm caused several pieces of paper to flutter from the table across the room to fall on to the floor. The remaining pieces of paper spilled over the edge of the table and joined the rest of the slivers of paper.*

Leo began to whine, and Dan fearing that he might jump up gave him a warning look. He was afraid to move in case the séance was broken.

"Careful!" Rachel admonished. She stared at the hodgepodge of paper on the floor. "Help me spell LESTER. My energy is erratic. We can't do much more now with this mess. But I can see some of the characters we need."

Pooling their strength they foraged through the muddled mess of paper on the floor and eventually managed to float up the name L.E.S.T.E.R. and lay it on the table.

Phil got an unexpected jolt in his stomach, though it eased off very quickly. Gavin stared at the name in wonder. "I think she wants us to ask Lester to look in Maxwell's locker. But we can't do that. It would be asking him to breach his privacy and we have nothing to go on to convince him to do it."

Rachel looked at Laticia in despair. "Now what?"

Both ghosts were tired. All their activities during that day had demanded a lot of energy. Although they were rapidly learning to use their power, their strength came in waves. As each day drew to a close they found their vim waning.

"I think I will go back to the cemetery. You had better stay here." Rachel said. "I get bursts of uncontrollable energy when we mention Maxwell and Ryan then it fades again when I try to be rational. Today has been tiring."

Laticia agreed. "We've been making bigger and bigger demands on ourselves today. If I can think of anything I will let you know. I will keep an eye on these."

Phil felt a cold shiver as Rachel left. He noted how Leo who had been lying contentedly near the window had suddenly become agitated when the letters had started to float haphazardly. Now the dog raised his head and gazed towards the window from where Phil supposed Rachel had departed. Yet he could still sense a presence of a ghost.

Meanwhile Laticia propped herself at the opposite end of the room to rest. She looked down at the scattered fragments of paper on the floor in exasperation.

It seemed to her that trying to bring Rachel's killers to justice was not going to be as easy as they had thought. The police would take a lot of convincing to arrest Ryan and Maxwell. Casting her eyes around the room she noticed on Gavin's shoe two stray characters A and B. She supposed that when the greater part of the alphabet fell off the table those unused pieces had remained together unshuffled. She looked for the letter 'I'.

"We're losing contact." Phil said. "Yet I can sense something lingering." The other two men grunted their agreement. Then Gavin looked up and saw a small piece of paper soar in the air before disappearing under the table. He bent down to see the name ABI emblazoned across his shoe. "Maybe not." He raised his head excitedly and bumped it on the table. "Ow." He put up a hand to rub his head. "Look at my foot."

Bemused, Phil and Dan obeyed his excited command.

"What do you suppose that means?" Gavin asked. He lifted the three pieces of paper and laid them out in front of them. A.B.I.

"Maybe we are not alone after all." Phil whispered. "Laticia are you still there?"

For her part Laticia felt she had done all she could. If she tried to answer they would ask more questions and her earlier vim had dissipated. Unlike Rachel who seemed to be able to control her vigour, most of the time, Laticia expended her vitality in strong bursts which then weakened her. She felt too lethargic to search through the pile of muddled paper on the floor. It had been a lucky fluke that she had managed to draw their attention to Abigail. In any case she didn't know what else she could do. The necessary 'I' lying idle on top of the paper pile had also been a stroke of chance. She withdrew again to a corner and watched.

The three men waited expectantly. Their eyes in turn sought each other's looking for clues. Each of them reading hope mingled with wonder. When it became obvious that no more contact with the ghosts were imminent, Phil slumped back in his chair. "So." He uttered the word slowly. "Abigail. What does that tell us?" He directed his attention towards Gavin.

"The girl with the glittery blonde hair who works on Sundays at the supermarket." Gavin replied.

Phil nodded.

Dan looked from one to the other. "She's the girl you saw in the pub yesterday with her friend and the aggressive man Ryan?"

"Yes with his girlfriend Nicky." Phil confirmed. "And Abigail. Somehow they are all connected."

"And we are back to the bloody jackets again." Gavin observed. He amended his statement soberly. "Bloody in the cruellest sense of the word."

"Tomorrow, I think we should go to the police with our suspicions." Phil said. "Somehow we have to convince them that they should re-interview Maxwell and find out where Ryan lives."

Dan fetched the bottle of brandy and three glasses. "I think you are right."

Chapter Eighteen

Chance Encounters

Rachel made her way to the graveyard. She had mixed feelings of elation and exasperation. She quickly found her mother and their group of new friends in the crypt.
After she had related to them all the outcome of the second séance there was an awed silence.
"So basically you have discovered the identity of your killers and you have told your father and brother, but they still haven't got the evidence." Stefan said.
"Yep." Rachel said with feeling. She was weary.
Anna said nothing. She was glad to know that at last she knew who had killed her daughter. She still felt the same grief and anger of a year ago, when the police had told her of Rachel's death. In her mind she turned over how to help Rachel force the police to arrest the two men involved.
"Bloody bastards!" Desmond said. Big Steve and Margareta nodded in agreement.
"So what now? Another séance?" Margareta asked.
Rachel shook her head. "I don't think so. Obviously if that's what they want Laticia and I will participate, but I don't think it will help now. What else can another séance achieve? We have told them all we know except Ryan's address, but we don't have

the facility to do that. In any case what good would that do? They can't go knocking on his door accusing him of murder."

"Somehow we have to get the police involved." Anna said.

Everyone agreed.

"You could accompany them to the police station tomorrow and you and Laticia must try to figure out how to guide them to the bin bag in Maxwell's locker." Big Steve suggested.

"Easier said than done." Rachel said. "It takes a lot of concentration just to move pieces of paper around. Forcing an officer of the law to investigate two men who were not prime suspects, and without evidence is going to be very difficult. Even when Laticia and I join forces we are limited in what we can do."

"Talking of Laticia. The guards are on alert to find her. She must be careful not to be found or they will take away her pass. Where is she?" Margareta asked.

"She's resting in my room at home." Rachel replied. "I am going back to my coffin now to get some rest too."

Anna accompanied Rachel to her coffin. On the way she mentioned that though the guards were on the lookout for Laticia she was hoping that she could come to the graveyard the following day to help with a project that Stefan was hoping to carry out.

Despite being tired, Rachel grinned. "Does this involve mobile phones mother?"

"Yes. But don't be so cynical. We are working on a plan which just might work."

Rachel yawned. "Have it your way. Good night."

Anna sashayed to her own coffin and made herself comfortable.

In her own sarcophagus Rachel lay down in the soft silk folds. Before she closed her eyes she shifted her gaze to the inanimate mobile phone and managed a grin as she thought of her mother's optimism. She wondered what she had in mind for Laticia and herself. Another question that mystified her was Stefan's conviction that he could use his old engineering skills as a computer consultant to make the mobile useful again. He was obviously very knowledgeable about many things, but using mobiles to contact the living? Anyway, she thought he was studying to be a solicitor before his accident. And just before she dropped off to sleep, she puzzled over what could be Saint Winefride's part in the scheme?

Gavin slept soundly and woke up eager to get his plan into action. He had spent several hours the night before discussing it with his father and Phil. They hoped to present their case to the police without making themselves look like idiots.

In his usual methodical way, Dan wrote down each topic he wanted to suggest to the police that they should investigate.

Without mentioning the suspects' names, at least to begin with, they felt that Dan should take the lead. He would inform the police of the old overgrown railway goat track. Then he would point out that the path leads to St Winefride's well. He hoped to plant in the minds of the police that one or more of those members of the sailing club, could have slipped out unseen, assaulted Rachel and then returned to the club.

Expecting the police to be sceptical about this, and all three agreeing it was unwise to admit that they had held a séance, Gavin and then Phil would each take it in turn to strongly support Dan's theory. Their decision not to mention Maxwell's and Ryan's names straight away was because they didn't want to appear to the police that they were desperate for results and were randomly accusing people.

They hoped that once they had the attention of the police detectives, with the outline of a conceivable theory, they could then make strong hints about jackets, lockers and bin bags.

Phil was surprised when Dan parked the car in a different part of town where he was expecting to see the police station. Dan had turned the engine off at the side of the library. At least the building he saw in front of him used to be the library, but it was now called a hub.

Gavin caught Phil's expression of surprise and explained that both library and police station had undergone an overhaul and both institutions were now housed in the same building. An annex had been built at the side of the library to accommodate the police.

"What happened to that lovely old building that was the police station?" Phil asked. "Please don't tell me it has been knocked down."

Gavin shook his head. "No. It's a residential care home. The building was sold off. At least the new owner has been sympathetic about the façade."

"Well that's some consolation I suppose." Phil remarked.

Inside the police headquarters, the desk sergeant recognised Dan and Gavin Bellis immediately. He acknowledged them with an inclination of his head whilst they sat down to wait in the small reception area. Sergeant Ward was taking down information from a middle aged woman about a lost gold watch. When she had left, the sergeant shook Dan and Gavin's hands and guided them to a small office at the back of the reception desk. It had an opaque window centred in the dividing wall, so he could check if anyone entered the station. He left them for a few moments and they could hear him ask a police constable to take his place at the desk.

"I'm afraid Detective Inspector Barker isn't here. Is there anything I can help you with?" The sergeant knew that there had been no progress on solving the murder of Rachel Bellis, but was not at liberty to tell her father and brother that. He knew that Mrs. Bellis had died recently and his heart went out to the family. Two tragedies in just over a year was a lot to bear. Dealing with bereaved families was something he had become used to over the years but it didn't make it easier. He was just as sensitive to grief as he had always been.

"I'm sorry to hear about your wife." Sergeant Ward began.

Dan bowed his head acknowledging the sentiment but refused to be drawn into conversation about his late wife. He needed to stay focused. "Thank you. We are here about Rachel. Has there been an arrest?" Dan knew very well that there hadn't been, but it was a way to introduce the delicate subject of his daughter's murder.

"I'm afraid not." Sergeant Ward reluctantly admitted.

Phil suddenly lurched forward holding his stomach and knew instantly that a ghost was listening. His heart began to thump excitedly against his chest.

"Are you alright?" The sergeant asked. "Do you want some water?" He looked at Phil intently. "Don't I know you from somewhere?"

"No thanks. I'm fine." Phil replied. He straightened up. The pain had gone but he knew that in that small room they had invisible company. He felt comforted with that thought. He risked a glance at Gavin and then Dan, and witnessed a glimmer of a smile twitching their faces.

"I never forget a face. Part of the job you see." The sergeant was saying.

"Maybe you knew my father Trevor Redwood. He used to be a part time magistrate. We do look alike though he is thirty years older than me!"

"That's probably it." Sergeant Ward agreed, though something about Phil was troubling him. He felt there was more to it than that. He put it aside for now and concentrated on the matter in front of him. He needed to reassure the Bellises that the police were doing everything within their power to find the murdering bastards who killed their lovely daughter. He wondered how to put it diplomatically that nothing new had turned up but the case was still open.

Whilst the officer was considering an opening line, Dan took the initiative to explain the reason for their visit. Quietly he pulled out from the breast pocket of his shirt the piece of paper on which he had written down his thoughts. Reading from it he made the first point.

Sergeant Ward listened politely. "Yes I remember that old railway track, but I didn't realise it was still there. The boat club and the new boat shed, as you know was built only a few years ago. I suppose most people have forgotten its existence. Not many people go for walks like they used to do. Too easy to get in the car these days." He gazed at Dan squarely. "I suppose it is feasible someone from the boat club had discovered it and used it as a short cut or a place to have a sneaky fag." He grew silent as he realised that Dan was suggesting someone had returned to the boat club via that path after having violated Rachel. That would indeed create the perfect alibi.

"But we interviewed all the employees at the sailing and rowing club. The manager Lester somebody or other provided me with a list of all those who were scheduled to work that night. I passed it on to the DI and he said each one tallied with the list."

"Lester Price." Gavin supplied the name. "We know the police interviewed everyone but did they cross check with the employees?"

The sergeant frowned. "Cross check?"

"What I mean is, did you ask each employee to verify the whereabouts of each other? You know, corroborate their timetable. For example, I know that during the evenings after the members of the public have left the lake, that the employees split up to do various tasks. There are jobs to do outside, such as cleaning and storing the boats, and other equipment. Some employees work alone, or in pairs, at various parts of the building. Sorting things out and what have you." Gavin pulled at his ear nervously as he tried to think of something to get the sergeant engaged.

"Did a worker notice a colleague was missing? Someone could easily slip away for an hour. If they used that track."

"Hmm. I suppose that's possible." The sergeant conceded. "I'm sure the detectives would have considered checking that fact if they felt they had a suspect, but I believe they regarded all the employees to be above suspicion. They interviewed two of them here and they were cleared. I believe they also spoke to the yacht owners and members of the public who had used the facilities that day."

"So would that mean they wouldn't have checked the lockers of the employees for blood stained clothes?" Phil ventured to ask. He wondered when he should mention Maxwell.

The sergeant was surprised at such a direct question. "If the detectives had reason to believe there was evidence in the lockers they would have got a warrant. I'm afraid they didn't. Why do you ask? Are you suggesting that there is evidence in one of the lockers? Have you discovered something we've missed? That's impossible. How would you know that and not us?"

Sergeant Ward turned his face towards Dan again and tried to be gentle.

"Look I know you want results, so do we, but we can't just go blundering in to that sailing club and ask to look in every locker without a good reason."

"Not even if we gave you names?" Dan asked. He felt he was losing ground. He'd managed to convince himself that the evidence was in the locker.

Sergeant Ward shook his head. "Not without a good reason." He was intrigued.

"What names? Are you just making wild guesses?"

Dan was indignant. "I'm desperate for justice for my daughter, but I'm not stupid to apportion blame on just anyone. I know that two men were responsible for Rachel's murder. One of whom I know is Maxwell Briggs and works at the lake boat club. I also have reason to believe he is hoarding a blood stained jacket in his locker!"

Both Gavin and Phil nodded their heads in agreement with Dan's statement and all three stared defiantly in to the sergeant's shocked countenance.

Sergeant Ward recognised Maxwell's name but didn't want to share that knowledge.

"But where did you get this information?" The sergeant asked. "I can't accuse this young man of anything without evidence."

"The evidence is in his locker." Dan reiterated.

Sergeant Ward sighed. "But how do you know that? I need more than a flimsy theory that something incriminating him is in his locker."

"But it's possible isn't it?" Gavin persisted.

"Anything is possible, but I need more than this." The sergeant repeated. He made his mind up to bring the meeting to an end.

"I promise I will pass on this information to detective inspector Barker, but I am doubtful he can do anything with it. That man was already questioned here at the station on the night of the murder."

"The other man's name is Ryan, we believe." Gavin added defiantly. "We don't know his other name but no doubt Maxwell Briggs could tell you."

"And does this Ryan work at the sailing club?"

Dan bit his lip whilst Gavin looked at Phil.

"We don't know where Ryan works." Phil admitted.

The Sergeant wrote everything down and then got up from his chair signalling that the interview was over. He pressed his lips together ruefully and sighed. "I will pass this information on but I don't have much hope. I sincerely want to help but we have procedures to follow, you know."

"Yes, yes I know." Dan agreed solemnly. He followed Sergeant Ward out of the room. Gavin and Phil trailed behind him. Both young men appeared deflated.

Outside the police station, Dan looked at his watch. The time was ten past eleven. Across the road he saw a café. "Come on let's get a coffee and talk things over."

Laticia and Rachel remained in the police station. They watched Sergeant Ward studying his notes. He shook his head frowning. It seemed that he had reached a decision not to pass on the information. In an instant he had crumpled the piece of paper and thrown it in the bin. A second later he retrieved it again. The fact that Dan Bellis had given him the name of two suspects niggled him. He wondered why an honest man like Dan, and his son for that matter had actually suggested the names of Rachel's attackers. He smoothed out the crumpled note, and stared at it for a while. Then sighing, he made a fresh copy of the names and put it aside to deal with later. The least he could do was to run the names through the police computer. He assumed it had already been done with Maxwell Briggs, but he would double check. As regards Ryan without a surname it would take forever. "But in any case not today." He muttered.

The original piece of paper containing information about the locker, the jacket and the old railway line path he tossed back into the bin.

Sergeant Ward got up from his desk to resume his duties and strode towards the door. *Simultaneously Rachel and Laticia retrieved the crumpled note and brought it back to the desk.*

Out of the corner of his eye, Sergeant Ward saw the crumpled note settle on his desk again, though he hadn't seen it soar through the air. His brows knitted in confusion. He was convinced he had thrown the note away. Picking it up, he threw the note away again. However the note didn't reach the bin. It hovered over the top, and as the sergeant stared, the creased message swayed from side to side in front of his eyes at barely an arm's length.

"What the fuck is going on? Is somebody having a joke with me?" The sergeant bellowed. He stretched out his hand to grab the document, but each attempt to get it ended in him pinching at thin air. He turned around to look for an explanation. No-one was in the room; the window was closed and the small fan in the corner of his small office was switched off. He sat down again trying to work things out. Was he going mad? He began to sweat though he told himself he was being foolish. Was there a ghost in the room? Impossible. He recalled his wife Christine telling him that after attending a séance with her friend Susan, years ago, they had both witnessed pieces of paper flying across the room. He had dismissed it as rubbish or some kind of trickery. Then, like a thunder clap jolting his brain he suddenly remembered where he had seen Phil Redwood. It was he who had held the séance at Susan's house.

"Hell fire!" Sergeant Ward breathed out loud. "Is that where they have got these names? They've had a bloody séance."

Rachel let the crumpled note fall on the desk.

For a few minutes Sergeant Ward contemplated the notes in front of him. He wasn't convinced that séances produced anything of value, yet something nagged him. What if there really was something in it? He wiped the sweat from his face and picked up the phone. Before he could change his mind he had pressed in the number of Detective Inspector Carl Barker. He knew it was going to take some convincing to get him on board, but what if there was some truth in what Dan Bellis had claimed?

Rachel and Laticia stayed long enough to listen to Sergeant Ward's telephone conversation and then they sashayed out of the station. For a few seconds they were undecided whether to try to get on a bus back to the village, but then noticed Dan's profile in the coffee shop across the road. The two ghosts made their way to the café.

"For goodness sake don't rush in like you usually do and upset Phil." Rachel warned.

Laticia tried to put the brakes on her exuberance but not enough to arrive unobtrusively. Phil felt an all too familiar though lighter twinge in his stomach and knew that he was being observed by an unseen phenomena. He advised his two companions of the fact.

"We have company." Phil grinned. "Of the supernatural kind." He supplied the extra information as Dan and Gavin looked around the café for someone they knew.

"Rachel?" Gavin asked with surprise.

Phil nodded. "I think she is here with her friend."

"How can you tell?" Dan asked in wonder. He was having difficulty accepting that his dead daughter's ghost was present in the café.

"It's hard to explain. I just know." Phil remarked. He picked up his cappuccino and sipped it.

"I wonder what they have been doing." Gavin said. "I'm not convinced the sergeant will pass on our information." He stirred his Americano dispiritedly.

"We've done what we can." Dan said. "There's little more we can do. It's up to the police now." He drained his coffee and got up. "I need a cigarette. I'll see you outside."

Later that afternoon Gavin and Phil took Leo for a walk into the village. They took the path that wound its way in front of St. Winefride's well. Before passing through the kissing gate into the town square, they paused to stroll into the graveyard. Gavin stood at the top of his mother's freshly dug grave. As yet there was no headstone. He and his father had already agreed that they would eventually get one erected. Phil stood aside with Leo and let Gavin have a few minutes alone. For a little while the dog stood still, then for no apparent reason began to bark frantically at Gavin. The dog had sensed the presence of Anna who had come to position herself at the side of her son. She was aware that her arrival at the graveside was the cause of the commotion that Leo was making, but unsure if the dog could actually see her. If he could, she wondered, could he hear her. She tried a command.

"Quiet Leo!"

The dog cocked his ears back. He looked perplexed. Anna was impressed. Leaving Gavin for a few seconds she re-positioned herself at the side of the dog. Leo instantly began to wag his tail excitedly. Phil witnessed this performance in puzzlement. He began to suspect that Anna's ghost was somewhere nearby. Yet he had no perception of her himself. He thought that was peculiar, especially in the light of what had been happening to him over the last few days. Maybe it was because she had only recently passed over, he mused. A few seconds later he was re-joined by Gavin. Together they walked almost by mutual silent agreement towards Rachel's grave. This time both of them stood reading the headstone. Leo was stock still, so Phil guessed that Rachel was not around. His eyes scanned the graveyard as he wondered where Laticia's place of rest could be.

As they walked along the path leading towards the lych gate they saw Stefan Kadinsky's brother Anthony with his wife Diane. They were tidying up Stefan's grave. They shook hands.

"I'm sorry to hear of your mother's death. So soon after Rachel's." Anthony began.

Gavin nodded his thanks and in return added his own condolences regarding Stefan.

"It was a relief to give him a proper funeral." Anthony said. "We had to wait several months before we got the rest of him."

Anthony, desperate to turn the conversation away from his bereavement, directed his attention towards Phil. "Stefan told me a while back that you had gone to live in Transylvania."

Anthony's wife looked up from deadheading some of the flowers to smile at Phil and Gavin. "I've never been, though I would like to go sometime. " She confided. "Anthony still has some elderly relatives living there. He also has some cousins in Bucharest."

"I love it." Phil said. "Actually it was Stefan who put the idea in my head. My wife Clare is there at the moment. She loves it too. Though I think she wants to come back here to live eventually."

Anthony sighed. "Yes, my brother loved it too. He was always going back there whenever he could get time off work. He did a lot of research on the family history, and I believe he learned some of the Romanian languages too."

"Interesting." Phil replied. He had never got round to learning the old languages, though he was indeed fascinated by the linguistics and culture of Transylvania.

There fell a heavy silence, and for lack of something else to say or do Anthony and Diane patted Leo's head and made a fuss of the dog. Eventually they parted and Phil and Gavin made their way to the town square just as the church clock struck three thirty. As they passed the bakery they almost collided with Abigail and Nicky. Both women were carrying take away coffees and a bag each containing cakes. Gavin could see through the flimsy paper that Abigail carried a custard tart. It looked like a Portuguese version of the ones that seemed to be available in every cake shop in town these days. He couldn't tell what sweet fancy Nicky had chosen.

Abigail spoke first. "Hello." She smiled encouragingly and Gavin felt an inexplicable lurch in his chest.

Both men returned the greeting. Out of politeness Nicky smiled too. She seemed more relaxed without Ryan hanging around in the background. The two women had their blonde hair streaked in some kind of pink glitter. Abigail's hair was long and she'd pushed it back off her face with a multi coloured bandeau tied in a knot on top of her head. Both of them were pretty Gavin observed. He made a nervous tug at his ear.

"Is this your afternoon snack?" Gavin asked. He and Phil fell in step with the girls as they walked briskly up the street away from the bakery.

"Kind of." Abigail replied. "We get a fifteen minute break so we have to be quick. The bakery always serves us first, because we have to get back to work. Sorry we can't stop." The two girls obviously used to their routine, and determined not to let anyone distract them, quickly outwalked Phil and Gavin, though Abi turned her head back to say 'bye'."

Both men stood on the corner of Brook Road and watched them walk along the narrow pavement under the railway bridge. They rounded a sharp bend and then became out of sight.

"I suppose we could stalk them." Phil suggested idly. He knew as soon as he said it that it was a ridiculous idea, but he was running out of inspiration. He was surprised when Gavin agreed. "OK. Let's go. They can't have gone far. If they are on a tea break."

"Actually, I meant hang around here until five o clock or so to see where they go home. That way Nicky might lead us to Ryan. There's a bus stop just over there. They may need to get a bus."

Gavin was taken aback. "Oh no, that's creepy. That's an hour and a half, maybe two hours hanging around looking suspicious. Besides they might not get a bus or come back down here to go home. I meant let's walk under the railway bridge and see if we can spot where they go. They're out of sight now, but if we hurry we might see them walk up the road."

"That's creepy too." Phil said. But even as he spoke he was matching his steps with Gavin's as they walked the length of Brook Road towards the railway bridge. Cautiously they rounded the corner and looked up the road. There were various shopfronts on both sides of the road, but Nicky and Abigail were nowhere to be seen.

"Didn't Emily say that there was a Beauty shop or something up here where she thought she had seen Abigail working?" Gavin remarked.

"Yes. I'd forgotten. Right. Let's just saunter up there and have a look. I could do with a haircut before I go back on Wednesday, maybe they do men's." Phil laughed.

"I suppose I could have a trim too." Gavin said wryly. He slowed his pace. "Let's not make it obvious. Leave it half an hour, otherwise they will know we have followed them. Then we can casually saunter up there and pretend we didn't know they worked there."

Phil grinned. "I get your drift. But maybe we should wait until tomorrow to make our visit seem more authentic. We can check the place out on the internet. There can't be many beauty salons in Holywell. By the way who is your usual barber? Looking at the length of your hair I don't think you have a regular one." He laughed.

Gavin smiled ruefully. I had it trimmed in some place in Chester for my mother's funeral, but I suppose I could spare another few centimetres."

"Easily." Came the amused reply.

"Let's not forget the real reason for going to a beauty salon. I'm not desperate for a haircut. The plan is to find out more about Ryan."

Whilst Phil and Gavin changed tack and headed for home, *Rachel slipped into the cemetery to find Anna. Together they sashayed across to the crypt. Already seated there was Stefan, Big Steve, and Margareta."*

"Where's the rest of the mob?" Anna asked.

"Probably hanging around St. Bruno's statue or St. Winefride's tomb." Margareta said. "They like to mingle with the tourists. Lots of the spirits do it, especially the modern dead ones like us. No doubt Tomtit will try to cause some mischief. Winefride usually positions herself on the roof of the cathedral along with her medieval spirit friends. They like to watch the crowds from above. Anyway, never mind them, how did you get on at the police station?"

Rachel related what had transpired at the police station then finished up with the conversation she and Laticia had heard Sergeant Ward make to detective Barker.

"It was obvious that the detective inspector was sceptical about the information, but what was good about it, was the fact that the sergeant didn't mention to the detective inspector that he reckoned Phil was a psychic. When the DI asked how they got the names of the suspect, the sergeant answered that he was told that it was a theory they had, and they had been adamant that they knew.

The sergeant said he felt they had been holding something back. That seemed to convince the DI, to follow up their theory, but he didn't promise to do anything straight away as he had a heavy work load as it was. However, he confessed that he had no other leads so he might as well see what he could do. He would give it some thought. He would check out the goat track anyway."

Anna sighed. "Well at least they have names to play with. I wonder if the sergeant has looked on the police national computer to find anything on that horrible Maxwell Briggs and that bloody Ryan."

"Laticia is in the police station now shadowing Sergeant Ward. She promised to report back to me at home as soon as she can." Rachel replied.

"Let's hope that at least one of them has a criminal record. It might help things along." Anna said. "Meanwhile we have a task for you and Laticia too. We just hope it isn't too risky for Laticia though." She took a deep breath. "Rachel, I have taken Stefan to your coffin so that he can look at your mobile. And before you get mad this is the plan. Stefan you had better explain."

Trying her best not to laugh, Rachel turned her attention to Stefan. She didn't know whether to be annoyed or not with her mother for allowing him into her coffin, but he seemed such an inoffensive sort of chap, so she decided to say nothing.

"I have looked at your mobile and I am delighted that it is a small simple and light weight version." Stefan began.

"Yes. I had a very basic one just for text messages and emails, plus of course the internet. I had been thinking of replacing it with something more up to date. But, I had a tablet and a lap top, I just wasn't sure what to get."

"Well, I'm glad you didn't." Stefan's face stretched into his peculiar collage of a

smile, making Rachel think not for the first time that the tiny fragments may not keep his fine features together, but of course, she reminded herself, they always would.

"If you and Laticia can use your strength to disassemble the parts, Tomtit and Winefride will help us to energise them so that you can send a message. We don't know how long the energy will last. If it works that is." He stopped talking whilst fixing Rachel with another lopsided stretchy grin. She looked dumbfounded whilst her mother wore a triumphant expression.

"What?" Rachel managed to say. She burst out laughing. "What did you say about Tomtit and Winefride? Impossible! I can't believe you think we can do that. Anyway, Laticia and I have only just discovered how to raise paper, there's no way we can remove bits of metal. We tried to open a metal locker door and that didn't work."

Stefan sensed her scepticism and self-doubt but engaged her with his patient kindly face. Even through the mishmash of his patchwork countenance Rachel could detect a kindly and patient man.

"It's worth a try. The metal of a locker door is much thicker and bigger. You don't really need to lift the mobile cover, you just need to press the catch at the top to release it. Your combined strength would probably do it. Once the cover is off you may be able to slide it down to release the sim card and possibly the battery, though that is heavier I grant you. Didn't you just say you managed

to dislodge a shoe? If you can't lift the battery we may be able to get round that if you can remove the cover. It would make it easier for Winefride if we have separate pieces."

"Winefride? But, what is a ghost from the dark ages going to do? They didn't have mobiles in those days!" Rachel managed to splutter the words out through choked back laughter at the image of a seventh century ghost fiddling around with a twenty first century electronic device, albeit a basic one.

"Water from the well." Stefan replied confidently.

Rachel couldn't hold back her mirth and she let out another burst of laughter. "Water? Are you insane?"

"Please Rachel, have some trust in him. Won't you please try? You have nothing to lose." Anna pleaded with her daughter.

Behind her mother's anxious face Rachel saw Desmond and Tom Titanium sneak up to the little group. Other spirits from various past decades hung around too. It seemed they were all aware of the plan. Rachel sighed. "I will ask Laticia to come tomorrow afternoon. It's her last opportunity. She's going to Barbados on Wednesday. It will be a risk if she is seen hanging around here though."

"Tell her to come at two o clock." Tom Titanium advised. "The guards change over at that time. They will be too busy talking for half an hour. They won't see her. In any

case I don't think they take the job very seriously. It's not often that the guards have to obstruct anyone. He glanced meaningfully at Big Steve. "Still, best not to take chances. Go straight to your coffin. We will meet there."

As Rachel glided away to join Laticia at the police station she wondered just how many spirits and ghosts were going to cram in to her coffin.

Chapter Nineteen

Technicalities

After Gavin and Phil left the house with the dog, Dan felt a wave of depression overtake him. Now he knew the identity of his daughter's killers; always supposing that the information via a séance was viable, he wanted to see justice. He had been sceptical when Gavin had suggested Phil hold a séance, but his scepticism had been swept away when he had seen those pieces of paper flying around the room. Surely it really was Rachel trying to communicate. The information she had relayed seemed genuine.

It had seemed strange that Anna had not tried to communicate, but he deduced without any logical reason to believe his own analysis, that Rachel had something to prove and Anna didn't. He shook his head in bewilderment as he realised he was making up his own theories about rules for the dead. He allowed a twitch of wry amusement to trace his lips.

Dan wanted action from the police. He wanted them to arrest Maxwell and his accomplice so that he could finally rest. For the past two days he had had to restrain Gavin from going down to the boat house to thump Maxwell, and yet now he wanted to do it himself. Sighing, he went outside to the garden shed and got out his fishing tackle. He still hadn't carried out his promise to Anna that he would resume his hobby. Maybe that would help him calm the rising anger frothing away in his stomach and sending nasty tastes of bile to his mouth. His grief was still raw. The painful knot in his stomach would sometimes loosen then tighten again. His throat would become dry, he was perpetually thirsty. Sometimes he was unable to concentrate on what he was doing.

At his old favourite spot near the lake, and not far from where Rachel's dying body had been found, Dan busied himself with putting bait on his fishing rod. Eventually he was ready to cast his line. Half an hour passed, sitting on an uncomfortable bench and without a bite. As the time slipped away, he became more and more dejected. He reeled in his rod with a view to re-casting, but instead he chanced a fleeting glance towards the spot where he knew Rachel would have been assaulted. Instantly his chest and stomach tightened making him feel as if a lump of lead had tunnelled into his core. A deep heavy feeling of loss gave way to a pitiful cry that ripped through him. Unexpunged grief and heartache held back for so long overcame him in a torrent of tears. Helplessly he found himself sobbing uncontrollably for his dead wife and daughter. A piteous howl tossed itself across the water and he realised, as his dripping eyes momentarily blinded him, that the sound was coming from himself. Taking in a lungful of air he tried to breathe properly. A few minutes passed, then feeling emotionally spent he fumbled for his handkerchief and began to wipe his face. He removed his glasses to swab away droplets of moisture. In the act of replacing them he felt a hand on his shoulder and he jumped nervously.

"Hello Dan. Are you alright? No of course you aren't. Can I do something for you?"

Dan turned to see Lester Price sitting at the side of him on the bench. He nodded. "I'm fine."

"I can see you needed to get things off your chest, but I was worried." He made a move to get up. "Sorry I'm invading your privacy."

By this time Dan had his composure reset. "No, don't go. You're right. I needed to let go. I'm alright now. Nothing like a good cry, as they say." Dan made an attempt to make light of his grief. He felt foolish. Caught out. Embarrassed. "I just haven't been able to do it. Thanks for stopping. It's very kind of you." He managed a smile through his wet cheeks and reddened eyes.

"Grief is a strange thing. It affects people in so many different ways." Lester offered. He repeated the often quoted line in an effort to reassure Dan and to try to restore his dignity. Lester got up and stepped back a few paces to give Dan some space. He understood that he had invaded Dan's privacy, but the noise he had been making had made him think an animal was in distress. He had only wanted to help.

"Aren't you working today?" Dan asked. An image of the locker room at the sailing club penetrated his thoughts. Should he ask Lester to intervene? He heavily contemplated the notion.

"Day off today." Lester said. "Household duties. He said with a bashful grin.

"It's a question of closure." Dan said not listening properly. He was more preoccupied with the contents of Maxwell's locker. He chose his words carefully.

Lester was sympathetic.

"I understand. I take it the police are no further forward in getting Rachel's killer. You've had a horrific year."

Dan shook his head. "We went to see them yesterday. We hope we have given them some new ideas. You know. Some new lines of inquiry."

Lester leaned forward and put his hand on Dan's shoulder again and squeezed it. "If there's anything I can do please don't hesitate. I have to go now."

"Actually, there is." Don said. Lester hesitated. Then Dan changed his mind. Thoughts ran through his mind about contaminating evidence. Perhaps it would be wise to leave Lester out of it. For now at least.

"No, no never mind. Forget it." Dan said.

"If you're sure." Lester lingered for a few seconds and Dan again shook his head. "No. I'm fine now. Thanks again for stopping."

With a heavy heart Dan packed up his fishing gear and made his way home. At least he had made a start in keeping his promises to Anna.

Rachel joined Laticia at the Police station. "Any developments?" She asked.

"Nothing much to tell since our sergeant here telephoned Detective Inspector Barker and relayed the information about the old railway footpath. As you witnessed earlier, Sergeant Ward seemed to have had an epiphany. He guessed we had a séance. After you went to report to your mother and the rest, he rang his wife. He asked her to confirm whether it was Phil that had conducted a séance that she attended years ago. When she did he got excited and rang Barker back again to say that Phil was the son of an ex magistrate. I suppose Ward thought, that the extra information might convince Barker to act sooner rather than later. But our dear sergeant didn't mention that Phil is a psychic." Laticia grinned.

"Ward probably didn't want to risk being laughed at. He reiterated his previous comment that it was a hunch he had that they knew something. Barker again said he would look into it, but whether he will, I don't know." Laticia shrugged. "If he hasn't made a start in the next two days, you'll have to try to convince him yourself. I'm sorry I can't be around much longer to help. The opportunity of a lift to the airport with Gavin and Phil is too good to waste."

"I agree. But before you go, I have a job for you to do tomorrow." Rachel explained about the mobile phone event to take place the next day in her coffin.

"You can't be serious." Laticia laughed. *"This I have to see. At least we might see our Saint Winefride in action."*

Rachel agreed. We will need to rest to conserve our energy.

Having found the name of the beauty salon on the internet and ascertained that barbering was a treatment on offer, the next day, Phil and Gavin made their way to *'Walsh's Hair, Beauty and Complementary Therapy Salon.'* Outside the building they tethered the dog to a nearby lamp post. Gavin stroked Leo's head and whispered a reassuring promise that they wouldn't be long. The dog cocked his head to one side intelligently then settled himself down on the pavement.

"Good boy." Gavin encouraged him. He knew that after five minutes Leo would start reminding him in no uncertain terms that he did not want to be left outside alone on the pavement.

"Let's go." Gavin said and followed Phil into the salon. The shop front was the fourth business set in a terrace of eight. Next door to the salon was a stationers. The other side sold mobile phones.

The interior of *Walsh's* was very wide and the shiny laminated flooring seemed to stretch endlessly towards the back. Gavin quickly assessed that the ground floor salon was the full length of the building. There was a stairway at the centre of the salon with a sign on the door marked 'Massage and Facials on the first floor.' The ground floor space was dedicated to hair washing and styling plus there was a nail bar. At one of the styling chairs, Abigail was busy cutting the hair of a client. She had her back to the door and didn't see Gavin and Phil make their way to the reception area which took up a corner near the street window.

"Can I help you?" A woman with an Afro hair style threaded with shiny gold strands addressed them with a smile.

Gavin cleared his throat and stared through the window at Leo who seemed to wag his tail encouragingly. "Are you able to fit in a haircut today or tomorrow?"

"If you can wait fifteen minutes, we can fit you in. Do you also want a haircut?" The receptionist turned her gaze on Phil who was intently examining a stylist magazine on the little table by the door.

"Yes please. Though I am happy to wait. We need to keep an eye on the dog you see." He pointed to Leo slumped lazily on the pavement.

Both men were told to sit down and wait. They watched the receptionist step towards Abigail where they assumed she had been told she had another client waiting. As if on cue Abigail turned around to see who was waiting for her and her face curved into a grin when she saw Gavin and Phil sitting patiently. At that point, Leo decided to bark, and Gavin went out to pacify him. He decided to stay with the dog until he was told it was his turn. After another ten minutes, Phil came out of the shop to tell Gavin that the receptionist had said Abigail was ready for her next client. "You're up." Phil said. "I think we will both get Abigail, but you go first. Those two other stylists or whatever you call them seem to be busy with perms and colours. They'll take ages."

Gavin threw Phil a puzzled look. "You seem to know a lot about it."

Phil grinned. "I do. Clare and her friends spend ages having their hair done. Go on. I will watch Leo."

"If I didn't know any better, I would think you were following me." Abigail said with a wry smile as she washed Gavin's hair.

"It's sheer chance that you are cutting my hair." Gavin offered. It was half true he thought. He had hoped to find a way to talk to her, and this encounter was turning out better than he could have hoped. He pulled at his ear absently. Abigail noticed the gesture. She shoved a towel over his head and began to rub his hair dry. She playfully ruffled his hair and then examined his ear.

"So when did you have your ear pierced? She asked innocently.

"A few years ago. It was the result of a drunken afternoon." He confessed. She frowned and he elaborated. "A friend's stag party that started with ear piercing and tattoos."

Abigail laughed. "So where's the tattoo?"
"Top of my arm. Very small rose. Sheer tokenism I'm afraid. They had to hold me down."
She laughed again. "Wicked! So you kept the ear-ring."
Gavin nodded.
"Don't move your head now. Do you want a trim, or do you want more taken off?" she ran her hands through his hair that covered the back of his neck. The sensation sent ripples of desire through Gavin's body which gave him a jolt. He wasn't expecting to get such a reaction. Yet he knew he was attracted to her.
"About an inch. Or should I say 2.5 centimetres? I think it probably is too long." He answered. He spoke quickly to hide his embarrassment. She smiled back at him through the mirror. "I understand both metric and imperial. Our clients use both." She laughed and Gavin felt more at ease.
Despite the fact it was only ten days ago that he had had his hair trimmed in a salon in Chester he felt it was worth having more cut off to enjoy the feel of her fingers on his head. In the mirror he caught a glimpse of Phil outside with the dog and he tried to focus on the real reason he was there.
"You have nice hair. Abigail said.
"Thanks. Does your friend Nicky work here too?"
Abigail nodded. She was concentrating on cutting.
"Day off today then?" Gavin persisted.

"No. She's upstairs. Keeping her head down." She bit her lip as if regretting having spoken and despite trying to engage her in more conversation, she refused to be drawn. Eventually, she led him to the receptionist where she left him to pay. See you again perhaps." She grinned and returned to her work station to wait for another client. "By the way the ear ring suits you."

Gavin felt too embarrassed to say anything in reply. His stomach was buzzing with tugs and wrenches making him feel breathless. He swallowed hard to get his emotions in check. Pulling out his wallet he paid for his haircut and left her a generous tip.

Peering through the window from outside, Phil witnessed the body language between Gavin and Abigail. He chuckled to the dog. "There's definitely some chemistry going on there Leo." He ruffled the dog's head then straightened up again as he waited to change places with Gavin.

Phil examined his friend curiously as he stepped out of the salon looking lovesick. Phil slapped him on his shoulder. Intuitively he knew not to mention Gavin's lovelorn expression. He could see the man was fighting his emotions.

"Any info?" Phil asked.

Gavin shook his head. "Not much. Nicky is here but working upstairs. Keeping her head down Abigail said. Sounds suspicious to me. Maybe a bruised face? Or am I reading too much into it?"

"Do you think Ryan's hit her?"
Gavin nodded. A worried expression spread on to his face. "Seems likely."
"Right. My turn." Phil handed the dog's lead to Gavin.
Abigail smirked when she saw Phil make himself comfortable in the client's chair.
"I really think there is some conspiracy going on with you two." She said to him.
"Don't you believe in coincidences?" Phil asked innocently.
"Sometimes."
"In my experience they occur more than you think."
She sniggered. "Really?"
"So is your friend Nicky here?" Phil asked. He liked to get to the point quickly.
"Why are you so interested?" Instinctively she was drawn to Phil's wedding ring. He saw her glance.
"Just wondering."
"Your friend asked me the same question. For your information she is working upstairs today."
"I see." Phil said. He decided to say nothing more, hoping that Abigail's curiosity might start a conversation. With a bit of luck she would ask the questions instead of him. It worked. A few minutes later she paused cutting and after a cautious glance behind her to see if no-one was listening, she asked him. "Do you both fancy Nicky or something? She's got a boyfriend you know, and he wouldn't like it. And you are married I see."

She looked a bit disappointed. Phil guessed that she was peeved because both he and Gavin asked about Nicky and had not shown any interest in her. If only she knew he thought.

"No, not really. It's not like that. Just interested."

"Is she in some kind of trouble?"

Phil took a deep breath. "She might be. Why do you ask?"

Abigail sighed and dropped her voice to almost a whisper. "She asked to change her timetable today so that she could work upstairs. She has a bruised face. She is doing massages. Less eye contact with the clients you see."

Phil's eyes locked on Abigail's in the mirror. "What happened?"

She made no reply so Phil mouthed to her one word in as a question. "Boyfriend?"

Abigail shrugged. She sighed but refused to be drawn.

"She should go to the police." Phil said carefully to the mirror.

"She won't."

"Then dump him."

"She's too scared to do that."

Phil frowned. "That sounds like even more a good reason to go to the police." He kept his voice low. Abigail glanced again over her shoulder to make sure her supervisor wasn't listening.

"It's kind of complicated."

"Everything alright?" The supervisor came behind them. "Our trainees are very competent. As we advised you when you booked, they are not fully qualified, but Abigail is one of our best trainees."

"Fine. Everything is fine." Phil said. He watched the supervisor walk away.

"Listen." Phil whispered urgently. "Can we talk? Get a coffee or something later? It's very important I talk to you."

Abigail bit her lip. "I get a break in half an hour. Nicky and I usually get takeaways from the bakery, but she won't come with me today. She doesn't want to be seen with her face like that."

"We'll see you there later. Thanks." Phil got up and Abigail led him to the reception desk to pay. He too left her a generous tip.

Outside he grinned at Gavin but said nothing until both men had walked down the street. "We've got a date with Abigail." Phil said as they strolled under the railway bridge and were back near the town square.

"How did you manage that?" Gavin asked incredulously as Phil led the way to the bakery where they had seen both Nicky and Abigail a few days earlier.

They selected a table and chair on the pavement and sat down outside the bakery.

Phil smirked enjoying his friend's discomfort. "I have a way with women."

"Bastard!"

Quickly Phil related what he had learned. Gavin drew a deep breath. "So the murdering fucking swine is knocking Nicky about too."

"Yes." Phil got up to order their coffee. He returned with a couple of cupcakes as well as their drinks.

When Abigail joined them twenty minutes later she looked warily at both men. Gavin pulled up another chair to the table and self-consciously she sat down.

"Thanks for coming." Phil said. "We'd like to ask you a few questions about your friend and her boyfriend."

"Are you detectives or something?" The worried expression deepened. Her eyes widened and once again Gavin felt attracted to this woman.

"Not really." Gavin replied. He cleared his throat which somehow had got hoarse when Abigail had arrived. "But before we chat, can I get you a coffee? Something to eat?"

"A latte please."

"Fine. Cake or something? Sandwich?"

"A custard tart would be nice." She smiled at him and Gavin's heart hurtled into space.

Whilst he was out of earshot, Phil gave Abigail some bare facts. "Gavin's mother has just passed away. And a year ago his sister was murdered."

Abigail blinked as she registered the news. "Oh my god. How awful. Poor guy. That's terrible."

"Yes it is. The thing is we are trying to find out who killed Rachel."

"Rachel?" Still somewhat stunned from receiving such shocking news Abigail frowned as she began to think over what Phil had told her. "Gosh I remember the murder. She was found near the lake wasn't she?" Involuntarily she turned her head towards the direction of the water's edge even though it wasn't visible from where they sat.

"Yes. That's right."

"And the police haven't found the killer?"

Phil shook his head. Before he could say any more, Gavin returned with Abigail's refreshments and two more coffees for himself and Phil. He could tell from the concerned expression on her face that Phil had told Abigail about his bereavements. He was glad. It saved him having to explain. So far he had managed to bury his grief about losing his mother, but he knew that he would have to deal with it soon. He had promised her he would find Rachel's killer and he was determined to concentrate on that. The grief for that was still lurking heavily in his stomach.

"I take it Phil has told you the reason we want to talk to you?"

"Not all of it." Phil said. "Just about Rachel and your mum."

"I'm so sorry." Abigail said. She touched his arm. It felt like an electric current running through him. The contact seemed to affect her too. Her eyes were misty with concern.

Phil took charge of the conversation. "The thing is Abigail, we have discovered a few clues which makes us believe your friend Nicky could be in danger."

Abigail sipped her coffee through the takeaway lid and stared at Phil over the top of it. "How come? Do you mean because of Ryan?"

"Yes!" Both men agreed loudly.

"But why Ryan? Oh god, you don't mean you think he is the murderer." Shock washed her face. She put down her coffee, spilling some on her overall. Nervously she brushed off the drips with the back of one hand and then reached for the serviette at the side of her pastry which as yet she hadn't touched.

"You said yourself you think he hits her. Why won't she go to the police?" Gavin asked evasively. Both he and Phil had agreed not to mention the séance if they could manage not to.

Abigail sighed and fingered her custard tart absently tearing it into bite size pieces.

"I wish she would. She told me a while ago, her father had been violent and she had to get away from the family home. He's dead now. I suppose she got fed up of the police coming to the house and didn't want to start that up again."

"Surely she can see that if she doesn't do anything now it could get worse?"

"Yes. I've told her that. But she said he's kind most of the time, and that he's just possessive."

"Giving her a black eye isn't being kind." Gavin said.

"I know. I told her that too. According to her, this was the first time he had physically hurt her. Yet I've seen bruises on her arms where he has got hold of her, too tight I reckon. Nicky doesn't seem to think that's abuse. She doesn't want to admit it. But, I think he is too rough." She dropped a piece of tart into her mouth.

They both watched her eating, each trying to think of what they should say next. Abigail sipped her coffee and her eyes searched the faces of both her companions.

"Do you think she would talk to us?" Phil asked.

"I don't know. I suppose if I tell her it's about helping you guys find a murderer, she might. I'll ask her when I get back." She picked up her half-finished coffee and stood up to get ready to go. "I have to get her a coffee to take back. Give me your mobile and I will let you know what she says."

Surprised at the request Gavin hastily wrote his number down on the serviette. She put it in her pocket. "I'll call you later. Thanks for the coffee and stuff."

Both Phil and Gavin got up too. They hung around until Abigail re-appeared from the bakery with her takeaways. She waved, and suddenly Phil stopped her. "Just a thought, do you know a guy called Maxwell?"

Abigail grimaced. "Do you mean Ryan's mate? The baron?"

"Baron? Oh you mean dealer I suppose!" Her scathing announcement confirmed Phil's suspicions that drugs was the reason for Maxwell's shady behaviour.

"I don't know him but met him once when he and Ryan picked Nicky up from work. He tried to sell me something to help me relax – Huh! I knew what he meant. I got the impression he had a stash somewhere."
"Does Nicky use?"
"No. She hates them, but she suspects Ryan is involved in some way. Look I have to go."
Before they could ask any more questions she checked her mobile for the time and ran past them in the direction of the railway bridge. "Sorry!" She called over her shoulder.
"Well. A bit of progress!" Gavin commented as they headed towards home.
"Yes. But I'm not sure where it's leading us. We seem to have the evidence and the names of the murderer and yet we can't tell anyone how we know. It's very frustrating."
"Yes. At the moment though I'm more frustrated that we came out without coats. I think it's going to chuck it down any minute." The grey sky which earlier that morning seemed to have promised to clear up, had suddenly darkened. A light wind also made its presence felt as it rifled through their clothes. They both quickened their pace only glancing over the wall at the cemetery as they passed. They were within a hundred yards from home when a freak shower drenched them. Dan handed them towels for their hair whilst he rubbed Leo's back and wiped his paws.

"So much for our new hair styles!" Gavin laughed self-consciously. Dan looked up in surprise. "What have you two been up to?"
Whilst they explained to Dan their encounter with the beautician, the two ghosts were busy ensconced in Rachel's coffin. Alongside them was Stefan, Tomtit and Anna. At the end of the coffin lay Rachel's mute mobile phone, still in the same position it had occupied since being laid to rest there with Rachel's corpse just a year ago.

"What we're hoping you can do is disassemble all the parts of the mobile." Stefan explained.

Rachel, still sceptical of the plan, looked at him incredulously and then at her mother who was plainly excited at the prospect.

"Why?" Rachel asked.

Laticia looked on inquisitively. Rachel sensed a gleam in her eye. "We could try." Laticia offered.

"If you can arrange all the parts separately, especially the sim card and the battery, and any other pieces, like the keypad or the camera and the sensors, we can get them all powered individually before re-assembling them." Stefan explained. "That's if it works." He grinned sheepishly.

Rachel rolled her eyes. "And just how is it going to be powered?"

"Please try." Anna begged her daughter. "Stefan has spoken to Winnie and she agreed that she will help. In fact she has

already started to do the first stage of her part."

"And that is?" Rachel asked, still not convinced, though she was aware that Laticia was game. She also reflected that the saint was now referred to as Winnie. It was almost as if her mother and the saint were huge friends!

"At the moment she is hovering full length over the magical spring water. She will draw as much energy from that healing source as she can and will then transfer it into the mobile parts. So you will need to be able to put them together again very quickly so that we can test it." Stefan advised her.

"How are you going to test it?" Laticia asked. She was getting really excited. Rachel stared at Stefan then at Laticia open mouthed.

"Good question. For some reason Gavin always keeps his mobile in his back pocket of his jeans. Phil does too." Rachel said. "So they would easily be able to get at it when we contact them. Always supposing it worked!" She added sarcastically.

"Let's hope it will." Anna said patiently. "Your father always puts his mobile on the coffee table when he isn't using it. All you would have to do is go there and wait to see if your name comes up on the screen."

"And give him a heart attack in the process!" Rachel retorted. Despite her scepticism she was warming to the idea. Her father was getting used to dealing with the

supernatural, he may not react as intensely as she feared. Besides she doubted if the experiment would work.

Anna shook her head and more or less reiterated what her daughter had been considering. "I think his recent experiences in participating in two séances will protect him from a detrimental reaction."

Resigned to what she thought was a pointless exercise Rachel agreed. "Alright. Let's try. Are you ready Laticia?"

Laticia nodded. "First of all we have to unclip the case cover at the top."

"OK."

Together both ghosts concentrated on the top of the mobile. Rachel could feel Laticia's energy binding with her own, yet nothing seemed to be happening to the mobile. Anna was watching her daughter's face earnestly. "Keep going. Don't give up." She held her daughter's gaze and willed her to go on. Rachel felt her mother's confidence and hope radiate towards her and she summoned up another burst of energy. Laticia too felt inspired by Anna, and a few seconds later, their combined effort rewarded them with a click, as the mobile case jerked up and slipped easily on to the pink silk lining of the coffin.

"Wow. Even better than I hoped." Stefan was ecstatic. Laticia and Rachel were exhausted but exhilarated.

"Give us a few minutes." Laticia said excitedly. All four of them gazed at the innards of the device.

"Removing the sim card shouldn't be too difficult." Stefan suggested. "The battery will probably take more effort."

"In that case, I think we should go for the battery first." Rachel said. Laticia agreed.

"When you lift out the battery and then the sim card do you think you could lay them in a line?" Stefan asked.

"We'll try our best." Rachel replied.

"Think of revenge!" Laticia said to Rachel. The combined rage of the two ghosts achieved the result they were looking for. Both ghosts were gratified to see the separate components of the mobile click out of place. It took a bit more effort to re-arrange them in the position Stefan had requested. Unable to get the battery to lift, both ghosts concentrated on pushing and shoving it along.

To the delight of those in the coffin and to Rachel's astonishment, two more great efforts from herself and Laticia produced the desired results. All the parts were assembled the way Stefan had hoped.

"This is going to be exciting." He said. His companions agreed.

Anna gloated.

Rachel admitted she was impressed with their exertions.

Laticia was smugly enjoying their display of power.

"If we do manage to charge it up, we may only get a few minutes time with it." Rachel commented. "Besides what are we going to

do with it, if it does work? We can't speak. We will have to text."

"How long did the battery last when you were using it?" Stefan asked.

"A couple of days. Sometimes longer if I didn't google anything or send emails."

"Well if we can charge it up, maybe you will have the same amount of time." Stefan said. He made no comment on the other part of her question.

"I wanted to text your father we are alright and solving the crime." Anna said forlornly. She was beginning to realise that even if they did charge the electronic device, it would be of no use to her. Even if Rachel had managed to make just one contact with the living, that would have to be by text. Only Rachel or Laticia had the power to press the keypad. Once Rachel's four week permission to roam finished, they would lose contact forever.

Rachel was sympathetic. "I understand mum. It will be fine. Dad would appreciate a text and help him to get on with his life." Despite herself, Rachel was getting excited about the prospect of sending a text.

Anna smiled at her daughter. Grateful that she understood.

"I think Laticia had better stay here for a few hours to wait for Winefride. Then we can put the thing to the test. As you know Laticia is leaving tomorrow for Barbados, we don't want her to get caught sneaking around the graveyard at this late stage." Anna said.

"Right. This is what I suggest." Stefan said taking charge. He was enjoying himself.

"First Tomtit is going to lie in his coffin for a few hours to try to get his titanium parts to generate some energy into his bones. Then when Winefride is ready he will come over here with her so that their combined energy sources help to energise the mobile.

"Winefride will hover over these parts and allow her influence from the spring water to flow into them. "Rachel you go home and keep watch over your father, then come back later tonight about ten o clock to help Laticia re-assemble the parts. Then you can both go home to wait for the test text."

"Right. I just want to stay to see Winefride in action first. I can't miss that."

Stefan understood her excitement. "Fine."

It was seven o clock that evening when Tomtit and Winefride appeared. No-one except Stefan had actually seen her close up and the females gasped to see how small she was. Her clothes were strange. A dark green silk robe was thickly pleated, billowing into soft folds from her waist downwards. The same fabric draped her arms and chest. The high neckline was edged with lace. On her head she wore what looked like a square of white linen the size of a handkerchief edged with more lace and jewels.

The saint spoke to Stefan in the language that they both understood. The rest watched as he explained what he wanted her to do. Tomtit wafted close to her. She regarded him warily. Her demeanour appeared to be haughty, but Rachel realised she was probably intimidated by so many spirits who were clearly not of her century. She supposed for someone like Winefride it would be like being in a science fiction film of the future. Rachel smothered a desire to laugh at the thought of it. She admired Stefan's easy manner as he soothed the saint.

Stefan assured Winefride that Laticia and he would be there to supervise the proceedings. The saint took up position to hover just a few inches off the ground over the mobile parts. Tomtit hung as closely as he could trying not to cause the saint any alarm. Quietly, Stefan indicated that Rachel and Anna should leave the coffin. They would all meet up again at ten o clock.

Chapter Twenty

Departures

Gavin and Phil had ordered pizzas and were putting together a huge salad in the kitchen when Rachel arrived home. Dan was setting the table in the dining room and Rachel poised herself in the corner to watch him arrange knives and forks and place mats. The place mats were old ones depicting various London tourist attractions. The colours were faded now and very worn. Several times Anna had tried to throw them out but Rachel had always persuaded her to keep them because they reminded her of family trips to that famous city. Dan opened a bottle of red wine and then put some glasses out. When the doorbell rang he went to answer it and brought back four takeaway boxes.

"They're here!" he called out to the kitchen. Phil came in with three warmed plates and helped Dan take the pizzas out of the boxes. The extra one contained garlic bread.

Gavin brought in the salad and a bowl of home-made coleslaw. Dan poured the wine. "Let's make a toast to Phil." He said. They chinked glasses. "Thank you for all that you have done Phil. We may not have convinced the police, but now we know who Rachel's killers are we can keep an eye on them, and who knows, soon we may get justice."

"I'm only sorry I can't stay to help further." Phil said sipping his wine. As he did so he felt a slight breeze behind him, Leo suddenly raised his head and Phil guessed Rachel had entered the room. She positioned herself on one of the empty chairs at the side of Phil.

Dan cut into his pizza. "I have had my eyes opened about the supernatural. Who would have thought it of a diehard cynic like myself?"

"Well even I have been astounded." Gavin said before he shoved a forkful of salad into his mouth.

"I've learnt a lot myself." Phil said gratified. "I've never used my skills in a murder case before. Rachel and her friend were very communicative."

"Funny how Anna wasn't with her though." Dan commented.

You are in for a surprise dad. Hopefully. Rachel mused. Her eyes swept the room looking for her father's mobile phone. She'd looked in the lounge on the coffee table as her mother had suggested but it wasn't there. It was on top of the television. With a bit of luck he would leave it there. She had never known him to use it much, so she assumed it would probably stay there all night. She just hoped it would remain charged, not that it would matter that much. Any text he got would get to him eventually.

After their meal, Phil went upstairs to pack his things. Gavin washed up, whilst Dan got out three clean glasses from the fridge to put on the table along with a bowl of ice. Gavin told Dan about making contact with Abigail and how he hoped they could talk to Nicky.

"If Nicky agrees to talk to Gavin, it might lead to something. Perhaps speed things up a bit?" Phil remarked on his return downstairs.

Dan sighed but made no comment and when Phil sat down again he went to the kitchen to fetch a bottle of Vodka from the freezer.

"I think we should try this vodka with you, seeing as you brought it." Dan said with a wry grin.

"Fine by me." Phil said. He took the proffered glass and sipped it slowly. "Very nice." His companions agreed.

Having digested this news about Gavin's possible conversation with Nicky, Rachel lingered for another hour, then made her way back to the cemetery. She arrived just as Winefride was leaving. She emerged from the coffin just before Rachel entered it. Anna was hovering nearby desperate to get in to the coffin. The saint gesticulated a curt farewell with a nod of her head to Rachel and then departed, her ghoulish clothes swaying behind her. Inside the coffin Rachel and Anna witnessed three delighted faces, but there was nothing to suggest that the parts were now live.

"Come on Rachel. You have work to do. I hope you are sufficiently rested." Anna was excited.

Laticia grinned. "I'm ready." She glanced at Rachel who despite misgivings in getting involved with this episode, was also feeling a wave of excitement.

"Alright. Let's do it." Slowly and steadily using their combined strength the two ghosts began to shove and push the pieces of the mobile together again. When the last piece – the cover - had been clipped on, they all gazed expectantly at the device. It still appeared to be dead. Suddenly Rachel realised that they hadn't switched it on. She caught her mother's hopeful expression, then hovered closer, and summoned up some energy to press the on button. For Anna's sake, Rachel fervently hoped they would get some activity. To her astonishment the familiar sound of Beethoven's fifth symphony came to her ears as the mobile now charged came to life.

"We did it!" Anna cried. The rest of the group dropped their jaws in astonishment. Tomtit began to do a little dance.

"Oh my god." Rachel said. "I don't believe it."

"Quick. Let's send a message to your father." Anna appealed desperately to her daughter. Obligingly Rachel prepared herself to press the buttons. She was amazed that all her old contacts were still visible. "Make it snappy mum. What do you want me to say?"

"Anything! Oh. No. let me think. Just say we are together and not to worry."

Enthralled by their success, they all watched as Rachel concentrated and willed herself to press the keys needed to send a message on the mobile. Eventually she pressed send.

"Do you think I should turn it off now? To save the battery?" Rachel said.

The group solemnly agreed.

Stefan and Tomtit, dumbstruck at the possibility of contacting the living electronically, said goodbye to Laticia, then wafted away smugly to their own resting places.

"Goodbye Laticia. Thanks for all your help. I hope you will be happy in Barbados." Anna said gratefully.

"I will miss you guys." Laticia said.

"See you tomorrow mum. As soon as I know that dad has got the message I will come and tell you."

The bottle of Vodka was half full when the two ghosts returned to the house. Dan and Phil were relaxing on armchairs, whereas Gavin had propped himself up with cushions and lay on the sofa with his feet up. The news was on the television, but neither of the men were taking much notice. In fact Dan had turned down the sound. His eyes were drooping and it looked as if he might fall asleep any second. Rachel scrutinised his face. He looked less strained that night. She wondered what effect the text message would have on him. She hoped it wouldn't frighten him. As Rachel gazed fondly at her father, she

realised that he had moved his mobile phone from off the top of the television. *Laticia searched the room to look for it.*
"Where will it be?"
"Let's look in the dining room." As they sauntered across the room Leo who had been asleep, woke up and began to whine. Phil heard him. Simultaneously he felt a slight breeze around him.
"I think we have company." Phil advised Gavin warily.
"Are you sure?" Gavin sat up straight.
"Absolutely. I may have had a lot to drink, but I know when there is a presence in the room. Leo knows it too."
Gavin jerked his head towards the dog. Leo had followed the ghosts in to the dining room. Phil put his glass down and got to his feet. "I wonder where he is going."
Suddenly alarmed, Gavin jumped off the sofa. He was just in time to see his father slump back in his chair. His vodka glass was precariously tilted in his hand. Gavin saved the glass from falling and put it on the coffee table.
Quietly both men followed the dog into the dining room. Leo sniffed around the two ghosts as Gavin and Phil curiously observed the dog's behaviour. A light was flashing on the mobile signifying a text message.
"I think it's here." Laticia said smugly.
"Wow." Rachel replied.
Gavin noticed his father's mobile and the flashing light. Absently he picked it up. His

look of astonishment made him clutch the back of a chair to steady himself. "No. This can't be right. Someone is playing tricks."
"What is it?" Phil asked.
"A message from Rachel! Impossible!"
Phil grasped the device from Gavin and read the text. "Bloody hell!" He turned around him. Little did he know that Rachel was facing him.
"Rachel if you are in this room, and I think you are, can you give us a sign, something to say you sent this text?"
"Are you mad?" Gavin said incredulously. "It's a hoax!"
"I'm not so sure." Phil said.
Rachel looked at Laticia despairingly. "What can we do?"
"I could punch him in the stomach." Laticia offered.
"No! Don't do that! Gavin will need to see something visual." Frantically she scanned the room. Then her eyes fell on the empty pizza boxes on one of the dining room chairs. "Look. Let's move those boxes. They are very light. One each."
Easily they raised the boxes into the air and let them float over first Phil's head then Gavin's.
"Now what?" Laticia asked. "Shall I drop mine on the table or what?"
"Yes. I think so. They both looked shocked."
"Oh my god. Rachel is that really you?" Gavin asked. He gasped when in reply

Rachel moved one of the boxes in his direction.

"Did you send the text?" Phil asked. *Again Rachel moved the box towards Phil.*

"Bloody hell. This is uncanny." Phil said excitedly. "How the hell did you do that?"

No reply.

"Too complicated a question." Gavin said recovering himself. "Rachel, can I send you a message? I still have your contact details, just like dad kept them."

Rachel looked at Laticia for inspiration. "What do I say?"

Laticia shrugged. "Say yes. It's worth a try."

The pizza box was raised again to Gavin.

"This is beyond anything I've ever seen before." Phil said. He sat down next to Gavin who had slumped on to a dining room chair. He watched his friend take out his mobile from his pocket and send a text to his sister. They waited several minutes but he received no response.

"Rachel are you still there?" Gavin asked.

Pizza box was raised again.

"Maybe it's just a fluke and she can't do it again." Phil suggested. He was breathing heavily. The excitement, the wine and the vodka were having a strange effect on him. The presence of the ghosts were also making an impact.

"I know why she can't answer! Gavin called out suddenly. "Her mobile is in her coffin!"

He was gratified to see the pizza box raised again.

"Bloody hell!" Phil said again. He turned around as he heard a sound from the other room. Then Dan stood in the doorway. He yawned and covered his mouth with the back of his hand. "It's getting late. I'm going to bed."

"Dad…" Gavin was on the point of telling him about the text, but thought it might be better to wait until the next day when his father was more alert. "Goodnight. We are just going to bed too. Have you decided to come to the airport with us in the morning?"

Dan yawned again. "What time are you leaving?"

"About ten thirty. Plenty of time to have breakfast."

"OK. Goodnight." Dan strode past them to the stairway. "Don't forget to move the pizza boxes away from Leo. You know he might go foraging in the night, if he can smell left over food."

Gavin grinned. "Will do."

"I suppose we'd better get to bed too." Phil said. "Much though I would like to have a last séance with your sister and possibly her friend, I'm too tired to concentrate."

"Yep. This has been an interesting end to your visit."

"Yes and we need some bloody rest too!" Laticia agreed.

Rachel smiled. "I'm exhausted too. Come on let's go upstairs. At least you know what time you will be leaving tomorrow. I just hope I have enough energy tomorrow to do things without you."

"You'll be fine. Our power is intensifying, I can feel it. Just a question of learning how to channel it. Anyway I'm too tired now to try anything else."

Neither Gavin nor Phil had difficulty sleeping that night. The excitement and the effects of the alcohol bestowed them with peaceful slumber.

At breakfast the next morning, Gavin waited until his father had eaten his cereal and toast and was on his second cup of coffee before he told him about the text message.

"Dad, whilst you were snoozing in the chair last night, we had a late visitor, possibly two."

"Oh, yes. Why didn't you wake me up? Who were they? The police?" Dan looked hopeful.

"Nothing like that. It was the invisible kind. Ghosts!"

Dan swallowed a mouthful of coffee quickly. "You don't mean Rachel? And your mother?" He asked wistfully.

Gavin shook his head. "I don't think mum was with her. Somehow I think, if she could have found a way to you she would have come."

Listening in the doorway Rachel witnessed her father's disappointed expression. She was waiting to discover his reaction to the text message before she disappeared to let her mother know. She intended to get back to the house so that she could travel in Gavin's car to Manchester airport. Laticia hovered behind Rachel waiting for Gavin to give Dan the news.

"Dad, I have your mobile here. It has a text on it. Before I give it you, I want you to know that this isn't a hoax. No-one is playing nasty tricks on you I promise."

Dan looked alarmed. "What do you mean son?"

"I mean the text is genuine. I don't know how it happened, but it is." Gavin carefully handed the mobile to his father. He was so emotional he half expected it to break. Last night he'd taken the mobile and put it on charge in his own bedroom. That morning before breakfast, he'd already checked it twice, worrying that the text might disappear before he could show it to his father. But the message was still visible.

Dan took the device from his son with trepidation. He seized his reading glasses from his shirt pocket then read the text. His face blanched. "What's the meaning of this? It's impossible!" He glared from Gavin to Phil and back again. "Are you sure you haven't played some evil trick on me?"

"Dad, I swear I wouldn't do such a thing. Please believe me. She was here. She confirmed it. The message is genuine!"

Dan laid the 'phone on the table and got up. His stomach lurched with shock and mixed emotions. He stepped towards the window and looked out into the garden in an effort to hide the tears that misted his eyes. In his mind he recalled the message: "**Dad, I am with mum. We r fine. We luv you xx**

Rachel was devastated that she had upset her father. She desperately wanted him to believe the message was genuine. Her eyes fell on her father's crumpled handkerchief lying on the chair. Impulsively, she forced it upwards and across to Dan. Without turning his head he took it to wipe his eyes. He had thought Phil or Gavin had handed it to him, but when he turned around to face them they were still sitting down at the table. He frowned. He hadn't heard them move. Both of them looked astonished.

"What now?" Dan asked.

Phil had been observing Leo's tail twitching. The dog's eyes were bright and watchful. He cleared his throat. "I believe Rachel handed that handkerchief to you."

"Oh dear. Now what have you done?" Laticia said. "Don't waste all your energy, you know I won't be here to help you."

"I have to do something to convince him before I go." Rachel replied. She eyed the clock on the wall, it was nine o clock. She had some time yet. "Something small."

"Have another cup of coffee dad. I will put some extra sugar in it. You've had a bit of a shock. We couldn't believe it either last night, but I promise you it is real."

Dan watched his son put the spoon into the sugar bowl, then stare incredulously as grains of sugar became elevated above the table. They formed a line then a heart shape before disappearing into Dan's cup.

"Nice one." Laticia said. "But conserve your energy!" She implored.

Bemused, Dan fixed his gaze on his two companions who had been as transfixed as he was when they saw the sugar spectacle. A glimmer of a smile edged its way on to Dan's face.

"Wherever you are Rachel, thank you." He sipped his coffee whilst Phil and Gavin shook their heads in disbelief as they tried to come to terms with this new unexpected phenomena.

"Oh my god." Gavin said. "What else can you do Rache?"

"She's gone." Phil said. "I felt her breeze past me. And look at Leo. He's been agitated all morning. He's settled again now."

Laticia had returned upstairs to wait.

As arranged, Anna and Stefan were waiting in Rachel's coffin when she reappeared. They eyed the mobile helplessly as they waited. They both looked at Rachel anxiously as she crept in beside them. "It worked!" She spoke the words as she floated towards the 'on' button. With a little effort she switched on the device and was rewarded with a flashing light telling her she had a message. In fact there were several messages. Old ones from the day she was murdered. She ignored them and went to the most recent one. "Gavin sent a message from his own phone." She explained. It was a simple message. "**Is this really you**?"

Anna and Stefan were gleeful. Rachel laughed. "Well mum, I didn't think it would work but wow!" She proceeded to tell them the reaction from her father, brother and Phil.
Anna's face was wistful.
Stefan was ecstatic.
"I must tell Gavin not to text me any more, we need to save the battery." Rachel sent a short abbreviated message to Gavin then switched off the mobile.
"Good idea." Agreed Stefan. I doubt very much Winefride will do it again. It took ages to get her to understand. When you are from the 7th century, it's hard to accept 21st century technology. It's a lot to take in. She is dealing with the future and we are dealing with the past. To her it's just bits of metal and magic."
"It is really!" Rachel said. "I must fly. Literally. See you later." She returned home in time to find Phil loading up his bags in the boot of Gavin's car.

Dan was sitting in the back of the vehicle. At the side of him Laticia arranged herself on the seat. Rachel swept in beside her. Before Phil got in the car Gavin passed his mobile to him so that he could read his latest message. He took care not to let his father see it. The poor man was still recovering from shock. Gavin himself was having difficulty coming to terms with receiving a message from "the other side" as he referred to it. Phil handed the mobile back. "Wow" he mouthed to Gavin. Rachel had texted: **ltd power save bat**.

Phil and Gavin had agreed that they wouldn't park the car at the airport, so at the Departures entrance, they dropped Phil off. "Cheers. See you Dan. Let me know how things go with the hairdresser." He winked at Gavin who rolled his eyes. Dan gave Gavin a quizzical look but said nothing.

Laticia slipped out behind Phil. "What's that about?"

Rachel grinned. "I've no idea. Maybe Gavin has fallen in love?"

Laticia waved a last farewell to Rachel. "We probably won't see each other again. Good luck. You still have three weeks of roaming time."

At that precise moment Detective Inspector Carl Barker was looking at the case file of Rachel Bellis. It was very slim. He recalled the case vividly. Poor young woman barely nineteen. Found covered in slime from the lake, almost dead from her injuries. They had interviewed the two young lads who had found her, and also the two men from the sailing club who had arrived a few minutes later to help. All four suspects had willingly gone down to the station to make statements. The first two had freely handed over the outer clothing they were wearing for inspection that same evening. A few spots of blood on one of the two rescuers clothes had aroused some suspicion and he had been detained for more questioning. Apparently he had pulled the girl out of the lake. Eventually he had been allowed to go home. The outer clothing of the other two hadn't looked suspicious. All four men had been cleared. So too had Emma the friend of the victim. Apparently she had arranged to meet the victim, and had actually arrived at their meeting place. Too late apparently.

The detective shook his head in frustration. It seemed as if the whole unpleasant incident had been choreographed and for a while he suspected Emma of having arranged for someone to attack Rachel. That line of inquiry had gone nowhere. They had interviewed Rachel's boyfriend Josh and they had also interviewed the employees at the boat house who had been working that night. They'd had no reason to search the boat shed nor the club itself. Their efforts had been concentrated on the two young men who had found Rachel, her friends and family.

Past experience had shown the police that the first person on the murder scene turned out to be the killer. On the other hand, very often the killer turned out to be a member of the victim's family. At one point they had suspected the father and the brother. Forensics after months of waiting for the report had not provided them with any clues. The only DNA was of the victim. The short time she had been in the muddy water had ruined any chance of finding any other DNA from the rape. Her jeans and underwear had been savagely removed before the sexual assault had taken place.

The police had found them easily enough the next day. They had been tossed into the water and were floating close to the edge where Rachel had been found.

Detective Inspector Carl Barker re-read the report again and then studied the note he had taken from the desk sergeant. A new line of inquiry was suggested. He mulled over it. He acknowledged that if the old railway goat track was still intact, it was possible for those two men from the boat house to have committed the rape then return to the boat house completely unseen. They would have had time to change their clothes and leave the normal way.

Yet there was a third guy, Lester Price who vouched for both of them. The detective sighed. There was no harm in looking at that old railway line path. But he would still need hard evidence. He doubted that blood stained clothes were going to be easy to find. At the time of the murder his officers had searched the ground and public bins looking for abandoned blood stained clothes but had found nothing.

He might have a word with Lester Price again. Barker sat thinking about the case, looking for something he might have missed. Then he remembered, that Lester Price had not been working that night. So how could he have vouched for those two men from the boat club being where they should be? Was there a deputy? Sighing, he closed the file and made a decision. With a bit of luck he could leave work earlier today. The training course he was due to attend should finish around four o clock. It shouldn't take too long to check out that old path. Then he was going home for a well-earned rest.

After they had returned from Manchester airport, Gavin parked his car on the driveway outside the house. He and his father strolled into the kitchen neither of them speaking. They hadn't spoken much during the journey home. Both of them were occupied with thinking about the weird text message from Rachel. Gavin, was doubly staggered at having received two text messages. He decided not to tell his father about the second one from Rachel.

Dan put on the kettle to make them some coffee. *Rachel slipped out of the car and left them to chat. She intended to do some snooping. First place to start was the boat house locker room. Before she did that, she slipped into the cemetery to make contact with her mother and the group of spirits she had come to look upon as her friends.*

Chapter Twenty One

Discoveries

Aware that Laticia's departure, would place more pressure on her single use of power, Rachel was keen to explore just how much she could do on her own. She hoped to create an opportunity to allow her to look properly in the bin bag lying in Maxwell's locker. If it still contained his blood stained jacket, she would have to try to get the police to find it. That was going to be difficult, and she had no idea how to pull it off. She stayed at the cemetery longer than she had intended to, answering questions and going over the evidence with her companions whilst they hung around in the crypt.
"Has that Abigail made contact with Gavin yet to fix up a meeting with Nicky?" Anna asked.
Rachel shook her head.
Anna frowned. "Maybe that Nicky doesn't want to be bothered, because she is afraid."
The others agreed. "She may even know something that she's not telling." Margareta suggested. "If there's blood on the sleeve of Ryan's jacket, she may be suspicious."
"She may have washed it." Desmond said.
"Not all the blood would have washed away." Margareta said. "It stains."
"Even after a year?" Desmond said.

"Yes. I've seen a few detective programmes on the telly, they can spray some stuff on it and shine a bright light on it to find traces of blood stains." Rachel agreed.

Anna nodded. "Yes, I believe it is called Luminol, but I'm not sure if it is available in this country. I've only seen it on American TV.

"I've been dead too long." Desmond said. "I didn't know about that."

"Yep. I think they have been using that stuff for years." Big Steve added. "I've seen 'em use it, the forensic teams, I mean in British films."

They heard the church clock strike three o clock.

"I'm going to hang around in the boat club for a few hours. Then I'm going to Nicky's house. I'll call home later to try to find out if Gavin has had any messages from Abigail. But tonight I will rest in my coffin." Rachel informed her group of friends.

"See you later. Good luck." Anna called.

It was the week before May day bank holiday and the staff at the boathouse were expecting a lot of visitors. The weather forecast was good, so there was a lot of activity going on in preparation for the week end.

Rachel slipped into the locker room at three thirty just when some of the staff were either taking a break or changing their shifts. Some of the employees worked part time. There was no sign of Maxwell. She hung around idly watching the workers change their footwear and outer clothing. At four o clock Rachel found herself alone again until her prey came into the room. Rachel wondered whether his lone entrance was deliberate. He looked furtive. Stealthily he opened his locker. Above the two hooks inside the locker where his jacket hung, there was a shelf which was stacked with two brown cardboard boxes. They were a similar size to those that usually contained shoes. Cautiously Maxwell took down one box and retrieved several small plastic packages which Rachel guessed contained cocaine. 'So, he is definitely into drugs.' She muttered. She expected him to snort some, but then realised that he was not a user but a pusher. He stuffed several small packages into his pockets, but then hesitated. Probably, Rachel figured, because his pockets were bulging.

Casting another watchful glance around the room to make sure he was still alone Maxwell bent down to pull out a small rolled up rucksack. The movement dislodged his boots where he had dumped them carelessly on top of the black bin bag at the bottom of the locker. Both slipped out of the locker falling one over the other and landed on to the floor.

Rachel seized her chance and managed to force the first boot to slide a little distance across the floor. Somewhat exasperated Maxwell bent down on the floor to attempt to put both boots together. He was slightly impeded because he was still holding the rucksack. He straightened up again to shove it under one arm before trying again.

A fresh surge of energy founded on her hatred of the man helped Rachel to dislodge one of the pair of shoes that had also been resting precariously on the bin bag. It tumbled with a thud to the floor and landed at Maxwell's feet. She was delighted that this time her efforts paid off. The shoes' pair toppled down on its own accord settling behind where Max was standing.

Max cursed, and whilst he was preoccupied with gathering his footwear, Rachel easily forced the bin bag to topple on its side. Quickly she pushed her head through the thin plastic of the bin bag to examine the contents. She was exultant when she saw that the blue fabric she had seen during her earlier attempt was indeed a jacket. Furthermore there were obvious signs of blood spatters down the front of the scrunched up garment. Some blood had seeped into the cotton fabric that held the metal zip together. "My blood!" She realised with anger. One of the sleeves had been crumpled backwards whilst in the bag. It had a dark trail that appeared to be congealed blood running down the stitching of the seam. Max had evidently shoved that piece of clothing into the bin bag quickly and just left it there.

Triumph mingled with hatred ran through Rachel's thoughts as she watched this monster re-packing his things. Max hurled both the boots and the shoes on top of the bin bag again, not bothering to fasten it properly. Rachel's loathing consumed her, causing a surge in her energy levels. She guessed that the night Maxwell and Ryan raped her they had been dealing with drugs. How many victims they had at their mercy was difficult to assess, but judging by the amount of cocaine he had stashed away, she guessed they had a lucrative business going. Maxwell and Ryan wore expensive clothes. Maxwell's job at the boat club didn't pay high wages, she knew. For him, she guessed the job was just a cover.

Once Maxwell had packed his rucksack he put it back in the locker. *Rachel assumed he had made it ready to retrieve later when his shift was over. She followed him out where he wore a cheerful grin as he greeted Lester at the reception desk.*

Together they both went outside to work on the boat maintenance.

For a few minutes Rachel hovered in the reception room, wondering what to do next.

She came to the conclusion that she could do no more at the boat club and decided to hover over the old railway track to the town. Maybe Maxwell would use it again later. Then she thought it might be more useful to hang around the beauty salon to see if she could pick up any information from Abigail and Nicky.

Just as Rachel emerged from the boat club, Detective Inspector Carl Barker parked his car in Holywell town square. He walked across the square, passed through the town gates and made his way to the network of various footpaths. Choosing the one where he believed would lead him to the old railway goat track, he soon came to a standstill where he gazed around him. He wanted to check the distance between that track, and the lych gate of St. Winefride's cathedral. Satisfied with his findings, he turned his attention to the entrance to the track. It was indeed overgrown with bushes and branches. He put on some thick gloves and pushed back two heavy branches of an ash tree. They yielded quite easily and the DI's expectations were heightened when he noticed some trampled weeds and broken branches of young saplings just beyond the ash tree.

It was evident that someone had walked through here quite recently. The path still wasn't in a fit state for most walkers though, he observed. He realised that the entrance had been deliberately left concealed with greenery to deter ramblers. This notion was confirmed when after a few tentative steps he noted that the vegetation lessened. Someone had gone to the trouble to cut back the lower parts of the undergrowth, yet allowed weeds to grow wildly higher up so that they created a thick green roof. In effect, it was a secret tunnel.

The DI took a few photos with his mobile before proceeding. As he progressed, he checked the time on his mobile so that he could measure how long it would take to

walk down to the sailing club. Through the vegetation he could glimpse the top of the building. Half way down the path he unknowingly passed Rachel. *She gazed at him with surprise. She passionately hoped he was investigating her murder. She had never met the detective, but looking at his clothes and his intent expression she guessed who he might be.*
Satisfied with his findings, Detective Inspector Carl Barker returned to his car. Tomorrow, he planned a different approach towards solving the murder of Rachel Bellis. The men from the Sailing club may not be as innocent as they had first appeared.
Meanwhile, Rachel made her way to the beauty salon. Abigail was with a client, but Nicky was nowhere to be seen. Unfamiliar with this salon, Rachel hovered around until she noticed the stairway leading up to the massage room on the second floor. Venturing upwards, she found Nicky giving a client an Indian head massage. Rachel was appalled when she saw the bruises around Nicky's eye. She guessed that was the handiwork of Ryan. No doubt she had told her employer that she had walked into a door or given some other pathetic excuse. Rachel decided to wait and follow her home. She also hoped that she might be able to listen to some conversation between the two friends. Her hopes were realised when later she followed them both towards the bus stop.

Abigail lived locally but accompanied Nicky to the bus stop. Before she left her to walk home, Abigail asked Nicky if she had reconsidered talking to Gavin about Ryan.

Nicky shook her head vehemently. "I honestly don't know why he wants to talk to me. I don't remember anything about that night when his sister was killed. It's nothing to do with me."

Abigail was growing more and more worried about her friend. Couldn't she see that Ryan was probably mixed up in the murder in some way or other? She herself wasn't prepared yet, to accept that Ryan was responsible for Rachel's death, but she felt he may know something. She was hoping he may have made some comment to Nicky, even some slight remark which may help Gavin. She certainly didn't like Ryan's friend Max. Personally she felt that if anyone was capable of murder, then sleaze ball Max would be that person. When Abigail's thoughts turned to Gavin, she felt a warm glow. He seemed like a nice guy and she wanted to help him.

"I just thought it wouldn't harm to have a chat with him." Abigail tried to persuade her friend.

Nicky shook her head. "And if Ryan saw me talk to him, he would just get jealous and take it out on me."

Abigail sighed. She was sick of hearing about Ryan and his jealousy, but her friend wouldn't admit it was a problem. Time for direct action. She took a deep breath and pointed at Nicky's bruises. "Is that how he works off his jealousy? Hitting you in the face?"

Nicky looked about to cry at Abigail's sharp accusation. She hung her head and said nothing. Fortunately for her the bus arrived and she got on it. "See you tomorrow." She muttered, leaving Abigail looking on exasperated.

Rachel decided to follow Abigail. She thought she might try to contact Gavin. Rachel wanted to hear their discussion, it might help her think of a plan to get the police involved. She could go to Nicky's later.

Instead of going straight home, Abigail chose to stroll to the cemetery. She soon found Rachel's grave. She stood observing it for a while, memorising the dates and trying to recall anything she had done that day. Nothing came to mind but she had her old diary at home. She would check to see if there was anything of significance in it. Unlike some of her friends she didn't keep a 'Dear diary', but she was meticulous about appointments, anniversaries and birthdays. Later at home she discovered that the date of death 20th March was the week before Easter. She and Nicky had exams that week and then Nicky was going to stay with her mother for Easter week end. So Nicky wasn't around when Rachel was killed. Abigail recalled that she herself had gone on a hen night in Chester with the girls from work. She decided to 'phone Gavin.

"I've been to see your sister's grave." She told him when he answered her call. "I've been racking my brains trying to think what I was doing that night. It wasn't far off Easter. I remember Nicky saying something about going away for a long week end to see her mother."

Gavin was surprised and pleased to hear from Abigail again. At first he was unsure what to say. Even though he couldn't see her, she seemed to have some hold on him. "I see." He said stiffly. "That's a shame. There might be something she knows that could help me."

Abigail was a bit affronted by Gavin's cold voice. "Why do you think she could help you? Do you really suspect her boyfriend?"

"Actually yes."

"How do you think he could be involved?"

Gavin breathed deeply contemplating how much he should tell her. He decided to trust her. "Phil and I have reason to believe that my sister's blood could be on her boyfriend's jacket." As soon as he said this, he wished he hadn't. What if she told Nicky and in turn, Nicky told Ryan. He would try to get rid of the garment. There was silence on the other side.

"Abigail? Are you still there?"

"Yeah. Yeah. Sorry. I'm gob smacked. But how do you know? I mean what makes you say that? Oh my god. You can't be serious."

"This is why I would like to talk to her."

"I've asked her. She's refused. She said she doesn't know anything."

Gavin sighed. "Alright. Thanks for trying. But please, don't tell her what I have said will you?"

"But shouldn't I warn her? She might be in trouble herself."

"Do you think she is in danger?"

Abigail was frightened for her friend and didn't know what to say or do. "I don't know. She might be though if you think he is violent."

Even as she spoke Abigail finally recognised that Ryan was a dangerous man. A look at the state of her friend's face was evidence enough. Gavin knew it too, but neither of them mentioned it over the 'phone. Gavin didn't know how to reply. Abigail spoke again which made him feel even more anxious. "Look, I will ask her again tomorrow when I see her in work. Maybe she will change her mind."

"Alright. Thank you. But promise me not to mention the jackets. It could be important evidence."

Abigail promised she wouldn't. She said she wanted to help. Gavin was reluctant to hang up but felt there was nothing more to say. Later he wished he'd invited her out for a drink to chat things through. At least he had her mobile number now. Maybe he could call her later.

Listening to the conversation Rachel became exasperated with her brother. Why didn't he invite Abigail out for a drink? He was clearly attracted to her. She left Abigail and went to find Nicky.

In Nicky's flat, Rachel watched the young girl make herself something to eat. She put it on a tray, there being no table, and sat on the sofa in front of the TV. It appeared that both Nicky's flat mates were out and the girl was alone. Rachel made herself comfortable on the sofa too. Together they watched several quiz programmes and Rachel was impressed with Nicky's knowledge. As she observed her intelligent and bruised face, Rachel found it difficult to believe how this smart woman could allow a brute like Ryan to treat her so badly.

Around eight thirty the thug himself arrived, and after an embrace he sat down beside Nicky on the sofa and putting his arm around her he pulled her to him. He seemed to be cheerful so Nicky decided to confide in him. Afterwards she regretted every word she had spoken.

"Do you remember about a year ago or more, about that girl who was murdered near the lake close to St. Winefride's well?"

Nicky frowned when she felt Ryan's muscles tense against her chest.

"What of it?" He asked.

"Her brother has been asking people if they know anything that might help him find the murderer."

"That's up to the police, isn't it? I thought they closed the case."

"I don't think so. But anyway this Gavin wants to talk to me."

"Gavin? Who's Gavin?" Ryan pulled away from Nicky and sat up to face her. He gripped her arms tightly.

"Gavin Bellis. He's the dead girl's brother." Nicky replied nervously. She could see that Ryan was immediately jealous. She wondered how she would ever get him to trust her. She still clung to the hope that he wouldn't turn out like her father.

"What does he want to talk to you for? Do you know him?" A notion that Nicky may have known Rachel dawned on him and his hold on her arms tightened. "Did you know his sister?"

Nicky shook her head. She was annoyed, and he was hurting her arms. "No. Of course not."

"Then why does he want to talk to you? Anyway how do you know he wants to talk to you?"

"Ryan let go my arms and I will tell you." He released her arms and she crossed them rubbing each one with her hands.

"I don't know him. He's been talking to Abi and he asked about me. He's that guy we saw in the pub the other day. Do you remember? His friend was with him, the one who picked up my jacket off the floor. Well, your jacket actually…"

Ryan got hold of one of Nicky's arms again and this time pushed it behind her back.

"Ow. Ryan you're hurting me."

"I don't want you talking to him. Do you hear me? Stay away from him."

"He only wants to find who killed his sister. What harm can it do? Ryan stop it."
But Ryan didn't stop. He was frightened. He took out his fear and anger on Nicky. He slapped her face hard and punched Nicky's chest and stomach, ignoring her cries and pleading for him to stop.
"Stay away from him." When she was half conscious and bleeding, she fell to the floor clutching her stomach, promising she would not talk to Gavin. He held her head and made her repeat it. "Promise you won't talk to him!" She nodded and whispered the words "I promise!" Coldly her assailant dropped her head on the floor, stepped over her and left, slamming the door behind him. Nicky slipped in to oblivion.

Outraged, Rachel felt helpless. She bent over Nicky. She was still breathing but seemed to be gasping for breath. She could see instantly that Nicky needed to get to hospital. Rachel hunted for Nicky's mobile. Even as she did this, she knew it was unlikely that she had the capacity to use it. It was probably in her bag, and Rachel had no ability to open it let alone search in it. She would have to leave her. Could she alert Nicky's next door neighbour? Slipping through the door, on to the landing Rachel placed herself outside the door of the adjacent flat and with all the energy she could muster she caused the doorbell to ring. It rang for a good while before a woman wrapped in a towel came to the door. She had obviously been in the shower. "Hello?" She seemed puzzled to find no-one on the doorstep. She glanced at Nicky's door but saw it was closed, and so she retreated into her own flat. *Exasperated, but determined Rachel again applied pressure on the bell.*

"Is there someone playing tricks on me?" The woman asked. Nervously she pulled the towel closer around her and opened the door again, just a fraction this time. She saw no-one. Curiously, she knocked on Nicky's door with the intention of asking her if she had been trying to contact her. She knew that no-one could get through the security lock downstairs. Only she and Nicky occupied the flats on this floor. She rang the bell and rapped on the door for good measure. When no-one answered, she was about to move away when she saw the letterbox slightly flutter. This had taken a great deal of effort on Rachel's part. It barely moved, but it attracted the attention of the neighbour nevertheless. Rachel hung around watching the neighbour, willing her to look through the letterbox. Overcome by curiosity, the neighbour did just that. She bent down and peered through the letterbox. She gasped when she saw Nicky's bloody face on the floor. Again she rapped on the door. Louder this time. "Nicky! Nicky!" she called.

Returning to her own flat the woman dialled 999.

As soon as the police arrived and an ambulance had taken Nicky away, Rachel

returned to the cemetery and told her mother what had happened.
"I must tell Gavin somehow to go to the hospital. We have proof now, that Ryan is a violent and dangerous man."
"Could you text him?" Anna said.
"I'm going to try."
Together they glided to Rachel's coffin. First she rested for a few minutes, then concentrating hard, she summoned up some energy to press the on button. "There's still a light on it. So the battery is not dead yet." Rachel's hatred for Ryan galvanised her strength sending potent surges of energy. She sent a message to Gavin hoping he would understand. **Nicky hsptl call Abi.**
"I don't want to waste the batt so I will turn it off. I'll go home now and see if he has picked up the message. If he hasn't I'll have to find some way of telling him what's happened."
Anna looked hopeful. "This unfortunate event may lead us to the outcome we are looking for. I just hope we are not the cause of poor Nicky's pain."
"I think something like this would have happened sooner or later mum. It's not our fault. But will she testify?" Rachel said sighing.
"But surely she will." Anna said.
Rachel shrugged. "I'm not so sure. She's scared of him. Look what happened to Laticia. Her husband promised to behave, and then he killed her."

Gavin was talking on his mobile to Abigail whilst pulling on his raincoat. It had started to rain outside. Dan was staring at him in disbelief. He had seen the text message from Rachel and was deeply shocked. More by the communication from Rachel, rather than because of the assault on Nicky. He was of course very sorry that Nicky had been attacked.

"OK if you don't trust me, I will see you at the hospital." Gavin was saying. He closed his mobile and seized his keys from the coffee table.

"Abigail is going to get a taxi to the hospital, but first she is going to ring Accident and Emergency to check that her friend has been admitted. She can't understand how I know and she doesn't. She won't let me give her a lift."

"Well I'm not surprised." Dan said sipping a glass of Vodka. "It's a shock for us both. How can you tell someone that you had a text message from someone who is dead? I can't believe it myself, yet I know it's true. God help us." He turned to his son. "Are you sure you can cope with this?"

"It's something I have to do dad. I have to keep going. Maybe when it's all over I will be able to give in to this weight that seems to follow me around. He thumped his chest and saw his father's face slump with worry. Gavin knew his father worried about him. He recognised his own grief reflected in his father's face. A feeling of helplessness, anger, pain and guilt that he experienced when Rachel died and now again for his mother. So far he had managed to put the loss for his mother on hold, but he knew sooner or later he would have to give in to it. Only his promise to find his sister's killer was keeping him going. That and his need to be close to his father.

Rachel watched them both. There was nothing she could do to help their pain. But she was glad that her brother and father were looking out for each other. She followed Gavin out to his car. He started up the engine just as his mobile rang. It was Abigail.

"I've rung the hospital. They've confirmed Nicky is there. They won't tell me anything else. Gavin can you pick me up? I haven't enough cash on me to pay the taxi. I don't want to waste time running to the cash machine. And it's raining! My mum is out and my two sisters haven't got much money on them, so I can't borrow."

"What's your address?"

They arrived at the hospital twenty minutes later. Abigail explained to the staff nurse that she was a close friend and that Nicky's family lived several miles away. She'd rung Nicky's mother and she was on her way to the hospital.

"Do you know how this happened?" The nurse asked?

Abi shook her head. "No, but I have my suspicions."

The nurse held Abi's gaze but said nothing else. She sighed. She had witnessed incidents such as this before. "You'd better have a word with the doctor. Tell her as much as you can. Your friend is in a bad way and she is unconscious."

It was several hours later that they moved Nicky to a bed on to another ward away from Accident and Emergency. Nicky's mother had arrived and was planning on staying the night with her daughter. Gavin took Abigail home.

"I will go and see her tomorrow after work." Abigail said sitting in the passenger seat beside him. "I hope she will make a complaint to the police. I wouldn't mind betting Ryan did this."

"It seems likely." Gavin agreed. "Has this happened before?"

"Not like this no. The more I think about it the more I realise that something was wrong and I didn't see it. There seems to be a pattern. She takes a day or two off work every now and again and says she has a cold, then returns to work clutching her stomach. When that happens she seems to walk as if she has bruised her ribs. Sometimes she complains of a pain in her arms or shoulders, yet she manages to get her work done. I've never known her to be admitted into hospital before. Nor have I seen her looking like she does now." She turned towards him her eyes wet and weary. "God I can't believe it." She took out a paper tissue and wiped her eyes before gazing at Gavin again. "You still haven't told me how you knew she was hurt."

Gavin felt uncomfortable. He fixed his eyes on the road ahead. "You'd never believe me if I told you."

Abigail regarded Gavin with a frown on her face. "I'm open minded."

Gavin was unsure what to say. Abigail sensed his reluctance to talk and so helped him out. "It's late, and I'm tired. Never mind, you can tell me another time. I'll call you. Thanks for the lift. And thanks for telling me about Nicky. Good night."

Gavin drove home with mixed feelings. He felt sorry for Nicky, but felt this incident might help the police track down Rachel's killers. He shuddered when he thought how his sister had suffered at the hands of those thugs Ryan and Maxwell. His thoughts turned to the text message from Rachel. It was incredible. He would have to tell Phil about this latest development. He doubted that he and his father would have got so far with this investigation without his help. As he again reflected on the events of the evening a thin shred of pleasure mingled with his emotions. This was due to the fact that Abigail was going to call him again.

Chapter Twenty Two

Developments

After Ryan had stormed out of Nicky's flat he had called Max and arranged to meet him at the *Black Raven*.
"If this is about that bloody jacket again, I've told you. Forget it. The police have got nothing on us."
Ryan didn't tell him about his assault on Nicky, but he told him that Gavin was making inquiries.
"So what? He can't prove anything. He doesn't know about the jackets. No-one knows. Forget it."
However the next day Max began to think about moving the bin bag from his locker and getting rid of it for good. It was over a year now. He doubted the police would still be searching for bloody clothes.
That lunch time Max waited to be alone in the locker room. He removed his boots and shoes off the top of the bag and dragged it from the corner of the locker to just inside the door. The bag was showing signs of wear and tear due to the constant pushing around it received from Maxwell's shoes and his wellingtons. The tiny rips on the side had widened but it was still intact. He took off his wet wellingtons and threw them back in the locker, then put on his shoes.
Checking that no-one was in sight, he turned the bin bag upside down and

emptied the soiled jacket out of the bag on to the bottom of the locker. He screwed his nose in disgust at the pungent smell. After another glance over his shoulder to make sure he was alone he furtively rolled the jacket into a small bundle before returning it to the bin bag. Squeezing the bin bag into a tight parcel he held it under one arm. With the other arm he shoved his wet wellingtons into the corner which had been occupied by the bin bag, in order to make space to replace his boots in the locker. Turning the key in the door he left the building and quickly strode to his car. After driving the short distance to his home which he shared with his parents and younger brother he dumped the bin bag in his bedroom. He planned to get rid of it later when it was dark. Satisfied with himself he returned to work.

That afternoon Detective Inspector Carl Barker decided to pay the boat club a visit. Detective Sergeant Chloe Watson went with him. They spoke to Lester Price first even though he was above suspicion. The DI had taken some time to check this man's alibi again before calling at the sailing and rowing boat club.

"So the night you were in London, who was in charge?"

"No-one actually. I was only off that one day, so as all the staff know the ropes, there wasn't any need for a deputy manager."

"So when we made our initial inquiries and you confirmed that Maxwell Briggs and

Jamie Weston were here, it was because you knew that was their rota?"

Lester nodded. "Yes. That's true." He frowned. Is there anything wrong Inspector?"

Detective Inspector Carl Barker shrugged but kept his thoughts to himself. He told Lester that he wanted to interview Jamie Weston and Maxwell Briggs again.

"Of course Inspector, I will get a message to them both over the PA system to tell them to come up to reception. It shouldn't take too long, I've just seen Maxwell go down to the locker room to get changed. He's on a different shift today. He's due to finish at four thirty." Lester glanced at his watch. The time was four twenty. "If you could just wait here. Jamie Weston is outside patrolling the lake, so that could take a bit longer. I'll have to get someone to replace him."

When Lester informed Maxwell a few minutes later that the inspector wanted to talk to him again, he appeared unruffled. The police officers who stood a few metres away in the reception area observed his demeanour. Neither of them spoke.

Maxwell was brimming with confidence, quietly congratulating himself on his swift action to move the incriminating evidence. He followed the detective inspector and Sergeant Chloe Watson into the meeting room that Lester had allocated for the purpose of interviewing Maxwell. He slouched in a chair opposite DI Carl Barker and grinned lasciviously at DS Chloe Watson.

"We are following a new line of inquiry." The DI informed Maxwell. He scrutinised his suspect's face as he added the words "into the murder of Rachel Bellis."

Max didn't flinch.

A tough one here. The DI mused.

"We are looking for clothing which may provide us with some evidence." Detective Sergeant Chloe Watson explained. She was careful not to mention a specific garment whilst she delivered her statement to Maxwell. She held his eyes steadily with her own. Maxwell, still relaxed and revelling in his foresight to remove the soiled clothing from his locker, maintained an air of arrogance. He met the sergeant's gaze and tried to flirt with her.

"And you think my jacket may be the one you are looking for? Surely not." He winked at Chloe but she wasn't having it. She'd met too many cocky types like this before.

"This will be the jacket that the club provides for you. Is that correct?" The detective sergeant asked casually.

"Yes. All the employees get jackets." Maxwell replied.

"Do you still have the one you were wearing a year ago?" The DI asked. "Most outdoor jackets last several years, and I have reason to believe that the ones supplied here are of very good quality."

Carl Barker took his time. His approach was deliberately slow and meaningful. He had come across this arrogant type too many times before in his long police career. His suspicion was aroused immediately, when he noted that Maxwell, had mentioned the specific item they were looking for. He exchanged a brief glance with his sergeant.

"Yes. They are of good quality. And yes I still have mine." Maxwell said enthusiastically. He was enjoying himself.

"Do you think we could see it?" The inspector asked.

"Yes. It's in the locker room. I've just hung it up. I was getting changed you see. I finish my shift in a few minutes. I can go and get it for you."

"If it's alright with you we will come down to the locker room with you."

"OK. No worries." Maxwell replied.

The police officers followed Maxwell down the corridor. As they passed through the foyer, the detective inspector and detective sergeant paused a while to study the view afforded by the high window. A tangle of buddleia bushes, lanky stems of ash trees and other uncultivated vegetation met their vision. Threaded through that labyrinth of undergrowth, thick brambles lashed out their prickly thorns as they weaved and coiled an uninspiring web amidst the foliage. All of it naturally concealed the old railway goat track. Only by looking very closely could a person detect a narrow path through the shrubbery. The thick flora would be enough to deter most people from attempting to walk through it. Chloe stood at the side of the DI to look at the overgrown scenario. He'd briefed her earlier of what he'd discovered. Neither of them displayed any concern, nor did they speak. Maxwell's stomach churned when he saw them gazing outside.

"Who looks after the shrubbery at the back of this building?" DI Barker asked in a dispassionate tone. He examined Maxwell's face as he asked the question.

"I'm not sure." This was actually the truth. Maxwell had no idea who maintained the outside area of the building.

"There used to be an old railway line at the back here, didn't they?" Chloe asked innocently.

"I don't know." Maxwell replied. Anxious to get the police officers away from the window, he gesticulated the stairs leading down to the locker room. "This way."

He was beginning to feel uncomfortable. This line of questioning confused him. However on the way downstairs, he began to relax again as they continued to ask questions. They went through the routine of asking him to recall his movements on the night of the murder. He was familiar with these questions and able to tell them the same lies as those he told when they had originally interviewed him.

Leading the police officers to the locker room, Maxwell attempted to appear unruffled. Despite this attempt of bravado however, he began to display signs of nervousness.

Detective Inspector Barker scrutinised Maxwell Briggs's body language. He caught the sergeant's eye. She nodded but said nothing. They both felt that Briggs was not as innocent as he had first appeared a year ago.

When Maxwell unlocked his locker both officers were disappointed to see Maxwell's jacket hanging up without any obvious blemishes on it. With his permission they took it out and examined it. They both paid particular attention to the collar, sleeves and cuffs where they knew that if there had been any residual blood stains it would have been easy to detect on the seams of those three areas.

Maxwell began to relax again. When Detective Inspector Barker asked him if he had a spare jacket, he wanted to laugh out loud. He shook his head and turned away from the locker door concealing a triumphant expression outlining his face.

As his equanimity returned to him, Maxwell was caught off guard again when the police officers asked if they could examine the inside of his locker. He agreed with a forced calmness. Then he began to worry. He had removed the bin bag with the soiled jacket but had not considered hiding the drugs.

If he'd known, when he'd heard the intercom message asking him to come up to reception, that police officers were waiting for him, he would have moved the boxes somewhere else. He could easily have passed them off as cleaning products and taken them to a temporary place in the cleaning cupboard. It would have been simple to do, since the meeting room where the police had interviewed him was next to the equipment room. Whilst Max was silently cursing Lester for not tipping him off, Detective Sergeant Chloe Watson had moved forward to peer inside the locker.

At the base of the locker she could see the pair of wet rubber wellies which Maxwell wore when wading in the water to launch or retrieve the boats. Some recent droplets of water had fallen from the wellies to settle on the base of the metal locker. In his earlier haste to remove the bin bag Maxwell had not bothered to tidy up. A few congealed beads of blood had escaped from the contents of the bin bag. Drips from Maxwell's wet wellingtons had merged with the beads of blood and pooled into a light pink splodge.

"What's that?" Chloe asked genuinely interested. She bent down to look closer. Maxwell was dismayed. He also bent his head partly to hide his apprehension. Chloe listened whilst Maxwell attempted to explain that it was probably grubby water from the lake that had stained his rubber boots.

Carl studied Maxwell's body language. Something about that pink globule and Maxwell's demeanour didn't seem right. His eyes strayed over the rest of the contents of the locker where they fell upon the two cardboard boxes on the top shelf. The police officers had no warrant and so could only hope for the suspect's cooperation to allow them to look into the boxes. Instinctively Carl doubted Maxwell's assistance. The man was cocky and would probably come up with some kind of a ruse that the contents were highly personal. Either that or he would say he was in a hurry to go home.

So, whilst Chloe and Maxwell bent down to examine the rubber wellingtons, Carl deliberately leaned heavily against the locker as if to support himself. As he hoped, one of the boxes dislodged itself and tumbled down. Like a Giselle, Maxwell leapt up and swiftly caught it, but not before a tiny plastic bag holding white powder fell on to the floor. He snatched it up but was unable to prevent both officers seeing the small package. His awkward and desperate handling of the cardboard box caused three more samples to escape. One by one they cascaded on to the floor. Still clutching the box, Maxwell attempted to snatch them up. However, Carl and Chloe had, by that time, deduced the packages contained cocaine.

"I think you had better come down to the station, so we can ask you some more questions." The detective said. "You can bring those two boxes with you."

Suddenly, Maxwell panicked. He tried to make a run for it, but the DI barred his way. Maxwell tried to push past the inspector, but the detective sergeant anticipating what he would do, was too quick for him. Before he realised what was happening Chloe had handcuffed him. The DI radioed for a police car to take their suspect to the police station. In the meantime detective inspector Carl Barker and Detective Sergeant Chloe Watson still wanted to talk to Jamie Weston.

Chapter Twenty Three

Revelations

After two days of changeable weather, the sun had begun to shine on that particular Thursday afternoon. Mrs. Briggs decided to do some washing. As usual she searched the house for dirty laundry. She found the bin bag in Maxwell's room and after seeing the contents of it decided to give the jacket a wash. She was used to cleaning up after her two sons so thought nothing of the state of the garment, though she did notice it seemed to have a lot of mould on it. There was also an unpleasant smell.

Her washing was hanging on the line when the two detectives arrived at her house. Within minutes another police constable arrived with a warrant to search Maxwell's bedroom. He handed it to the DI.

"What's all this about inspector?" Mrs. Briggs asked anxiously. "Is my son in trouble?"

"I'm afraid so. At the moment I can't tell you anything else."

Mrs. Briggs nervously led the police officers to her son's bedroom. They saw the empty bin bag and carefully examined it. They couldn't detect anything incriminating in it, though it reeked of an unpleasant odour. They could see it was old and creased. Chloe put it in an evidence bag. They hoped to find inside samples of coagulated droplets of blood. They expectantly searched the bedroom for the jacket.

Do you know if there was anything in this bin bag? Detective Sergeant Chloe Watson asked Mrs. Briggs gently.

"Yes. A smelly dirty jacket. I was going to soak it in a stain remover. I can't think how it got to that state."

"Where is it? Can we see it?" The detective inspector asked. He tried to conceal his excitement.

Mrs. Briggs led them to the kitchen. She picked up the soiled jacket from a chair at the side of the sink. "Here it is, though I don't know why you are interested in it. The thing stinks."

"Can I take it with us?" The DS held out her hand for it.

"I can't think why, but if you want it. Take it." Mrs. Briggs said. She frowned. "Glad to get rid of it."

Chloe put the jacket into another sample bag. "Thank you for your help." She said smiling.

"So have you spoken to my son?" Mrs. Briggs asked. Fear was beginning to edge its way on to her face.

"Yes. He is at the station helping us with our inquiries." The detective said as gently as he could.

Mrs. Briggs sat down on the chair trying to overcome her shock.

"Why? What's he done?" Is it to do with that jacket? Is it stolen?"

The detective inspector looked steadily into the distressed woman's face. This was one part of the job he hated when unsuspecting parents discovered the truth about the horrendous behaviour of their offspring.

"I'm afraid so. I can't tell you anything more as yet. But thank you for your cooperation."

"When will he be home?" Mrs. Briggs asked.

"I'm not sure. Perhaps you could ring the station later. Here's my card."

The police officers left the house hopeful that they had the evidence to close the case on the murder of Rachel Bellis.

Earlier at the boat club the interview with Jamie Weston had revealed that sometimes he and Maxwell had to separate to carry out their duties. He confirmed that most of the time Maxwell was alone in the locker room whereas he was usually outside with two or three other colleagues. Both police officers were convinced of Jamie's innocence.

When they left the boat club to visit Maxwell Briggs' home, both police officers were unaware that Nicky was in hospital. At that stage of the day their investigation had no connection with Nicky.

Abigail had gone to work that morning and had explained to her employer that Nicky was in hospital though she didn't give her the salient details.

Gavin had spent some time talking to his own employers and was making plans to resume work the following week.

Rachel spent most of her time at the side of Nicky's bed hoping she would regain consciousness.

Nicky's mother was also at her bedside in the hospital. She had been to Nicky's flat to collect her bag and her mobile. She had also packed a few of her personal things.

Ryan was in work. He was a fork lift truck driver at a warehouse on the outskirts of Holywell. He had tried during his break to contact Max but he wasn't answering his texts. His mobile was switched off. He was unable to contact Nicky either. Ryan was feeling extremely stressed.

Maxwell Briggs was in an interview room waiting for the return of DI Carl Barker and DS Chloe Watson.

At six thirty Nicky regained consciousness.

Abigail phoned the hospital after she had finished work and was told that Nicky was awake and able to talk to her mother. Abigail then called Gavin on his mobile.

"Will they let us see her?" Gavin asked.

"I'm not sure. But if not, perhaps we can talk to her mother for a few minutes. We might be able to find out what happened."

"Right I'll pick you up in half an hour."

When they arrived at the hospital Nicky was sleeping naturally. "She's told me a little about what happened." Nicky's mother explained. "Do you know anything Abigail? I know you are very friendly with her. I can't believe this has happened. I've tried for so many years to protect her and now this." She broke down into tears. Abigail led her to the volunteers run café at the front of the hospital. Gavin followed and brought some tea for the three of them. Abigail introduced Gavin.

"Yes, Nicky has just mentioned your name." Abigail and Gavin exchanged a startled look. "Nicky said that Ryan thought you were having an affair with her. Is that true?"

Gavin was shocked. "Of course not."

"That's why he hit her. She said." Nicky's mother eyed Gavin thoughtfully.

Abigail frowned. "Mrs. Parry…"

"Please call me Meg."

"Meg, perhaps Nicky is concussed and probably hasn't explained things properly. Gavin wasn't having an affair with Nicky, he hardly knows her. Did she say anything else?" Abigail asked.

Abigail was trying to think quickly. At least they have now established that it was Ryan who hit Nicky. "Like what started the violence?"

"She mentioned something about a jacket. She said Ryan went crazy. Whose jacket is it?" Meg asked.

Again Gavin and Abigail exchanged glances. This time Abigail held Gavin's eyes. She seemed to seek permission to explain the whole story to Mrs. Parry. He nodded his consent.

"Mrs. Parry I have something very disturbing to tell you."

Rachel who had been listening to all this was pleased that at last Gavin was making some progress. She sincerely hoped that

Mrs. Parry would convince Nicky that she had to tell the police what had happened. In particular that the jacket in Nicky's wardrobe was Ryan's.

At that moment Ryan was at home sulkily watching the television. His parents had gone out. Wednesday nights was their cinema night as they got two for the price of one tickets. They were both in the 'over fifty club'. After switching channels and then checking his text messages Ryan decided to go out for a drink at the *Black Raven*. He thought he might find Max there. Maybe he would go and see Nicky later.

Whilst Ryan was drinking his pint, DI Carl Barker and DS Chloe Watson had just entered the interview room and were about to interrogate Maxwell Briggs. They had more pertinent questions about the murder of Rachel Bellis, the charge for handling large quantities of cocaine would come later.

Maxwell had just been advised of his rights, when the door to the interview room opened and a police officer handed a note to the DI. Carl motioned to DS Chloe Watson to go out of the room with him. Maxwell's face dropped. He had been in that room for several hours and was fed up. Now it looked like he was going to be abandoned again. Malevolently he hoped that this disruption was a new murder case to occupy the police officers' attention and that they would let him go. He was planning on leaving town as soon as he could.

Meanwhile he was going to deny all knowledge of the cocaine. He would say he was looking after it for a friend and had only just realised what it was. If necessary he would say it was Ryan's.

Outside the interview room the DI and DS scrutinised the note.

"Let's get to the hospital to see what this girl has to say. If she gives us permission to search her flat we won't need a warrant."

Before the detectives left the station, another police officer handed DI Barker a second note. "I'm not sure if this helps sir, but I thought I would tell you anyway."

Carl shared the note with Chloe. "Hmm. So two blue sailing club jackets along with other articles of clothing went missing from the sailing club a year ago. Very interesting." Carl muttered. They went outside and made their way to the hospital.

The two police detectives were surprised to see Gavin sitting on one of the seats outside the patient's ward. He was waiting with Abigail. Alongside them were Nicky's flatmates Amy and Jess.

Gavin recognised the detective inspector. They shook hands, and Gavin introduced Abigail. He told him that Abigail was a friend of Nicky and that he had brought her to the hospital. Gavin was unsure how much to tell the detective so for now he decided to say nothing. Abigail introduced the two flatmates who had been appalled to hear that Nicky had been suffering for so long without them knowing. Both girls realised that Nicky had been hiding her injuries and had not confided in them that Ryan was so violent. Carl Barker assured them all that after he had spoken to Nicky he would like to talk to Abigail, Amy and Jess.

As Carl walked away to see Nicky he wondered just how much Gavin Bellis knew about this particular case. He was shocked when he saw Nicky Parry. Her face was bruised, her arm was in plaster and apparently she had three broken ribs. Her lips were cut and swollen. Chloe Watson studied the patient with indignation and horror. She cast a sympathetic glance at Nicky's mother who was sitting at the side of her holding her daughter's hand.

Gently the detective inspector asked Nicky some questions. He discovered that this wasn't the first time Ryan had hit her. With the encouragement of her mother and friends she was going to tell the police everything she knew. Her mother supplemented Nicky's story with information she had gleaned from Abigail and Gavin. She made a point of telling them about the jackets.

Rachel was elated, but at the same time saddened to see the bruised state of Nicky's face.

After a couple of pints at the *Black Raven*, Ryan drove to Nicky's flat. He pressed the buzzer to her flat and though no-one spoke, the door opened. He ran up the steps to the flat. He didn't intend to stay long, he was going to seize that jacket which had been worrying him ever since that incident at the pub with those three men. He was going to drive somewhere with it and dump it in the sea miles away from Holywell. The door to the flat was open and Ryan barged in closing the door behind him.

"Nicky." He called. "Why didn't you return my text? Stop playing hard to get."

"She's not here." An unfamiliar voice spoke behind him. DS Chloe Watson barred the door.

"Who are you?" Ryan asked. "Where's Nicky?"

"She's in hospital because of you." This time DI Carl Barker spoke. He stepped out of Nicky's bedroom holding Ryan's jacket. Ryan wheeled around again and froze.

"What do you mean? She was alright when I left her."

"So you admit you were here last night?" Carl said softly. "I would like you to come down to the station with us so we can ask you some questions."

"What for? I'm not going to any bloody station. I only gave her a playful punch."

"So playful that she's fractured three ribs and has two bruised eyes. Not forgetting a broken arm." Chloe said coldly.

"And whilst we are in the station we would like to ask you where you were on the night Rachel Bellis was brutally raped and murdered." Chloe continued.

Carl scrutinised Ryan's reaction, as Chloe's words sunk in.

Ryan's face collapsed. "What do you mean?" He breathed quietly. His heart was hammering against his chest. Where's bloody Max when you need him.

"Maybe this will explain things." The inspector held up the jacket he had retrieved from Nicky's wardrobe.

Ryan turned to get out but anticipating his panic, Chloe remained against the door. He tried to push her away. She was unbalanced momentarily, but put her foot out to trip Ryan. He stumbled, yet was almost out through the door when Carl caught hold of him from behind with an arm hooked around his neck. "I don't think you are going anywhere except with us."

Chloe quickly recovered herself and cuffed Ryan.

Rachel watched the episode smugly from the comfort of an armchair. She followed the officers and Ryan down to the unmarked police car where he was bundled into and taken to the station.

"I suppose the police will have to wait for a forensics report on the jacket before they get any further." Dan said much later, when Gavin had relayed to him what the DI had explained to him.

"Yes. But I think they might get a confession out of Ryan. Despite his bravado I don't think it will take him long to crack under interrogation. That Maxwell is a much harder case. But if Ryan incriminates him and if they find Rachel's DNA on those jackets it could conclude with both of them bastards spending time in prison."

"Let's hope so." Dan agreed.

"In any case the police will get Ryan Barnes for GBH to Nicky, and they can get Maxwell Briggs for possession of cocaine."

"Hmm. Yes I suppose that's something, but I would prefer those two thugs went to prison for what they did to our Rachel." Dan said emotionally.

Gavin sighed. He felt the same way.

When Rachel related this conversation to Anna she was more philosophical. "Even if they can't prove they killed you, those horrible brutes will have a police record. They will probably do time, and who knows the police may find some more evidence. We've come a long way these last couple of weeks. So well done Rachel."

Rachel shared the same feelings with all members of her family. She was glad those two monsters were feeling uncomfortable under police scrutiny. She was ecstatic when two days later the police contacted her father to tell him that Ryan had confessed to the rape and murder of his daughter.

Whilst Gavin and Dan were pleased that the police were going to convict Ryan for rape and murder, they still hoped that there would be a breakthrough with Maxwell Briggs. The police had informed them that Ryan had incriminated Maxwell in the assault on Rachel, but Maxwell was still vehemently denying it.

In the meantime Gavin called Abigail to tell her the good news. He shyly offered to buy her a drink to celebrate and was delighted that she accepted. They agreed to meet in St. Winefride's Head hotel bar.

"Thanks for all your help. It's been a long hard road but we got there." Gavin had bought a bottle of white wine and they chinked glasses.

"I was pleased to help. My only regret is Nicky's horrible experience with that man."

"Yes he is a nasty piece of work. I think that relationship was doomed without our interference. But I am so very sorry too that my involvement has been to her detriment." Gavin looked despondent as he thought of Nicky. The outcome could have been so much worse.

"Don't be too hard on yourself. Leaving that jacket with Nicky was Ryan's undoing. It was just a matter of time. As regards Nicky, she has the chance to start again. I will keep an eye on her. Jess and Amy have also said they will too. They're so sorry that they hadn't noticed her suffering. I suppose they were just too busy with their own lives and she didn't want to tell them. She's had some bad luck. First with a violent father and then bloody Ryan. Her mother told me all about the past. It's like as if the violence has followed her around." Abi said as she gazed at Gavin.

Gavin looked into Abigail's troubled eyes and felt his heart beat wildly against his chest. He knew he was having really strong feelings of affection for this girl.

"Have you told your friend Phil about what happened?" Abi asked with a twinkle in her eye. I bet he's chuffed."

Gavin grinned. He was delighted that she had accepted that Phil's psychic powers had been instrumental in finding Rachel's killers.

"Yep he really is. He sends you his regards."

Abi smiled.

Rachel had divided her time between sitting at the side of Nicky's bed and watching her father potter about the house.

The early days of May, had brought some heavy showers keeping Dan and Gavin indoors. Despite the weather, Gavin, to give him credit had taken Leo for walks. He had also spent some time at his mother's graveside. *Anna had been touched to see him.*

"I must say he's losing that haunted look if you pardon the expression." Anna confided in her daughter sometime after Ryan's confession.

Rachel agreed. "Yes. I suppose it must be a load off his mind. He's going back to work on Monday."

The night before Rachel's four week pass to roam as a ghost was up, she planned on leaving a farewell message to her father and Gavin. The battery on the mobile was now dead and so she had to resort to something else.

The idea came to her on the morning of her departure. Her father and brother were eating breakfast cereal. Gavin had poured out some of the corn flakes in to his bowl and was about to pour some for his father when Rachel forced some flakes into the air. They fell on to the tablecloth where Rachel used her energy to forge a message.
Mesmerised, both men watched as Rachel managed to write the word BIBI in the flakes. The lettering was crooked and badly put together, but they understood what was happening. She then framed a large heart with the rest of the flakes and added her initials REB.
"Goodbye Rachel love." Dan said. He wiped his eyes.
"Goodbye Rachel. Rest in peace." Gavin added.
Back at the cemetery, the Assessors asked Rachel if her four weeks had been of value and she impressed them with her account of what had occurred during that time.
Her friends were also impressed. "The amount of times she heard "well done" from Margareta, Trevor, Desmond and Tomtit" were heartening. But unsurprisingly her mother was the most impressed and pleased. "I wish I could hug you." She said.
Rachel looked around her cronies. "Where's Big Steve?"
They all laughed. "Oh, didn't you know? He was given two weeks leave to roam. He

left yesterday to try to solve his own case."
They all laughed.

Six weeks later, DI Carl Barker called to see Dan Bellis.

"We've received the forensics report on those jackets and the residual contents of that old bin bag. We believe we have enough evidence to convict Maxwell Briggs. We've also got a witness who says he has seen him use that old rail track behind the boathouse. So fingers crossed, we will get him."

Later that day, Dan accompanied Gavin, Abigail and Nicky to Rachel's graveside. They had a bottle of champagne and some glasses with them. The weather wasn't particularly good for a summer's day but they didn't care.

"It looks like the police have enough evidence to convict Maxwell Briggs and Ryan Barnes for what they did to you Rachel. So we are celebrating. We hope you can hear us." Gavin said.

After one drink each, they strode over to Anna's grave. This time Dan spoke. "We kept our promise Anna. The police have caught those men who assaulted our daughter." They drank again and Gavin kissed Abigail. Together they stood hand in hand.

"It looks like romance is on the cards."
Anna said gleefully.
Rachel grinned.

THE END

Author's note

The town of Holywell in North Wales is the location for this novel, inspired by the famous St. Winefride's Well. For the purposes of the novel, I have re-arranged the geographical area that surrounds Holywell. Most of it is totally fictitious. There is a lake in Holywell, however it is several miles away from the town and nowhere near St. Winefride's well.

All the characters in this novel are fictitious. Any resemblance to those living or deceased is purely coincidental. Also fictitious are the names of the shops, streets, pubs and bakeries. Again any resemblance to those mentioned is a coincidence.

Thanks

Once again I must thank my sister Lesley for her help and support whilst writing this novel. I would also like to thank my friend Maureen and the members of Cardiff Writers' Circle for their feedback and support.

If you enjoyed this ghost detective story you may like

Restless Yew Tree Cottage
By Pamela Cartlidge

When Preston inherits his mother's cottage he converts it into a jazz café. Whilst his mother – Stella - was alive she claimed her cottage was haunted by Alwenna. This ghost had been the guiding spirit for Stella who as a clairvoyant had gained some notability as a fortune teller.

Accustomed to these past practises of his mother, Phillip, unperturbed continues with his plans. Soon the jazz café gains a good reputation. Things go awry when his long lost and troubled niece Amanda steps into the café.

Unaware that she has inherited her grandmother's extra sensory powers, Amanda unwittingly awakens the ghost's interest. When Amanda's mother and husband arrive at the Jazz café, Amanda and Preston sense a malevolence that appears to emanate from Alwenna.

Bluebells and Tin Hats by Pamela Cartlidge

Set in a small mining town in North Wales, this romantic historical novel traces the life of fourteen year old Louisa caught up in the clash of old and new traditions during the nineteen thirties.

Unable to change her mother's entrenched belief that working in service was her best career choice Louisa finds herself living and working away from home in a job she detests. Fortunately after two miserable weeks, one of her beloved brothers rescues her and takes her home.

Whilst struggling to change her destiny, the impact of a mining explosion in Gresford and the arrival of a young man from Liverpool changes Louisa's life forever. Running alongside the developing stages of romance, the years leading up to and through world war two pushes Louisa down a turbulent path of tragedy and love.

Rhubarb without Sugar by Pamela Cartlidge

In nineteen forty five, Louisa and her family, are hoping and waiting for the return of their loved ones from the war. To keep herself occupied Louisa attempts to carve a career for herself using her talents as an accomplished seamstress. Her flair for recycling and creating fashionable clothes has already won her admiration and respect.

As time moves on, the early nineteen fifties sees the end of fabric rationing, and facilitates the setting up of numerous clothes factories in Louisa's home town of Wrexham. These new developments run parallel with the changing dynamics of Louisa's personal life. Whilst she faces hard challenges in both her work and with her health, she also becomes entangled with a trial for murder.

Coming soon

The Keeper by Pamela Cartlidge

In 1970, Ruth, recently widowed, and mother of a two year old girl abducts three young children. From then on she embarks upon a hide and seek existence. Financially secure, and extremely intelligent, she needs all her wits to avoid both the police and the fathers of the abducted children.

Several years later, Ron, the father of the oldest abducted child is released from prison after serving a sentence for GBH. He tries to find his missing son. He locates Barry the father of the younger two abducted children. Ron wants his son. Barry is more interested in money. They make a deal to try to find Ruth and the missing children.

Printed in Great Britain
by Amazon